Praise for the Mysteries of Margaret Grace

"Gerry proves a resilient, enterprising detective and Maddie a delightful sidekick in this tightly honed mystery, where smalltown personalities get a gentle poke."
        —*Publishers Weekly* on *Murder in Miniature*

"A really interesting concept for a mystery story. Very appealing characters and a plot that will keep you on your toes. ...I highly recommend this to all fans of cozy mysteries."
        —*Once Upon a Romance* on *Monster in Miniature*

"...in turns a funny, thrilling, and heartbreaking murder mystery. Gerry Porter is a thoroughly likable amateur sleuth, determined to get to the truth regardless the cost. Young Maddie is laugh-out-loud entertaining.... The mystery is well-plotted and the tying together of the various loose ends is satisfying, making this a difficult to put down page-turner."
        —*Fresh Fiction* on *Monster in Miniature*

"Grace does a wonderful job of leaving clues hidden along the way. ...A charming cozy that will have you feeling like you're back visiting with friends you haven't seen in a while and anxiously awaiting the next time you get together."
        —*TheBestReviews.com* on *Monster in Miniature*

Mix-up in Miniature

Mix-up in Miniature

A MINIATURE MYSTERY

Margaret Grace

2012
PERSEVERANCE PRESS / JOHN DANIEL & COMPANY
PALO ALTO / MCKINLEYVILLE, CALIFORNIA

Copyright © 2012 by Camille Minichino
All rights reserved
Printed in the United States of America

A Perseverance Press Book
Published by John Daniel & Company
A division of Daniel & Daniel, Publishers, Inc.
Post Office Box 2790
McKinleyville, California 95519
www.danielpublishing.com/perseverance

Distributed by SCB Distributors (800) 729-6423

Book design by Eric Larson, Studio E Books, Santa Barbara

Cover photo by Richard Rufer,
at Shellie's Miniature Mania, San Carlos, California

10 9 8 7 6 5 4 3 2 1

LIBRARY OF CONGRESS CATALOGING-IN-PUBLICATION DATA
Grace, Margaret, (date)
Mix-up in miniature / by Margaret Grace.
    p. cm. — (The miniature series)
  ISBN 978-1-56474-510-1 (pbk. : alk. paper)
  1. Porter, Geraldine (Fictitious character)—Fiction. 2. Miniature craft—Fiction.
3. Women authors—Crimes against—Fiction. 4. Dollhouses—Collectors and collecting—Fiction. 5. Grandparent and child—Fiction. I. Title.
PS3563.I4663M49 2012
813'.54—dc23
        2011035732

To Richard Rufer,
my amazing husband and on-the-job IT crew

Acknowledgments

THANKS as always to my dream critique team: mystery authors Jonnie Jacobs, Rita Lakin, and Margaret Lucke.

Thanks also to the extraordinary Alameda County DA Inspector Chris Lux for advice on police procedure. My interpretation of his counsel through sixteen books should not be held against him.

Thanks to the many writers and friends who offered critique, information, and inspiration; in particular: Gail and David Abbate, Judy Barnett, Sara Bly, Margaret Hamilton, Mary McConnell, Ann Parker, Sue Stephenson, and Jean Stokowski.

Thanks to Shellie Kazan, proprietor of Shellie's Miniature Mania in San Carlos, California, and her staff, who allowed me to turn the shop into a crime scene for the cover of *Mix-up in Miniature*.

Special thanks to Meredith Phillips, my editor and co-crafter in the world of miniatures.

My deepest gratitude goes to my husband, Dick Rufer, the best there is. I can't imagine working without his support.

Mix-up in Miniature

Chapter 1

MY NEPHEW SKIP looked over my shoulder at the magazine I held. He read from the open page, stumbling over some of the abbreviations.

> NEW HOME LISTING: 1890 Victorian beauty: 6 br, 3 bath, orig wdwrk, stained glass, rare lghtng fixts, wall trtmnts, oak flrs, 2 frplcs, 2 wd stvs, bsmnt, attic, cottge w possible rental rm upstairs. Exclnt cond, some gutter repair rq. Exclnt val.

Skip shook his head, his Porter-family red hair catching the rays from my atrium skylight. "You already own six houses, Aunt Gerry, and, like, a gajillion shops."

"So?"

"Shouldn't you be selling some off, not buying?"

Intermittent bites from a ginger cookie slowed down his friendly rebuke. My kitchen, just behind us, still held the aroma of Skip's favorite snack, newly out of the oven.

"I have no duplicate shops," I said. "And some of my houses are very small. For example…"

I waved my arm in the direction of a beige-and-terra-cotta Pueblo-style dollhouse sitting on a table in my atrium where we'd settled for a brief visit. At one-half scale (one half inch of dollhouse for every one foot of life-size space) the whole house was barely two feet in width and in length. Adorable, especially after Maddie and I had painted all the doors and window frames a rich Santa Fe blue.

At eleven years old, my granddaughter was still a little shaky with a brush, but I liked the fact that you could distinguish her walls from mine. I couldn't predict how much longer she'd be happy doing projects with me. She'd already hinted that she might be calling me Gerry soon.

But on the home ownership issue, Skip had a point. Being Lincoln Point's youngest, sharpest homicide detective, he'd noticed how I'd maneuvered houses of different sizes, scales, and architectural styles into every available space. My four-bedroom life-size home had become one giant crafts room and miniature-real-estate show room.

Besides the half-scale Pueblo, I had five miniature houses in full, or one-twelfth scale (one inch of dollhouse for every one foot of real space), the largest of them a ten-room brick Victorian forty-two inches high. And of course I also displayed the standard "street of shops" pieces and assorted room boxes. None of my buildings were of the "playhouse" type that children might use or dolls might populate.

Time to 'fess up. I owned a lot of property. I was a regular mini–feudal lord. I closed the dollhouse magazine on the tempting ad for another miniature Victorian.

"Here's an idea," Skip said, working on his third cookie. "Aren't you part of that library committee that wants to buy a bookmobile for the town? You could donate one of your dollhouses to the auction for the fund-raiser."

That was Skip's way of reminding me of my lofty position on the committee: gofer for auction items. In particular, our chairman and head librarian, Doris Ann Hartley, had been prodding me to approach the biggest celebrity in our small northern California town, bestselling romance novelist Alexandra Rockwell, aka Varena Young, her pen name. I was to persuade Ms. Rockwell to donate her enormous museum-quality dollhouse, a Georgian mansion.

"You want me to ask for Alexandra Rockwell's award-winning mansion? Lord and Lady Morley's home?" had been my startled response.

"Who are the Morleys? And why do they have titles?" Doris Ann had asked. "I thought I knew everyone in town."

"That's the name of the dollhouse. Ms. Rockwell calls her hallmark dollhouse the Lord and Lady Morley mansion. That miniature must be worth a million dollars," I'd said, facetiously emphasizing *miniature.* "She's not going to give that gem to us to auction off."

"Of course she's not," Doris Ann had said. "It's just the start of a negotiation. You ask for that, then bargain to accept whichever smaller piece of her dollhouse collection she offers."

It was true that any one of Ms. Rockwell's dollhouses, featured often in trade magazines, would be an excellent auction item, far surpassing my own creations and those of all my crafter friends.

"So it's a trick? Ask for the biggest, most elaborate house, though all you really want is one of the smaller ones?"

"That's the idea."

No wonder I'd never get the hang of negotiating. No wonder I hated it.

"I'd rather donate all my houses than try to get one from the Rockwell Estate," I said to Skip now. Only a slight exaggeration, as my nephew knew.

Alexandra Rockwell was well into her eighties by any reckoning. She was purportedly a duchess, whatever that meant these days, and she'd become a franchise, publishing up to three Regency romance books a year for her legion of fans throughout the world.

Not just from nobility, I dreaded soliciting from anyone, even for a worthy cause like enhancing the reading pleasure of hundreds of Lincoln Point citizens who were unable to get to the library. My usual sales presentation went along the lines of "You probably don't want to do this, but—" Not a successful communication path for any venture, whether selling Girl Scout cookies, peddling raffle tickets, or asking outright for a charitable contribution. I'd explained to Doris Ann that making a cold call to negotiate with a novelist who was number one on the romance charts was not in my skill set.

Ms. Rockwell was known as well for her dollhouse collection, which she started as a young woman. But the lady was not the kind of miniaturist I hung out with. It was obvious that she didn't hang out with anyone in the lowlands of Lincoln Point— those of us who lived below the gated communities on the hill.

Most of us crafters stood in awe the few times Ms. Rockwell had visited our crafts fairs. She'd breeze in, accompanied by her assistants. Bodyguards? we wondered. She'd walk quickly through the aisles of handcrafted furniture and accessories, waving her long arms gracefully, pointing to what she wanted, always the most exquisite and expensive items in the exhibit room. A four-inch-long inlaid wooden coffee table by a craftsman who specialized in such pieces. A tiny, delicately painted ceramic vase. A miniature hand-woven reproduction of a unicorn tapestry. Pieces most of us coveted and saved up for years to buy.

One of Ms. Rockwell's aides would make the purchases as the great lady continued down the rows of tables, then disappeared through the side exit. No stopping to chat with the vendors. No checking out the snack bar to grab one of Mabel's mint-chip brownies.

Once Ms. Rockwell left the building, we'd all make guesses as to where in her collection she might place her purchases.

"She must be working on a half-scale late Regency," I'd said on the day not long ago that Ms. Rockwell bought a marvelous double-bow high-back elbow chair. "It would complement the period her novels are set in."

"You mean her crafter-in-residence is working on a late Regency," my friend Linda had responded, doubtful that anyone who didn't come to our crafters meetings had the skills to put a dollhouse together. It never did any good to remind Linda that if it weren't for noncrafters, we'd have very few customers at our fairs.

It wasn't the first time we'd engaged in speculation as to whether the famous Ms. Rockwell actually made miniature furnishings and built her dollhouses herself, just as there was a question about whether, as Varena Young, she still wrote her own books.

Susan, another member of our regular miniatures group, had had a different response altogether. "Don't tell me you actually read romances, Gerry," she said, a look of mock horror on her face. "A former English teacher who's always quoting Shakespeare reads Varena Young's bodice-rippers?"

I felt I needed to defend my reading habits. "I've read only a couple, to prepare myself for when I ask for her million-dollar dollhouse. And they're really not bodice-rippers. If they were movies, they wouldn't even be R-rated."

In any case, Alexandra Rockwell and her writer persona gave us all something to talk about in the sleepy town of Lincoln Point, where—far from the hubbub of San Francisco—there was little drama to everyday life.

Rock music playing in my backyard brought me back to present realities and the fact that I couldn't put off my negotiating task much longer. Skip's cell phone had rung.

My nephew, an apartment dweller with no yard, had gone out to inspect his patch of Brussels sprouts and kale in my garden. He now reentered through my patio doors, clicking his phone shut and ending our visit with his trademark "Gotta go, Aunt Gerry."

Once Skip left, called to duty on a Monday afternoon and toting a plastic bag bursting with cookies, there was nothing to do but steel myself to call the Rockwell Estate. Or was it the Young Estate?

I wondered how I should address the lady to increase my chance of seeing her. I wondered if it would matter.

I REFRESHED my tea and gave some thought to reneging on my bookmobile assignment. I recalled last week's meeting when Doris Ann had said, "You're the closest we have to a dollhouse expert, Gerry."

"Linda Reed is much better," I'd pointed out. "Unlike me, Linda makes everything from scratch."

Doris Ann sighed and gave me a look that, I had to admit, I understood. She was well aware that Linda was the Martha Stewart of crafters, never having built from a kit since she was old enough to use a wood sander. But we all knew also that Linda was at the low end of the tact and social skills spectra, just as likely to challenge or insult Ms. Rockwell as not. I might well have been the best the library committee had to offer.

A sad state, indeed, but it was time I took action.

I picked up my phone and dialed the number of the Rockwell Estate. A nervous shiver ran through me, just thinking of the winding road to Ms. Rockwell's life-size mansion high up on the edge of town. I wanted to see her home and her dollhouse collection, I realized, without actually having to ask for permission or, worse, a donation.

I knew what I was getting into. I'd driven past the checkpoints at the perimeters of the gated communities in the hills. Though he didn't live there, it was the scenic route I took to the home of Henry Baker, my BFF, or Best Friend Forever, as Maddie called him. Henry and I were still working out what the proper term was for our dating-after-fifty situation.

More than ever, traffic at the busy intersection between our homes was a nightmare, thanks to a huge construction project that promised to add tens of thousands more square feet of office space to Lincoln Point.

I waited through six rings for someone at the Rockwell Estate to answer. I was ready to count my blessings and hang up. A sorry excuse for a solicitor, hoping for no response. But a woman picked up the phone before I could escape. I heard a stern voice say, "Rockwell residence."

I was committed now.

I identified myself and asked to make an appointment with Ms. Rockwell. I tried to slur over the "Ms.," in case the lady of the house preferred to be called Miss, as were all the heroines in her romance novels, or Mrs., in the event that there was a Mr. of the house.

"Are you the Geraldine Porter from the library bookmobile committee?" the woman asked.

I gulped, bracing for either rude verbiage to put me in my place or an abrupt dial tone resulting from a quick hang-up. I had a flashback to my days of trying to sell ads to local businesses for my Bronx high school yearbook. I always came in last on the sales thermometer.

"Yes, I am. I'm sorry to bother you," I said, true to form.

"Wonderful." The tone had turned downright cheery. "Ms. Rockwell has been hoping you'd call. Are you free to stop in and visit with her, say, around three this afternoon?"

How old did I have to get before human behavior didn't surprise me every time?

Chapter 2

I WAS SO giddy on the drive to the Rockwell Estate, I needed to share my delight. I called Henry.

"I'm on my way to see Alexandra Rockwell," I said through the Bluetooth device clipped to my car's sun visor. "I told you about the novelist Varena Young, who's also a miniaturist. I'm passing right by your street."

"Why would you do that?" he asked.

"Remember I mentioned we want her to donate a dollhouse to the bookmobile auction?"

"I meant, why would you *pass by* my street?"

"I can stop on the way back."

For some reason I felt a blush coming on.

I'D taken the route through town, with streets at sea level at first, then, heading upward abruptly soon after I passed Henry's neighborhood. The first sign that I was leaving the part of town inhabited by ordinary folk was the immaculate, sprawling Lincoln Valley Country Club and Golf Course. Its vast, high-maintenance lawns were surrounded by trees, a few of which had turned a golden yellow and remained so even this late in the year.

A poor excuse for fall, my late husband, Ken, would have said.

With only two weeks till Thanksgiving, it was well past the height of the foliage season that Ken and I had enjoyed every year when we lived in New York. Each October, we took a foliage-and-picnic cruise to Bear Mountain, fifty miles north of our Bronx apartment. I missed the breathtaking vistas along the Hudson, the glorious red maples, the orange ash, the yellow poplars.

On this otherwise perfect, crisp fall day in California, I decided it was time to plan a picnic somewhere nearby, even if we couldn't reproduce the Adirondacks. I was sure I could talk a few relatives and friends into it.

I started the mental organization of the event as I drove. The weekend after the holiday should work, before the Christmas rush took over completely. I ran through the guest list as I drove past the fairways. My granddaughter, Maddie, of course—she who would miss nothing. Her best local friend, Taylor, who was Henry's granddaughter and Maddie's peer in the pre-teen set. My dear sister-in-law, Beverly, who was Skip's mother. Beverly's friend (as Henry was mine), Nick. Maybe Skip himself and his girlfriend, June, whom I'd ask to make her special potato salad.

Too many details to handle without paper and pen. And not enough seat belts—my little blue Saturn was filling up fast with my projected picnickers. We'd have to take Henry's van. Or charter a bus.

The road became dangerously curvy after the country club so I left my virtual party planning and focused on the sharp switchbacks. I wound my way up into the hills north of town, and reached a cul-de-sac with an imposing black wrought-iron fence at the end. The tips of the fence posts were sculpted into unattractive mythical creatures I didn't recognize. I thought normal birds or flowers would have been more welcoming, but then that wasn't the primary purpose of the fence.

A fancy check-in booth with a tiled roof stood to the left of the gate. I lowered my window and gave a uniformed middle-aged man my name.

"I'm here to visit the Rockwell residence," I announced. It sounded even better to me than the vainglorious "I'm with the band."

With no acknowledgment from the portly sentinel, the gates swung open and I drove through. More hills and more winding turns. I was at the edge of a nearly five-thousand-acre country club community, one of four such groupings in the upper regions of Lincoln Point.

The Rockwell residence was in Robert Todd Heights, site of the largest homes of the four neighborhoods. The other compounds were, in descending order of price tag, Edward Baker Heights, William Wallace Heights, and Thomas Heights. All named after Abraham Lincoln and Mary Todd's sons, in accordance with an unwritten town rule that, whenever feasible, we'd name buildings and properties after people and events in Lincoln's life.

I was now less than seven miles from my home, but light years away in terms of socio-economics. I'd tutored the son of one of my former Abraham Lincoln High students at their home in Thomas Heights, so I had some idea what was behind the ornate doors I was passing. Some were fronted by stained glass worthy of a church in Venice and fountains reminiscent of the plazas on the postcards of European vacationers.

Skip had said it more exactly when I told him where Ms. Rockwell lived. "From here to there, it works out to about a half million dollars a mile," he'd said. "And that's for the smaller homes. Figure twice that for Robert Todd Heights, where you're talking twelve, fourteen thousand square feet of living space."

The data were enough to intimidate me as I pulled into a circular drive in front of an enormous mansion in light stucco. The Rockwell Estate.

Before I got out of my car, I checked my hair in the visor mirror. Too late now for a salon poof-up procedure. The famed novelist would see my 'do at its limp best. In my good slacks and a relatively new sweater set, all in shades of brown and beige, I matched the stucco exterior of the house. And the dead leaves on the path.

I was a bit disappointed that I had to park my own car and open its door myself. I pictured a valet looking out a window at my Saturn and deciding it wasn't worth special handling.

On the way to the front door, I was newly overwhelmed by the size of Ms. Rockwell's home. My own residence, yard and all, would fit into one wing, like a dollhouse. At times like this I missed being able to hear the inevitable lecture from Ken, who was a respected architect. He would have pointed out the wise choices of curves on one element of the structure or the poor slant of roof on another. Sometimes his critique enhanced my enjoyment of a building; other times I wished he'd simply let me enjoy it in my own way, even if I liked something that was wrong about it.

The only feature of the Rockwell home that I recognized was the grand double set of curving steps that led to the front door, a conceit commonly seen in the Regency period.

I wondered if there was a protocol for climbing the left or the right steps to the front door. Was someone watching and judging? Deciding whether I was left- or right-leaning? Left- or right-brained? I took the steps on the right since they were closer to where I'd parked my low-end car. So much for heavy-duty analysis.

I used the high brass knocker, a lion's head, making my presence known. Descriptive passages from the latest romance novel by Varena Young, *The Rake in the Garden*, flitted through my mind. I imagined I'd soon be led through rooms filled with detailed marquetry on walls, end tables, and curio cabinets. Perhaps a snuff box here or there. Certainly a dark-paneled library with matching leather-bound classics.

As I recalled the adventures of Felicity, the heroine who fell in love with the Rake, the door opened. A tall, thin woman in casual business attire that included a sweater set much like mine except in shades of blue, stood there, smiling slightly. So far, so good. My clothes weren't out of line. Or did this mean I looked like a servant?

She held out her hand and gave me a practiced, controlled smile. "Laura Overbee, Ms. Young's personal assistant."

Not a servant. Overbee was a great moniker for a romance heroine, I thought. Maybe Ms. Young changed her staff's names to fit her world.

I shook Ms. Overbee's hand. "Geraldine Porter, from the library committee. Ms. Young is expecting me." I was surprised how easy it was for me to switch back and forth between the great lady's names, following the lead of her staff.

I knew I sounded too formal, but the bright, two-level entrance hall in front of me nearly took my breath away. A double set of curved marble treads and risers grew seamlessly from the marble floor and then met at the same point on the upper level. I stared at the white filigree newels and banisters on both sides of the stairs. A repeat of the pattern of the exterior steps.

Ken would have been impressed, especially at the openness of the hallway and the airy, modern look. Not at all what I had expected. No dark corners for trysts or nefarious deeds, just endless air and sunlight.

Ms. Overbee looked to be mid-thirties, the same age range as my only child, Richard, Maddie's father. She had a much stiffer, nervous air about her, however. She kept perfect posture while looking over her shoulder a couple of times during our brief introduction, as if I'd walked in on her attempt to steal tiny diamonds from the legendary dollhouse, wherever it was in this enormous modern palace.

Or, perhaps the important job of personal assistant to a famous writer was more stressful than that of an orthopedic surgeon at the Stanford Medical Center. (I'd trained myself to rattle off the details of my son's profession as if they were one word. Not that I was overly proud of him.)

"The household staff seems to be occupied at the moment," Ms. Overbee said, guiding me through one of three high, curved doorways to a beautifully appointed room on the left. The music room, I supposed, unless there was more than one highly polished grand piano in the house. "If you'll take a seat, someone will find Ms. Young for you."

I smiled and thanked her. I wanted to assure her I got her message: *Don't think I'm always relegated to lowly tasks like answering a knock on the door. A real servant will be attending to your needs.* I sat up straight and tried not to act as if this were the first magnificent home I'd ever visited.

A faint scent of rosewater filled the space, either from Ms. Overbee's toilette or from the many vases of fresh flowers that surrounded me.

Ms. Overbee walked away, her hands folded in front of her, in the manner of Mrs. Winfred Steeples, the dowager in Varena Young's novel, *The Last of the Steeples*. My, I'd absorbed more of this new-to-me genre than I thought. How would I explain this to my book club friends, who shunned genre fiction and read little other than the classics and winners of the National Book Award?

In front of me, on a large, pale floral carpet, was one of several low tables in the room. I wouldn't have described it as a coffee table, lest someone be led to compare this fine piece of furniture to the simple straight-legged version that sat in my own living room.

I thought how my dear Henry, who'd retired after a long tenure teaching shop at ALHS, and was an expert woodworker, would love to see this furniture and the light wood floors. I knew if I asked, he'd gladly make me a miniature replica of the lavish fireplace mantel that took up most of the far wall. Funny how the men in my life had the combined knowledge to build the doll-houses of my dreams—my late husband an expert on exteriors, and my new friend a master at interiors.

I might have gone on thinking about the virtues of Henry Baker, who'd gently broken through my firm belief that I'd never meet a man as wonderful as Ken Porter, but a swooshing noise interrupted.

Alexandra Rockwell, aka Varena Young, had entered the room. The faint rosewater air was replaced by a bold scent I couldn't place at first. An invigorating, spicy aroma with a touch of lemon.

Ms. Young wore a long, flowing, soft red dress. She might have been entering the stage of a great theater. Her neck, with its telltale rings of age, supported too many jeweled chains and pendants for me to count without staring. The same for the bracelets on her arms. Her brown hair was pulled back into a chignon.

Even in the middle of the afternoon, in her own home, meeting a plebian from downtown, Ms. Young was dressed like the women on the covers of her novels. I'd had a look at her author photographs, however, and guessed it had been many years since her last photo shoot.

I stood as she arrived at the sofa, her arms outstretched, offering both her hands. As tall as I was, she had a couple of inches on me. Ms. Young was definitely more relaxed and confident than her personal assistant, Laura Overbee. There was a certain security that came with wealth and fame, I assumed, and this lady exuded both.

"I'm Varena," she said, in a full, throaty voice that seemed to provide at least four-part harmony. "May I call you Geraldine?"

"Of course," I stammered.

"Would you like to see Lord and Lady Morley's home?"

Does a glue gun get hot? I wanted to answer.

"I'd love to," I said, not mentioning that I'd kept yellowing copies of every magazine spread and newspaper article written about Lord and Lady Morley's home, and that seeing it in person had been in my dreams for decades.

"Let's go back then, shall we?"

My friend Varena, as I now thought of her, ushered me out of the music room, across the entryway, where I stole a glance up at the sparkling crystal chandelier. This time I looked between the two sets of marble stairs, to a pair of curved arches and ultimately to immense glass doors that led outside. In spite of the brightness of the day, all the ceiling lights were lit, their circular reflections everywhere on the marble floor. The Green movement had not yet reached the lavish homes in Robert Todd Heights, but for the moment I forgave them their lack of environmental awareness.

Varena led me farther into the house toward a room at the end of a long corridor. On the way we passed more vases of flowers, set into alcoves, and more rooms with no doors, but simple, white arched openings. How many sitting rooms did one family need? I pictured myself turning them all into crafts areas. One room for shadow boxes. One for my miniature shops. One for construction work. One for display. I took a breath.

"What a beautiful home you have," I said, immediately regretting the clichéd remark. I squeezed my lips together to prevent further comments, but Varena's thank-you smile was as gracious as if I'd been the first to notice.

I wondered at the age of the house. Ken would have been able to tell me whether this was a redone old mansion or a relatively new construction. It didn't seem appropriate to ask. Neither would I give in to my curiosity about whether Varena was from old money or if she'd benefitted from characters like Felicity and the Rake to support this lifestyle.

Without further comment, Varena paused at the only solid interior door I'd seen. "Here we are. The Morleys have their own room," she said.

I caught a twinkle in her eye, which comforted me. I didn't want to think the grande dame had passed over into a completely fictional world where the Morleys were her only friends.

Varena opened the door, and the Georgian mansion—the term "dollhouse" didn't seem to fit—came into view, set on a low table in the middle of a dark-paneled room. Finally, my fantasy was realized and I was transported two centuries back. I changed my mind on the spot about the value of living in a fictional world with imaginary people.

I wanted in.

My breath caught at the light reflected from the tiny crystal chandelier in the Morleys' foyer, brighter than the life-size one out in the life-size foyer. I'd read that several tiny, real diamonds from Varena's jewelry collection had been placed strategically in the dollhouse chandelier. Rays bounced around also from the real silver cutlery and napkin rings on the polished dining room table, and from one or more jeweled objects in just about every room.

I could swear I saw a swarm of beautifully coiffed men and women gliding across the dance floor in the great ballroom. It wasn't hard to picture Felicity, in her voluminous gown, and the handsome Rake sitting primly on the intricate mahogany and green-cushioned loveseat against the wall. No body parts would be touching, of course, but flirtatious looks would pass between them and their hearts would swell with the music.

I nearly fainted from the heat of my thoughts. No wonder romance novels were the biggest sellers in the book world.

Cooling off, I followed Varena's mesmerizing voice. She pointed out the tiny books bound in leather and gold and a one-half-inch lapis lazuli statuette brought to her by a friend who'd worked on an archeological dig in the Fertile Crescent. Her finger, tipped lightly in a shade of red that matched her dress, stopped over a working, bubbling fountain in the courtyard.

"They tell me there are special waterworks underneath here, somewhere," Varena told me, shrugging her shoulders and waving her hand at the base of the dollhouse, as if the notion confused her and all she cared about was the effect of the tiny sprays of water.

I wanted to sit in front of the house and inspect every miniature working clock and feel all the layers of fabric that made up the window treatments. I wanted to sit on the Regency side chair with gold-patterned upholstery and take a sip of tea from the silver service set on an ornate low table.

Mostly, I wanted to know which, if any, of the marvelous pieces Varena was excited about were her own creations. I knew Linda would have asked the moment they met. I could hear her in my mind, asking simply, *Is there a chance in hell any of this is your work?* I was glad Linda wasn't here now to spoil my moment. Craftsperson or not, Varena Young had impeccable taste.

Every few minutes Varena stepped back, arms folded across all her chains and pendants, and smiled broadly. I could tell she enjoyed watching my delight in her treasures. Whatever had made me think Varena would be unapproachable just because she was never seen chatting with the locals at Willie's Bagels on Sunday mornings, and we'd never bumped into her browsing in Rosie's Bookshop?

I forgave her. She was too busy writing books, after all. And she was a crafter, or at least a crafts collector, a crafts lover, and therefore, "good people," as Skip would say.

Though I was happy Linda was at her nursing job, I wished Maddie were with me. I wished Henry were with me. I wished Ken were with me.

I'd had enough class to leave my camera at home, but I wondered about taking notes. I didn't want to forget a single detail of the dollhouse or its owner to share with my crafts group on Wednesday evening.

As for the bookmobile fund-raiser, if I had any doubts before today, I knew as soon as I set eyes on the Morley dollhouse that this building would not be gracing the auction table. I doubted it would even fit through the doorway to the exhibit hall.

I'd almost summoned the courage to ask my hostess if she enjoyed crafting herself. A diplomatic way to put it, I thought. But I was spared a potential faux pas by the arrival of a dark-haired woman in a plain blue shirtwaist dress and what my mother and aunts called sensible shoes. Not quite a uniform, but close.

"Excuse me, Miss Young," the young woman said. She stood in the doorway, wringing her hands in apparent distress. Were all of Varena Young's staff strung out? The two women I'd met who were in her employ were a sharp contrast to the smooth, stately Varena herself.

"Corazón, dear, not now. We can go over the menu later this evening," Varena said.

"I'm sorry, Miss Young. It's not for this weekend's party. I wanted to tell you, you have a guest waiting in the upstairs den."

I'd done enough tutoring of English as a second language to recognize Corazón's Mexican accent, which, though controlled, came through in the way she pronounced *you* and words containing *r*'s.

Varena's face took on a sternness I hadn't seen in the entire fifteen minutes that I'd known her. "I have a guest waiting right here," she said. I straightened my shoulders and felt my ego puff up a bit, even though apparently I wasn't on the guest list for that weekend party.

Corazón patted her thick hair, wrapped in a net at the back. She sighed audibly. "Miss Young, they tell me you must come now."

I felt sorry for the short woman who seemed to have too many bosses, and whose English pronunciation got worse as her stress level rose. I wanted to sit her down and work on the initial *y* sound, one of the most difficult to master for native Spanish speakers. "Think of your double *l*," I'd remind her. "The way it is in La Jolla."

Varena turned to me and bestowed an apologetic look. "Geraldine?" she asked, eyebrows raised, as if she were seeking my permission to leave me and attend to the upstairs guest.

"Please don't worry about me," I said. "I'm very grateful for the time you've spent with me."

I felt like a subject of the queen. In fact, I remembered, I was in the presence of a duchess. Only a rumored duchess, true, but that was more nobility than anyone else I'd ever stood this close to. The two grand houses, both the life-sized modern one and the modeled Georgian, had apparently sent me into a mode where I might curtsy at any moment.

"We still have business to do," Varena said to me. "If it meets with your approval, I plan to donate my midsize Tudor to your auction. I've already tagged it for your event. I'll show it to you when I come back. I hope it will be acceptable."

My breath caught. Another great fantasy had come to pass— I'd snagged one of Varena Young's dollhouses without even trying.

"Thank you, thank you," I said. Too late to take one back. Maddie's influence was showing.

"And, this might sound too forward, but wouldn't it be lovely if now and then I could drop in on your famous crafts group?"

Famous? My heart sang. I was ready to gush again when Corazón, whom I was beginning to dislike, interrupted again, this time with a simple "Miss Young?"

Varena gave a resigned sigh. "Wait here, will you?" she asked me, as if she truly thought I might leave, perhaps insulted that I was being offered only a midsize Tudor or that she wanted to join our crafting sessions.

I glanced back at the dollhouse mansion that I'd only begun to explore. "I'll be happy to wait," I said.

Varena walked past Corazón toward the hallway. I wondered who would have been ushered directly to an upstairs room for a meeting with the lady of the house. I pictured long hallways with bedroom after bedroom, bath after bath. And a sitting room for special guests.

I noticed that Corazón hung back. When Varena was out of sight, she came up to me.

"You might as well leave," she told me, in a near whisper. "It will be a long while."

"That's not a problem," I said. I had miles to go in the miniature mansion. "I'll wait."

Corazón leaned closer. "It's her brother upstairs."

I wondered why she hadn't announced Varena's brother out loud, and I wasn't sure how I was supposed to respond to this information.

"I'll wait," I said again.

Corazón turned and left the room, clearly not happy with me.

I wasn't usually this stubborn, but I was buoyed by having met the real Varena Young, who seemed to value my presence in her home. I felt privileged.

I imagined I'd make a very unpleasant rich person.

Chapter 3

WHAT A DAY I was having. I was now alone in front of Lord and Lady Morley's home. I thought of them as new friends, along with Varena.

I'd sometimes worried in the past about the extent of my immersion into the world of six-inch beds and half-inch pencils, but belonging to a crafts community set my mind at ease. It was normal for miniaturists to imagine living in their creations, inhabiting the detailed replicas that gave them so much pleasure. Or at least that was what we told ourselves.

Three floors, an attic, and a basement stretched out before me. I gazed at a lovely rose quartz floor, bordered with jade, in the Morleys' miniature drawing room. I studied a wooden spinning wheel, an ornate upright piano with mother-of-pearl keys, and a green cloisonné chair. I peered through a window from the outside of the house to get a different perspective and marveled at the way the copious, draped window treatments spoke of opulence.

For the first time I surveyed the life-size room I was standing in. Not only was the paneling as dark as that in the Morleys' dollhouse study, but several elements of décor were identical. A paisley area rug under the table that supported the dollhouse bore the same pattern as a rug in the miniature study, and one wall of the room held a vertical array of swords that was mirrored by the tiny ones over the Morleys' fireplace.

I ran my hand over the curved metal handle of the four-foot sword on the wall, the longest in the grouping, and then along

the handle of the four-inch replica in the Georgian. I was nearly
dizzy, straddling two worlds.

Crash/boom!

Had something fallen or broken? Not by my hand, I hoped,
in my trancelike state. The noise echoed down the hallway and
startled me. An earthquake? A temblor was always high on the
suspect list for any Californian, but nothing in my vicinity showed
any signs of motion.

The noise continued, now as loud voices.

I stepped into the corridor that led to the entryway. I could
hear the muffled sounds of two or more people arguing upstairs. The whole area around the grand staircase was open and
the sound traveled easily. I singled out Varena's rich voice, but
couldn't understand what she was saying. She sounded frustrated one moment and angry the next. At times a male voice
predominated—her brother, I assumed—but his words were no
clearer. I heard a pleading tone, then silence, then more subdued
voices.

I was embarrassed that I'd been eavesdropping on private
conversations in someone's home. As much as I was enjoying the
dollhouse room, I decided to make an unobtrusive, unescorted
exit from the property. I could always come back another day to
claim the Tudor.

Corazón had been right to encourage me to leave before
the visit-cum-fight started. Had she known that Varena and her
brother were about to have a knock-down-drag-out?

I cast one last glance at the Morley mansion, glimpsing a
charming shell chair with a turquoise satin cushion. I picked up
my purse—the best I owned, but the least expensive item of any
size, including all its contents, within miles—and left the room.

On my way to the front of the house, I heard more of the
argument upstairs, picking out odd words and phrases for which
I couldn't glean the context: "You're not fooling anyone," from a
soft male voice; "You'll never be more than a…" from a stronger
male voice, and something like, "After all these years…" from the
female voice. Possibly Varena's. I couldn't swear to any of it and
was glad I'd never have reason to.

The script could have applied to just about any family, I thought, at some moment in its history.

As I entered the area at the foot of the grand stairway, the argument appeared to have stopped completely. I stood still, waiting for another shoe to drop. I heard clocks ticking and a few bird chirps from the open patio door on my right. Nothing human from upstairs. I took a few more steps.

Still no more arguing. I considered rushing back to the Morley room to wait for Varena, pretending I hadn't heard a thing. There were so many details I hadn't examined at the Morleys' and I hadn't laid eyes on the Tudor, which I now thought of as mine. In fact, I'd already begun the calculations that would tell me whether I could afford to bid on it.

I could stay and wait, but I felt it would be awkward for Varena and me to resume our conversation as if nothing embarrassing had intervened.

Besides that, I was already slightly behind schedule for picking up my granddaughter at her after-school computer class in Palo Alto, about ten miles away. There wasn't a specific ending time for the extended program, but Maddie and I had agreed that I'd be there around four-fifteen. It occurred to me that I should have alerted my sister-in-law, Beverly, that I might need her as backup car pool, but I'd been too excited about making this trip to the Heights.

I heard not another peep from upstairs, and tempting as it was to tiptoe back to the Morleys' room and make myself comfortable, I let myself out the front door, got in my car without bumping into anyone on Varena's staff, and drove away.

MY regrets as I left Varena's home were legion. I'd meant to ask where she kept the rest of her dollhouses. Surely, they didn't each have their own room.

A strange feeling crept over me and I wondered if I'd ever be back. What if Varena already regretted her promise to me and decided not to give up the Tudor after all? I should have stood my ground until I had the house in hand. A small Tudor was usually one large room with a stairway to a loft. A midsize version, which I'd been awarded, would have at least three separate rooms downstairs and two or three upstairs, plus a standard loft under a thatched roof. A midsize would just fit in the trunk of my car.

I didn't look forward to giving my report to the library committee. "Even though I've met Varena in person, and we are now on a first-name basis," I'd have to admit, "there is no dollhouse in my trunk. All I have is a hasty promise."

By the time I got to sea level, I doubted even hearing the offer from Varena. I retrospectively picked apart her request for me to wait. What if she'd already regretted her offer and wanted to politely retract it? What if she interpreted the fact that I left as a refusal of her donation?

My stellar record of "least sales" and "worst negotiator" at any age was uncontested for now.

AS soon as I'd driven through the stretch of tortuous hairpin curves and was safely in the flatlands, I used my Bluetooth to call Henry.

"How did it go?" he asked.

I gave him a brief but exuberant summary of the grandeur behind me. I tried to remember the correct names for some of the wood-crafting features I'd particularly liked in the dollhouse: carved pillars, broken (that was a good thing) pediments, and Corinthian capitals topping the pilasters.

"So it's not strictly Georgian," he'd said.

"It was sumptuous," I said, annoyed at his critique. "I wanted to crawl inside and live there."

I told him about the duplicate walls of swords, and more to his interest, the metal tool rack standing in the basement of the dollhouse. Though most of the tools that hung from the two black crossbars looked modern—saws, wrenches, hatchets, long-nosed pliers, and the like—the display, with curlicued ornamentation, was reminiscent of a medieval torture rack.

"Did you get a donation for the auction?" he asked.

Why was Henry trying to annoy me?

"Are you hoping I'll drive right by your street again?" I

asked, sending an audible sigh toward the little green light on my Bluetooth.

His laugh brought me back to adulthood.

"Sorry," I said. "I'm rehashing my end of the conversation with Varena and coming up weak."

"You're too hard on yourself. Anyway, I've taken away any excuse you have for hurrying past my house again."

What did that mean? My one errand for the afternoon was to pick up Maddie. Her mother, my wonderful daughter-in-law, Mary Lou, was at a meeting of art gallery owners in Houston. Richard had taken the opportunity for a few days' leave from the hospital and accompanied her. It would give them a chance to spend some time together and visit old friends who'd moved there.

Maddie was mine for the next five days. The short commute from Lincoln Point to her Palo Alto school every day was hardly worth discussing when her parents asked if I could take care of her.

I realized Henry had chipped in, unsolicited, to help with the car pool arrangements. "You have Maddie?" I said.

"Yup. She was finished early and called about a half hour ago when she couldn't reach you on your cell. I told her you were with some VIPs."

"I hope she was polite at least."

"You know she was. And she couldn't get here too soon to suit Taylor. The two of them are collaborating on their science homework. Maddie has a great new book for a project on the conservation of energy."

I yawned deliberately. "How exciting."

"I know how that thrills you. Nice that their teachers use the same curriculum, though, isn't it?"

"And even nicer that they have someone who's not hopeless at science to help them."

"You're not hopeless. Just a little afraid."

"There's a lot to be afraid of."

"Are you almost here?"

"Five minutes."

"I'll put the water on for tea, then, and start dinner. Hope chicken and dumplings are okay."

It hadn't been that long since Henry and I had slid into making assumptions about our relationship. I couldn't pinpoint a day or a date, but somehow it had evolved that on a day like this, it would be natural for Maddie to call him to see if he knew where I was and for him to pick her up, and a matter of course that we'd all have dinner together.

I'd been a widow for several years and cherished Ken's memory, but I also liked this new relationship more and more.

I decided to forgive Henry his purist opening remark about the eclectic mix of styles in Varena's mostly Georgian dollhouse, and his reminding me of my inability to strike even the smallest of deals.

"GRANDMA, Grandma! I missed you."

Maddie nearly knocked me over with her battering-ram hug. Her heavy athletic shoes, running lights and all, knocked into my ankles. It had been almost two weeks since I'd seen her, which was unusual, but a nasty bug had attacked her respiratory system and had kept her out of school and also away from me.

"I missed you, too, sweetheart. Don't ever get sick again," I said, wishing I could make that happen.

Maddie reached into her jeans pocket and pulled out a tiny plastic bag. "I have a present for you. I didn't have time to wrap it, but I can't wait."

I took the small bag and watched her grin widen as I extracted a jewelry box, less than a quarter-inch wide. Inside were red earrings—tiny crystal and red glass beads, to be exact, but more exciting to me than genuine rubies.

I drew Maddie back into a hug. "You know how much I need these for the top of that new dresser. They're perfect."

"I didn't make them," she confessed.

"We won't tell anyone," I said, kissing the top of her head.

"Especially Mrs. Reed," she said. My friend Linda would be pleased to know that her unflinching reputation for do-it-yourself, and from-scratch, had spread to the next generation.

I didn't look forward to the day, one I was warned by the experts to expect, when it would no longer be cool to give Grandma this kind of welcome. But, ahem, my granddaughter was special, gifted, and very mature. It was quite possible she'd skip that rebellious phase. Taylor, four months younger, hadn't reached the coolness point either, so I had another powerhouse hug as I finally reached the front steps of her home.

"It's Uncle Henry's turn next," Maddie said. Her smile indicated that she knew exactly what she was doing.

I responded to a longer, gentler hug from Henry. I hoped there'd be no outgrowing those.

ATTORNEY Kay Courtland, Taylor's mother, brought the total to five for an early dinner. Kay was still in her business suit and pumps, dressed for her San Jose office, to which she'd have to return shortly, she informed us.

"I snuck out because I knew Grandpa's chicken and dumplings were on the menu," she said, looking at her young daughter. She dug into a full plate. "Don't worry, I promised Dad I'd take him a big helping."

"He's negotiating, right?" Taylor asked.

Taylor had learned the word, plus a few manipulation techniques from Maddie, who was the best negotiator in any age group. No matter what the issue, she was somehow able to work things around to what she wanted, all the while seeming to agree with everyone else. She certainly hadn't gotten that gene from her wimpy grandmother.

I mentally slapped the side of my head: Why hadn't we sent Team Maddie in to negotiate with Varena? She'd never have let Varena get away after her promise. Maddie would have walked out of the house, her skinny legs staggering under that Tudor, and plunked it in my trunk.

Kay addressed us all. "Bill's deep into merger negotiations with two big companies that want to swallow each other up. If we can keep them both happy, it'll be a great coup for the firm."

And I thought I had it tough, assigned to dollhouse detail. I gave an involuntary shudder, as if I'd suddenly been asked to help Bill seal the deal.

Taylor's parents, partners in their own downtown law firm, often worked late. One of the reasons a live-in grandfather was the perfect setup. The house had belonged to the Baker family since Kay was a toddler. More than once, Kay and Bill had come close to buying a home of their own, but no one in the group of four really wanted that, and for the time being, the combined Baker-Courtland plan was serving everyone's emotional and physical needs.

I tried to keep my description of my best dollhouse day thus far to a minimum, not monopolizing the conversation, but I couldn't help my verbal swooning over the Morleys' weeping-willow fountain and pool banked with flowers, which impressed even Kay.

"Too bad you couldn't take pictures," Taylor said.

"It'd be better if you just take us all with you, Grandma," was Maddie's predictable solution.

She pushed up the long sleeves of her bejeweled T-shirt, nearly identical to Taylor's, and mopped the last of the gravy on her plate with a small, deftly managed piece of biscuit.

Henry's turn for attention came when his daughter began a round of compliments. "I've made this recipe, Dad, but it never tastes as good," Kay said.

"That was the best chicken ever," according to Taylor.

Strange coming from her, since she'd eaten only a smidgen of meat while putting away three large dumplings. The same was true for Maddie, for whom a gourmet meal was pizza followed by ice cream followed by more ice cream. Though my plain brown hair was in stark contrast to Maddie's splendid red locks, the sweets gene was one she did inherit from me.

Henry was by far a better cook than I was. My specialty was baking, which was a lot more fun and smelled better. I wished I'd thought ahead of time to load my car with samples of my latest output of sweet things—chocolate pecan pie from a new recipe, and my special frosted triple-ginger cookies for which I humbly accepted prizes at bake-offs. I apologized to the group for showing up empty-handed.

"What? No dessert? I guess we'll all have to go to Sadie's." This from Maddie, the problem-solver, and the most loyal customer of Sadie's Ice Cream Shop.

"Or to my house," I offered.

"Your grandma always has tons of ice cream," Taylor mentioned, giving Henry and Kay a hint-hint look.

Dum, ta da dum, ta da dum, ta da dum.

My cell phone, the ring tone of which was regularly reprogrammed by Maddie, who refused to clue me in on how it was done. The current lively marching tune was the result of her being enthralled by the school band in her hometown as they practiced for a parade. I could think of many less agreeable tunes I'd had to live through.

I was tempted to let it ring through to voicemail, but saw that it was Skip. Probably June was working and he was calling around to find a good meal. Nothing would have pleased Maddie more than having her "uncle," technically her cousin-once-removed, join the dinner party. Skip teased her that as soon as he turned thirty, she'd lose interest.

"Hey, Aunt Gerry," he said. Not in a happy mood, I could tell. In fact, a very serious mood.

My throat tightened. "What's wrong?" I asked.

"How do you always know?"

"Just tell me it's not your mom."

"It's not Mom. She's totally over the episode from last week, good as new. She just called me from her assignment as a fake cop."

I breathed out and relaxed. Beverly's chronic heart problem was at bay for now. I rushed to her defense on other grounds. "Don't disparage your splendid corps of civilian volunteers."

"I wouldn't dream of it."

"So, then what is wrong?"

"It's about someone else's mom. It's Alexandra Rockwell."

It took a moment to reconnect the name Alexandra Rock-well with my new friend, Varena Young. "What's happened?" My head was dizzy with this convoluted loop, taking me back to the starting point.

"She's been murdered." Skip paused to let it sink in. "We took the call and got up here to Robert Todd Heights about an hour ago."

"Did you say, 'murdered'?"

My vision blurred for a moment. My cell phone seemed to be gaining weight as the seconds ticked by, as if the inanimate object had partaken of too many helpings of Henry's chicken and dumplings.

"Murdered?"

Why had I said the terrible word out loud? Twice. With my granddaughter and Henry's granddaughter present. I looked around at my table companions, all of whom had stopped eating and talking, their eyes widening.

I wished I could shrink my nearly six-foot frame into six inches and crawl into a dollhouse.

Chapter 4

I LEFT THE table before I further traumatized my family and friends and moved into the den, resigned to real life and Skip's awful news.

"Ms. Rockwell's—Young's—assistant found her in a room with this huge, I mean, huge dollhouse. I'm standing right outside the door of the room it's in. It's the biggest one I've ever seen, Aunt Gerry."

If Skip was trying to sidetrack me into discussing the merits of a dollhouse, albeit a magnificent one, it wasn't going to work this time. "Varena was in with Lord and Lady Morley?" I asked.

"Who are the Morleys? That name hasn't come up yet." Skip sounded understandably confused.

"That huge dollhouse. Morley's the name"—I almost said, "of the people who live there"—but switched in time to "the name of her largest dollhouse."

Had Varena gone looking for me? I wondered. If she were hurrying, she might have tripped on that beautiful long dress.

"Oh," Skip said, sounding still a bit confused, probably wondering why the name of a dollhouse mattered.

I guessed I hadn't trained him as well as I'd thought in miniature homes. But then, my dollhouses, the only ones he knew, weren't grand enough to need a name, especially not a noble one.

A tug at my shirt distracted me.

"Grandma? Grandma, is that Uncle Skip? Tell him I can help if he has a new case or anything."

I covered the mouthpiece with my hand. "In a little while,

42

Maddie. We're busy right now. Why don't you and Taylor serve dessert?"

"There isn't any."

Of course not. Hadn't we just figured that out?

Happily, Henry came into the den at that moment and picked her up, something I could no longer do. Her gangly body pretended to resist, her arms and legs flailing as he threw her over his shoulder. She couldn't contain the charming grin that said she was delighted at the game.

Taylor, who was letting her blond pixie cut grow out to Maddie's length, stood by in admiration at her "older" friend's boldness. I was glad to see Henry scoop his granddaughter up with his other arm, holding both girls for all of two seconds before letting them go. Still impressive for someone in his retirement years.

Back to my call. "How do you know Varena was killed, Skip? Couldn't she have fallen? That happens a lot at a certain age, you know."

Polite as he was, Skip didn't jump at the chance to remind me that he'd been a homicide detective for a few years now and could tell a murder from a non-murder, and that I should stick to baking and crafting.

"I'm here, Aunt Gerry, and I've seen the victim. I have to tell you it's pretty clear that she was murdered." He spoke without rebuke, in a slow, gentle tone that I appreciated.

"How...?"

I heard his familiar hesitation cough, signaling reluctance to share details. "Someone used a heavy object to...uh...kill her."

My arms had already turned weak; now I was in danger of dropping my newly burdensome phone on the floor. I looked out into Henry's dining room where the remnants of my dinner were visible. Bad idea. The chicken gravy had congealed in the shape of a brain, or a liver, or some other internal organ. Nothing that should see the light of day.

Varena. Heavy object. The juxtaposition was unthinkable. It was about time I stopped asking questions I didn't want the answers to.

I turned my head away, fighting back nausea, and met Henry's eyes. He put his hand on my elbow and all but sat me in one of the easy chairs. I wondered briefly if I'd have had such an intense reaction if I'd heard simply that Varena had died. What if I read a newspaper report in the next couple of days, or heard on the local news, that famous novelist and Lincoln Point resident Alexandra Rockwell, aka Varena Young, had succumbed to a heart attack or cancer, or had died of an undisclosed disease that she'd been suffering from for many years. I'd have been sad, surely, but not shocked or outraged, as if I myself had been attacked in front of Lord and Lady Morley's mansion.

Henry made a gesture that served to relay a message to Kay and the girls that they should start clearing the dishes from the table. That is, distract themselves for the time being.

This was a Henry moment, as I'd come to think of the times when he came through in a critical situation. Henry had the ability—talent?—to take control without being pushy or patronizing, to offer support in exactly the right measure while everyone else was dumbstruck.

I shifted in the soft leather chair, my eyes burning from holding back tears, my fingers sore from clutching the phone. How could the loss of someone I knew so briefly be affecting me this way? It must have been the dizzying speed of it all—I'd never gone so quickly from making a new friend to losing her.

"Aunt Gerry?" Skip's voice came from another world, perhaps the one inhabited by Lord and Lady Morley.

It occurred to me that if Varena had died of what we called natural causes, not only would I not be outraged, but I wouldn't be on the other end of a special phone call from my nephew, representing the Lincoln Point Police Department. And even with a determination of murder, I still wouldn't rate early notification. Unless there was another factor.

Why had Skip made this call to me directly from the crime scene? If he arrived only an hour ago, I must be one of the first to be notified of Varena's murder, outside of her own family and staff, I presumed.

"I'm here," I said finally. "Thanks for letting me know, Skip."

What else can you tell me? Why would anyone want to murder Varena Young? She seemed charming to me."

"Is this gigantic dollhouse I'm standing in front of the one you wanted her to donate to the library auction?"

Even in my deteriorating state, I recognized Skip's tactic of answering a question with one of his own. I'd learned to acquiesce. "No. Well, yes, but we knew that was out of the question," I said. "It's probably insured for way more than we could get for it at a Lincoln Point event. We would have been happy to have any of the houses in her collection, and"—I wondered if I were about to jinx the deal—"she offered us a midsize Tudor. I think."

"You think?"

"She did. She definitely did offer a Tudor, but she was called away before I could see it. When did this happen, Skip?"

"Not very long ago according to the M.E. Rough guess, a couple of hours, maybe less."

I looked at the tall mahogany grandfather clock in Henry's den, one he'd made in his own shop, of course. Six-fifteen. Varena might have been killed as early as four-fifteen? Had I narrowly missed running into a killer in the richest neighborhood in town?

"But that's very close to the time I left her home," I said. "I was there today. I left around three forty-five." I felt a chill all through my body. What if I'd been there? Could I have saved her? Would I have been a second victim?

"I know when you were here," Skip said.

"I don't remember telling you I was going to Robert Todd Heights today. I didn't make the call until after you left my house this morning."

"You didn't tell me. Ms. Rockwell's staff did. In fact, outside of the staff, you were the last person to see her alive."

I swallowed hard. I remembered the contentious loud voices, two definitely male, coming from the upper level of Varena's home.

"She left me for a meeting with her brother."

A pause. "Not possible. She doesn't have a brother. She has two children, a son and a daughter, both divorced. Alicia, the daughter, is a fashion designer; she's here now. We're tracking her son down. He's flying in from Washington, D.C. or someplace back east. There are also a couple of exes for the victim. But that goes way back and neither one is alive. No brother."

"She has a brother, Skip. Corazón, her maid or housekeeper, came to the Lord and Lady Morley room while Varena and I were talking. She interrupted us to tell Varena that her *brother* was upstairs." I made sure to emphasize the word.

I heard paper rustling and pictured Skip flipping through his spiral notebook. He preferred the old-fashioned kind that we used to call a stenographer's pad. I'd taken it upon myself to stay on the lookout for the outdated green lined pads and keep him supplied. I thought that I wouldn't like what he'd written on the pages this evening.

"Let's see. Corazón Cruz?" he asked. "She identified herself as part of the household staff. I spoke with her, and you know, I had a little trouble understanding her. She has a pretty heavy accent."

I got the message and I didn't like it.

"Her accent isn't that heavy, Skip. But I guess you did misunderstand her. I, on the other hand, am pretty used to Hispanic accents."

I knew my voice had risen. I'd come perilously close to scolding my nephew, as if he were eleven years old again and had skipped school to wander through Joshua Speed Woods. It was a good thing Henry had joined Kay and the girls, clanging away in the kitchen—to give me privacy, I knew.

Did I now have to remind this grown-up Skip that I'd been an ESL tutor since before he was born? Or that at least a third of the hundreds and hundreds of Abraham Lincoln High students I'd taught during my twenty-seven-year tenure had Spanish-speaking parents?

There was no way I'd misunderstood Corazón Cruz.

"Maybe she said something else," Skip said, still not hearing me. "Like, maybe another staff member, a guy, wanted to see the victim." More flipping sounds. "Laura Overbee, her personal assistant, and Paige Taggart, her research assistant, were both here all afternoon. Oh, and an old guy, probably close to the victim's age, who's her financial manager arrived around three-thirty. Quentin

Charles. Or Charles Quentin, I'm not sure, the way the first officer on the scene wrote it. Maybe one of these staff people sent
Corazón to get Ms. Young and she got mixed up."

He pronounced the housekeeper's name as an American
would: *Core*-a-zon. I wanted desperately to correct him: Cor-a-
son. If he couldn't say Corazón's name properly, with the accent
on the last syllable and the *z* pronounced close to an *s*, how could
he understand her? But I knew it wasn't a good idea to antago-
nize my nephew while he was in detective mode.

I couldn't contain a long, frustrated breath, however. Skip
had heard them often over the years. "May I please speak to
Corazón?" I asked, pronouncing her name like a native. "I'm
sure that if I could just have a minute with her, she'll remember
me and we can clear this up."

Skip caught himself, but I heard the beginnings of a laugh.
When you've helped raise a boy, you recognized his every sound
and tic.

Skip's father never returned from the first Gulf War. His Uncle Ken and I stepped in to help Beverly at a time when she was
often too devastated to take care of herself, let alone an energetic eleven-year-old boy. Skip grew up with our son, Richard,
as much in our home as his own.

Now that little redheaded boy was on the other end of the
line telling me I didn't hear what I knew I heard, that my ability
to understand a Hispanic accent was less than perfect.

Skip cleared his throat and apparently swallowed his laugh.
"Aunt Gerry, why don't we talk about this in person? We'd like
you to come downtown anyway, since you were the last—"

"One of the last," I said, thinking of the killer.

"One of the last people to see the victim. We'll need a formal
statement for the record."

"You sound as though I'm a suspect."

"You know the drill as well as I do, right?"

"Sure." I didn't intend to sound convincing.

"I'm leaving now and I need to make a couple of stops before
I go back to the station. I'll meet you there at, say, eight or so.
Can you do that?"

I grunted. "Of course, Detective Gowen."

I hung up and mentally canceled my plan to make an extra pecan pie, his favorite, for him before Thanksgiving dinner. If I kept that resolve to punish my nephew, it would be the first time.

HENRY joined me in the den carrying a cup of tea for me and a mug of coffee for himself.

"Perfect timing," he said, setting the drinks down. "Kay took the girls to Sadie's for ice cream to-go. They just left, so we have some time."

Another good Henry move. I stood and all but fainted into his arms, my head on his chest, not crying, not knowing exactly what I felt except that I was sad and confused. I felt a great loss at Varena's death and anger at the violence she suffered. Added to that, my frustration at Skip's denseness grew as I recalled our unsatisfactory conversation.

I tried to sink into Henry's comfortable embrace and believe everything would soon be clear.

After a few moments we settled on the couch. I took a sip of chamomile and gave Henry the short version of Skip's message.

"Strange," Henry said. "Was her English that bad?"

I bristled. "Not you, too."

"I'm kidding."

"Sorry. Maybe I am wound up."

"Let's talk about something else," he said. "Do you know how hard it was to get your granddaughter out of here?"

"I'm sure it wasn't easy. Did you have to promise to remember every word I tell you about the call from Skip?"

"Uh-huh. And it wasn't cheap, either—you're to persuade her father to get her a few million more RAMs, or whatever, of memory for her computer."

I laughed, picturing my granddaughter doing her best to co-operate, all the while negotiating and wanting to stay where the action was. "She has no idea what's going on, but she can smell a case from a mile away. I'm sure she offered her computer skills already."

Henry nodded, a grandfatherly grin on his face. "Do you think she's seriously headed for a career in investigative work? You've said she's been in this phase for quite a while."

"If so, hopefully it will be something that keeps her at a desk and not running around with a gun on her hip. It's bad enough that my only nephew does that for a living." My thick-headed nephew, I added to myself.

"Let me drive you to the station later. I don't like to see you driving alone when you're upset."

"I'm calmed down now," I said, only half-truthfully.

"You just found out someone you'd created a bond with was murdered, and you nearly witnessed it. It's dark and you don't know how close to the station you'll be able to park. Do you need any more reasons?" He took my hand. "Here's another. I'd feel much better driving you."

I thought how I'd been on my own in the years since Ken died, and essentially alone during his two-year illness. Ken's sister, Beverly, had been a great help, as was nurse Linda and all my friends, but at the end of the day, I was by myself and responsible for myself. I'd become used to it.

When Henry first came into my life, I resisted his solicitousness, but I was finding it easier every day to accept his steady, caring presence. I hoped I'd brought half as much to his life.

"Okay," I said, enjoying Henry's surprised look.

"Wow, just like that?"

I kissed his cheek, patted his nearly bald head, and prepared to slap a condition on my acquiescence. He gave me a look that said he expected nothing less.

"Just like that, but I need to make a stop on the way."

"You want to go home and change?"

"Not exactly."

Dum, ta da dum, ta da dum, ta da dum.

A call from Maddie on my marching-band cell phone.

I considered not taking it, but I knew Maddie's persistence and I didn't want to hear marching tunes all evening. One of these days I was going to learn how to silence my ringer. If she'd teach me.

"Hi, sweetheart. Lucky you, hanging around an ice cream shop. And on a school night."

Maddie blew a raspberry as only an eleven-year-old could. "Uncle Henry made me come. I wanted to hear about Uncle Skip's new case. It must have been a case, right? The way you were talking."

"You'll hear about it soon enough."

"Aunt Kay says she might have to do another errand but I think she's stalling. Can we come back now?"

"Don't forget to pick up Sadie's double chocolate for Aunt Beverly in case she comes by."

"Now you're stalling, Grandma. Nuts!"

I couldn't resist. "No nuts, just plain chocolate sauce for me." I heard an involuntary laugh. "Okay, okay."

Oh, dear. A *nuts* followed by a double *okay*. My poor granddaughter. These were standby expressions she'd abandoned a while ago. That she was reverting to her younger self was a sure sign of stress.

And I was about to make it worse.

"Let me talk to Aunt Kay, please, sweetheart."

I heard Maddie's loud, meaningful groan, then Kay's greeting.

"I have a big favor to ask, Kay," I said. I looked at Henry to be sure he was listening also, since this was the condition I was placing on letting him drive me around town. "I know you're anxious to get back to your office—"

"Not anymore. Bill called to say the deal's settled. *Ta da*. I married a genius. He's on his way home. What do you need?"

"I'm going to coax your dad into taking me on an errand. You can come home anytime but, sorry to say, you'll have to deal with Maddie when she finds out we're not here."

Kay laughed. "It's a good thing I've had practice with the little blond clone here. We'll be fine."

How had I managed to find a second unbeatable family?

Chapter 5

WHEN I RETURNED from a quick freshening up, Henry had
on his leather jacket and held his keys in his hand.

"Let's go," he said, holding out one of my warm coats that I
left at his house for emergencies. Another small advance in the
mutual domesticity that had evolved within the past few months.

"If you don't mind, I think I have time for an errand before
we head for the police station," I began.

"I know. I figured we'd be able to brush up on our Spanish
on the way to the Heights."

"How did you know?"

He gave me a sideways look. "When are you going to realize
how wonderfully predictable you are?"

"I need to pay my respects to my friend's family."

"Of course you do," Henry said, his expression telling me he
was aware of my full agenda.

I also had to find and talk to Corazón.

In my mind I was on this mission for Maddie as much as
for myself. Neither her parents nor I were happy about the fact
that she was so captivated by law enforcement, relishing "cases,"
a word she'd picked up when she'd barely reached the age of reason
and had loved ever since.

Her favorite trip by far in recent years was not to one of the
many California theme parks we'd taken her to at great expense.
No, her dream trip had been to the Lincoln Point police building
for a tour Skip had arranged. The treat, complete with snacks in
the officers' lounge, was part of a bargain she'd made when her
computer skills helped him on a case.

The best strategy to secure a gun-free future for my grand-daughter was for me to clear up the part of Skip's case that I was directly involved with and then withdraw, taking Maddie with me.

Thanks to my nephew's stubbornness, I never got to tell him about the argument I'd overheard between Varena and her nonexistent brother and another man. With any luck, the police would find the brother, determine what the fight was about, and solve her murder quickly.

For the rest, I hoped the library auction would benefit from one midsize Tudor given in Varena Young's memory.

A few small details to send the police in the right direction, and I was done. Then there'd be no case for Maddie or me.

"Corazón Cruz, be warned," Henry said as we buckled our seat belts.

I couldn't have said it better. His accent was impeccable.

THE Robert Todd Heights visitors' list hadn't been updated since I'd visited this afternoon, so we had no problem at the checkpoint. Henry drove his white SUV along the perimeter of the properties and into Varena's semicircular driveway where my own car had been only a few hours ago. Several other vehicles dotted the blacktop area now, a couple of which I recognized from the Lincoln Point PD fleet.

The stately ambience had been adulterated with crime scene tape and a uniformed officer. I'd expected this scenario and wasn't too worried about its cramping my style. Between the large pool of ALHS graduates who'd been my students before they entered the police academy, and the number of Skip's colleagues who'd benefited from my tins of ginger cookies, I had many friends among the local law enforcement community.

As we pulled up closer to the front door, I saw the first good omen—indeed the officer on duty was one of my former students, Renee Hirsch. When I saw her sashaying back and forth along the path, begging for a visit from an old, beloved teacher, I knew things were going my way.

I tapped lightly on the side window of the SUV as a way of pointing her out to Henry.

"Class of 2000," I said. "Not the most insightful student, but she wrote a very good paper on how the Great Depression impacted Steinbeck's female characters. A solid B-plus."

I knew that Henry, who'd taught shop at ALHS as many years as I'd taught English, would understand my shorthand and wouldn't be surprised that I remembered a thirty-ish alum.

"Kids?" he asked, trying to help me reconnect with her.

I thought back. "I've got it. What's that sport where they hit a ball that's sitting on a post?"

"T-ball. Go for it."

"Thanks." I opened the door to step out of his car.

"What do you want from me?" Henry asked.

"I'd rather you stay here for now," I said.

"I'll just walk around a bit so they know you have backup."

"Six-shooter drawn?" I asked.

"Whatever you need."

It was what I had come to expect.

I got out of the car and began another journey to Varena's front door, this time with a heavy heart.

Except for the sound of the wind, which had picked up considerably since this afternoon, it was deadly quiet on the hilltop. Traffic noises from the streets below were barely a whisper and the birds and the beasts that lived in the surrounding woods seemed to have retired early this evening, perhaps in honor of the recently, dearly departed.

I pulled my coat close and made my way to Officer Hirsch. I wondered who owned the vehicles that weren't unmarked Lincoln Point PD inventory. I knew very little about cars but I could tell spanking new from old and weathered, and ordinary hood ornaments from high end. I was back in top-of-the-line country.

My eyes were drawn to the east side of the house where I knew the Morleys' elegant miniature home was situated. I remembered one of the last things I'd seen before the fight broke out upstairs—place settings with delicate eggcups that, according to local miniaturists' lore, had been painted with a one-haired brush. Although those details seemed trivial now, I wished I were returning to see more of the dollhouse's treasures. I wished their owner were alive and vibrant in her red dress, as she had been this afternoon.

"Officer Hirsch," I said with a tiny salute, as Renee, all five-three of her, started toward me.

"Hey, Mrs. Porter?" she said, surprise and a touch of student-teacher intimidation in her voice, as if I'd come to collect much-overdue homework.

It never failed that students reverted to their classroom days and attitudes when they saw me, as if tests were never really over and a teacher could pull a grade and lower it, revoking a diploma, no matter how much time had passed. Over the years, the phenomenon had come in handy.

"Nice to see you, Renee. I read about your son's team taking the T-ball championship. That must have been pretty exciting."

"Oh, yeah, thanks. He takes after his father. I told him to go pro and make it possible for his parents to live up here."

"Not a happy place now, though," I said.

"I know." Renee took off her hat and swung it to encompass the Rockwell Estate, her expression turning serious. "Awful thing, huh?"

"Yes, I was here just this afternoon, visiting Ms. Young."

"I heard that."

Of course she had. I took a deep, sad breath. "I was hoping I could have just a minute to pay my respects."

I waved in the general direction of the yellow tape, as if that flimsy piece of plastic, and not police department protocol, were all that stood between me and my friend's grieving family.

"I don't see why not, Mrs. Porter. M.E., evidence people, everybody's gone anyway. Even your nephew, the Skipper."

How well I knew. "It would mean so much if I could make a short visit with anyone who's available."

"Tell you what, go right up and give a quick knock. I'll be over there a ways if you need anything."

"Thanks, Renee."

High school teachers' salaries were low, but you couldn't beat the perks.

———

FOR the second time today, Laura Overbee answered my knock. She was wearing a black sweater set this time, clearly following the protocol for mourning, and she wasn't pleased to see me.

"Mrs. Porter," she said, laboriously, as if I'd been trying to sell her a set of household brushes. She was understandably unaware how easily I could be dismissed. "Did you leave something behind?"

My first thought, which I held back, was, *Yes, I forgot to take the midsize Tudor my friend Varena wanted me to have.*

"I wondered if I could please speak to Ms. Cruz for just a minute?"

Forceful as ever, was I.

A heavy sigh from the much-beleaguered Ms. Overbee. "This is not a good time. I don't know whether you've heard, but Ms. Young has passed away."

Ugh. Why hadn't I thought of expressing condolences first?

"Yes, and I was so sorry," I said, a little late. "It's certainly a great loss for all of us."

"Indeed," said the stiff Ms. Overbee, who was too young for that usage.

She moved the door a few inches closer to its closed position. I forced myself to remember that this gatekeeper was young enough to be my daughter. She was slightly shorter than I was. Only my diffidence made her seem to tower over me.

For courage, I turned slightly to see Henry, bigger than both of us, a mere few yards away, and Renee a little behind him, armed.

I steeled myself, leaned in and wedged my elbow, laden with my clunky purse as leverage, into the doorway.

"I just need a few minutes with Ms. Cruz and I'll be on my way." I waved my hand in the direction of the lowlands, to where I would happily retreat after my brief interview with a member of the household staff.

Ms. Overbee's jaw tightened. I could tell she was struggling to maintain the decorum fitting her role. "Ms. Cruz is not here."

"Please, it's very important that I talk to her, Ms. Overbee. Can you tell me where I can find her or when she'll be back?"

Suddenly, we were not alone. Through the narrow crack Ms. Overbee allowed me, I saw a tall man come up behind her.

"Trouble here, Laura?" he asked. His voice was deep and carried an air of authority.

"Nothing I can't handle, Charles," she said, her flustered behavior not matching her words. "This is Varena's friend, Mrs. Porter."

He moved her aside and opened the door, showing his full height, eye level with me, but with higher and whiter hair. This must be the man Skip had mentioned as Varena's financial manager.

"Mrs. Porter, Charles Quentin here."

I took his hand and gave it a quick shake before he knew what was happening. "It's a pleasure to meet you," I said, in the manner of a Varena Young Regency romance heroine.

"Yes." He let out a grunt that sounded more like confusion than annoyance, but I knew he was on the edge. "If you must know, Mrs. Porter, Ms. Cruz is no longer in service here."

It sounded as though the Rockwell Estate had disconnected Corazón Cruz, as if she were a telephone number.

"Can you tell me how to reach her? It's very important."

Mr. Quentin—his bearing inspired me to think of him as Lord Quentin—sized me up. What exactly he was assessing, I didn't know. IQ? Threat level? Whatever the numbers, I must have measured up because he invited me into the foyer.

Barely.

He dismissed Laura with a wave and stood with me at the foot of the grand double staircase. No invitation to sit in the music room as Ms. Overbee had granted me this afternoon.

"You were visiting earlier today, Mrs. Porter. Is that right?"

"Yes, I was."

"We're very sorry you had to be here for this tragedy. I hope you didn't hear anything or were witness to anything that would upset you?"

"No, not at all. I left about a half hour before—" I paused and changed tack. "Ms. Young was about to give me—"

"Ms. Young was very generous and gave to many charities.

I'm sure yours is listed and will be taken care of once the estate is settled."

"But, I—"

"Now please excuse us while we deal with family matters."

One more try. "I would very much like to get in touch with Corazón Cruz," I said. "And then I won't bother you again."

"We don't expect any further contact with her."

"Perhaps you have an address where you'll send her severance check?"

"Thank you for stopping by, Mrs. Porter. Have a good evening." Charles Quentin led me to the door, his hand on my elbow. He closed the door on me with a smooth, firm motion.

First there's no brother, now no contact with Corazón?

As I stood on the wrong side of the enormous door with its lion's head knocker, the wind whipped around my head. I could have sworn I heard an owl in the distance. It was all too easy to think of Heathcliff and the moors. I nearly laughed.

Had I wandered into the land where Lord and Lady Morley dwelled?

HENRY drove off the Rockwell property and stopped at a lookout on the road home. The night sky was beautiful over the mostly dark hills, providing some comfort after a disheartening hour. No better place for us to sit and try to make sense of what I'd just been told.

I put my hand to my forehead, frustrated with myself. "Why didn't I think of asking Ms. Overbee or Mr. Quentin about Varena's brother?"

"From what you've said, neither one of them was inclined to answer any questions anyway," Henry said. "Look at the bright side. Neither one claimed that Corazón Cruz doesn't exist."

"True, but small consolation."

"Maybe she ran away because she killed the lady," Henry suggested.

"Or she witnessed the murder and is afraid for her own life."

"Is she illegal?" Henry asked. "She might have split knowing there'd be all kinds of law enforcement snooping around."

"I can't imagine Varena using anyone who wasn't here legally. She was too public a figure."

"Many a public figure has been brought down by just such an oversight," Henry reminded me.

"Good point. But wouldn't she have run sooner? Corazón has already been interviewed by Skip."

"The heavy-accent incident."

I made a face, close to one Maddie might have put on. "So he says. Maybe I can persuade him to give me her contact information since apparently he has no intention of using it."

"Another possibility is that Corazón was Varena Young's favorite and once she was gone, her kids fired the lady. For all we know, they fired all the current help, to bring in their own. It happens."

I nodded. Worth thinking about, though it seemed to me that would be pretty fast action. "Skip said Varena's daughter was there this evening and they were waiting for her son. I wish I'd met her children. Alicia and Adam."

"You worried about getting that Tudor?"

"That, too, I guess. But I'm still curious about the brother."

"It could also be that Corazón was lying, simple as that. Maybe as a way of getting you out of there so the family could be alone. You know, a brother is more important than you, that kind of thing."

While I considered Henry's new theories, a car pulled up alongside us, lights flashing, a security company seal visible on the side. Uh-oh, were we trespassing? Apparently admission past the checkpoint didn't mean you could wander around the exclusive Robert Todd Heights at will.

A uniformed man, too old to have been my student, got out of the vehicle, holding his flashlight high and at a sharp angle. If he was trying to blind us, it was working.

Henry rolled down his window. "Evening, Officer," he said in his usual cooperative, nonthreatening tone. "I'm Henry Porter. My wife and I just paid our respects to the Rockwell family. Terrible thing, wasn't it?"

The guard nodded, maintaining a suspicious look in his eyes. "You finish your business now?"

"Yes, sir. We were heading back when we stopped to take a look at the view and compose ourselves."

I dabbed at my eyes in support of Henry's narrative.

The guard rolled his tongue around his mouth and nodded again, seeming sold on the story. Either he was at the end of his shift and not interested in a complication or he judged Henry to be a model citizen. As long as he didn't arrest us, it didn't matter which. "Okay, well, you have a nice evening."

"You, too. Thank you, Officer."

Henry backed out of the spot and I let out my breath.

"'Henry Porter'?" I said.

He shrugged. "I figured if they checked, they'd see 'Porter' on the access list for today and wouldn't run my plates, which I'm sure the guy wrote down."

"Should I be worried that you slipped into a con so easily?"

"What did you think of the 'my wife and I' part?" he asked, turning slightly in my direction.

My pulse returned to its accelerated mode. I looked straight ahead as if I were the one responsible for keeping the shiny white SUV on the road.

Dum, ta da dum, ta da dum, ta da dum.

Maddie on my cell phone. I was never more grateful for an interruption. I clicked the phone on without a glance at Henry "Porter."

"Wait till you see what's here, Grandma. When are you coming home, home, home?" Maddie asked.

Oh, my. Were we entering a triplicate phase? What kind of grandmother puts an innocent, loving child through such misery? "Where are you and the other girls now, sweetheart?"

"Home. Your home this time, Grandma. Aunt Kay stopped by here so I could get my flash drive since you've been Away So Long."

That was Maddie's capital-letter tone.

"I know it seems that way, but we have just one more errand

and then I'll be home." I wanted to say, "Home, home, home," but didn't care to annoy my little darling further.

I'd nearly forgotten our real errand tonight was to get me to the police station. I didn't look forward to meeting Skip with no new evidence that Varena Young had a brother, one she may have fought with shortly before she was murdered.

"Wait till you see what's here," Maddie said, repeating the thrust of her message.

It was too late for a mail delivery or any other kind of shipping service. "What's there, sweetheart? A ton of ice cream, I'll bet."

"I don't think I'll tell you since you've been Away So Long."

"I guess I'll have to wait," I said, knowing there wasn't a chance that Maddie could hold out.

"Okay, okay, I'll tell you. It's a dollhouse. There's no box or crate or anything, just a humungous plastic bag. Did you order it, Grandma? Is it for us?"

Dare I think it? Varena's Tudor? She couldn't have had time to arrange a delivery before meeting her vicious end.

"What does it look like?"

"It's really big. It was outside on the step. It was just sitting there, and it took all three of us to push it into the atrium. It's a really cool house. All streamlined."

I hadn't been dreaming. Maybe Varena had arranged days ago for the dollhouse to be sent, long before our visit. Maybe Doris Ann contacted Varena herself or appointed someone else and neglected to tell me. I nearly cheered out loud.

I paused in my thinking. Maddie had called the house streamlined. I wouldn't have described a Tudor as streamlined.

"Is it a Tudor, Maddie? Remember all the different styles of architecture we saw at Shellie's store in San Carlos?"

"I know what a Tudor is, Grandma. It's the one with all the little brown beams everywhere on the outside and lead in the windows and the roof is thatchy."

Her Grandpa would have been proud.

"That's right. And you're saying this dollhouse is more modern?"

"Like, super-modern. There's a lot of furniture, too. It got all thrown around, so we're fixing it up. But even the furniture is modern. It's all glassy and plain. Like Frank Lord Wright."

Close enough.

More important was that Varena or her family had come through somehow and we had one of her dollhouses for our bookmobile auction. Tudor or modern, it didn't matter to me.

"The police station next," I said to Henry, my mood almost cheery.

What could go wrong now that there was a new dollhouse in my atrium?

Chapter 6

THE LINCOLN POINT police station was about as far as one could drive from the lavish homes on the Heights and still be within city limits. We housed our law enforcement officers and detectives in the oldest building in town, at the edge of Civic Center. City Hall stood in the middle of the complex, with the library on the opposite side from the police department. The set of three buildings, all large and white, screamed "government."

A quote from the man we thought of as our town's "founder," Abraham Lincoln, dominated the center portico: I MUST STAND WITH ANYBODY THAT STANDS RIGHT, AND STAND WITH HIM WHILE HE IS RIGHT, AND PART WITH HIM WHEN HE GOES WRONG.

"Tough love," Skip called it.

At eight o'clock on a Monday evening, the grand plaza in front of the buildings was lit by a row of streetlights along the perimeter of the semicircular Civic Drive. With both City Hall and the library closed, the police station's windows were the only ones with signs of life.

"Don't bother to park," I said, as Henry and I approached the end of Springfield Boulevard. "I'll get out in front of the station. Skip can drive me home when we're done."

"You don't want me to go in with you?"

I shook my head. "I'll be fine. If Skip's too busy to take me home, I'll call Beverly or Linda or—"

"I get it," he said. "If I'm in there with you, it will look too much like a date gone bad."

He'd read my mind. I had to stop underestimating Henry's propensity for razor-sharp insights.

"I don't want to impose," I said. A half truth.

"Here's an idea. I'll browse around Rosie's bookshop, and you can call me when you're ready to leave." He pointed to the corner opposite the police station. "She'll be open until at least nine. And if you're later than that, I'll start thinking about posting bail."

I finally agreed. Henry would have a good time with our friend Rosie Norman, who owned the only bookshop in town. And I wouldn't have to feel self-conscious with Henry on my arm, raising eyebrows.

One of these years I'd stop worrying about what others might or might not be thinking and the position of the town gossips' eyebrows. Probably the same year I became a good saleswoman, negotiator, and fund-raiser.

I'D been in the halls of the LPPD and in Skip's cubicle often enough, but never in an interview room by myself. I was as nervous as if I'd been caught wielding a blunt object or a butcher knife. I wished I'd brought supplies like a bucket of paint and a sewing kit so I could fix up the walls and the torn seat cushion. The whole building needed a going-over, but this room was the worst I'd seen. Also, the temperature seemed to hover around freezing.

The rooms for witnesses or visitors were much nicer. Was this the room the police used for number-one suspects? Providing the most unpleasant ambience possible? If so, why was I here?

As the minutes passed, my uneasiness grew and Henry's comment about posting bail seemed less a joke.

When the door opened at eight-thirty, I jumped, hitting my knee on the metal table.

"Ouch," said a broad-shouldered woman wearing a dark blue, loose-cut skirted suit.

I didn't think I'd ever seen her before. I figured her to be in her late thirties and tried to extrapolate her features back to her teens when I might have had her in class. As good as I was, I couldn't claim to remember absolutely every student I'd ever taught or every colleague of Skip's I'd ever taken cookies to, but I would have bet a few pieces of miniature furniture that I'd never given this woman a grade.

"You okay?" she asked, pointing toward my knee.

"I'm fine." Just a bruised ego. *Who are you?* almost slipped out.

She took a seat across from me and gave me a closed-mouth smile. "I'm Detective Rutherford, Detective Gowen's partner at the moment. I'm new in town, but I've heard all about you, Mrs. Porter."

I smiled back, sure that she had. I wished I'd heard about her. My considerable language skills seemed to have abandoned me and I mumbled something trivial about hoping what she'd heard were good things.

"It's Geraldine, and I'm glad to meet you," I added.

Where was Skip? And why hadn't he told me about a new partner—female at that? As far as I knew, Detective Rutherford was the first woman in the Lincoln Point Homicide Division. I'd been assigned the one detective I didn't know. Practice for her or intimidation for me? I couldn't wait to find out.

"I know you're probably used to special attention, Mrs. Porter, but this is a murder investigation and we have to take it by the book from the top." While mixing metaphors, Detective Rutherford adopted a prayerful position for her hands, beating a rhythm on the table with her steepled fingertips, keeping her thumbs crossed.

I stiffened. "Of course."

"How well did you know the victim?" Her fingers beat the table at "know" and "victim."

"Ms. Rockwell?" I asked, meaning, *She has a name.*

"Ms. Rockwell," Detective Rutherford granted.

"I just met Ms. Rockwell today, but like everyone else in town, I've known of her as Varena Young for some time."

"She was a duchess, I understand."

"I've heard that."

Detective Rutherford flipped through pages in a notebook. I suspected it was for show, that she was simply playing off a script she knew by heart and didn't really need help remembering the facts of the case.

For about a half hour, Detective Rutherford had me repeat what she must have known if she'd bothered to consult with my nephew. Why had I gone to the estate? What time did I get there? What time did I leave? What was the purpose of my visit, which, I didn't point out, was the same as "Why had I gone to the estate?" Did I see or hear anything unusual?

I took the "anything unusual" question as an opportunity to report on Corazón Cruz's message to me about Varena's brother and my subsequent overhearing of an argument possibly between him and Varena and another male.

"Yes, I have that here from Detective Gowen."

"Have you located her brother?"

"You also told Detective Gowen that you left the victim's residence around three forty-five?"

I gritted my teeth, resigned, but not happy. "Yes, I did."

"And you went straight home?"

"No, I went to a friend's home. He'd picked up my grand-daughter and I—"

"The name of your friend?"

I hated to give Henry's name and contact information to this loathsome woman, but I had no choice. "Henry Baker."

"I understand Ms. Young also had a very valuable dollhouse collection."

"That's correct."

It wasn't like me to answer just this side of monosyllables. I shouldn't have been intimidated by this woman. If she wasn't a former student, she was certainly of an age to have been sitting in front of me nearly twenty years ago, fretting over a pop quiz on comparing and contrasting the comedies and tragedies of William Shakespeare. I threw my shoulders back. She's the one who should be intimidated. I had to work on my confidence skills.

Detective Rutherford disentangled her fingers and sat back. She glanced at the ceiling and I followed suit. I wondered if she had the same thought about the spotty soundproofing, with tiles scattered over the ceiling and one wall, a project that was either coming or going. No wonder assorted wails and thumps from the hallway seeped through. With all my senses on high alert, I heard every groan and imagined handcuffed riffraff passing by outside the room.

"Did you kind of wish it were yours?" she asked.

"Excuse me?"

"You do dollhouses, right?"

Do dollhouses? Like Debbie does Dallas? I let out a sigh and bit my lower lip. "I'm a miniaturist, yes."

"So. The dollhouse collection. Did you envy it?"

"Excuse me?" I said again, this time more forcefully.

She sat back and put her hands in the shallow pockets of her jacket. "Did you envy Ms. Young's dollhouse collection?"

My inner English teacher cringed at her incorrect usage. Envy was directed toward people, not things.

"Are you asking if I'm envious of Ms. Young because of her dollhouse collection?"

"You tell me," she said.

I folded my arms, reeking of confidence. "No," I said.

I felt a growl at the edge of my throat. I scanned the bare room as if I'd missed something in the last hour. Skip, perhaps, standing in the corner, laughing at the prank. Maybe the woman was his latest girlfriend and this was his idea of a clever way to introduce us. I couldn't hold onto that idea very long, however. He and my neighbor, June Chinn, seemed a solid couple.

Even if Skip were uncommitted, I couldn't think of a worse match than Detective Rutherford—too serious and full of self-importance on the personality side, and too old and too solidly built in the looks department. Skip preferred slight, girly girls, as he called them, probably to annoy his mother and me, women who could hold their own in a teasing match. The woman grilling me was singularly not a teaser, large-boned, and looked like she could throw a mean punch. I doubted she'd ever played with a dollhouse or been fascinated by a four-inch-high working fountain.

"Any chance she willed one or two to you?" she asked.

I thought of the dollhouse that arrived in my garage a couple of hours ago. It had not been willed to me. And I hadn't actually seen it. All I had was hearsay from an eleven-year-old. I had no reason to assume the dollhouse had been willed to me from the Rockwell Estate.

"No."

Detective Rutherford breathed a heavy sigh. "Let's go back to the time of the crime, Mrs. Porter." She flipped through her small notebook. "Your meeting with the victim was in a room with a very large dollhouse."

No question, no answer.

"Did you touch anything in the room?"

"Yes."

Another heavy sigh. I expected the detective to slap handcuffs on me any second. "What did you touch, Mrs. Porter?"

"I handled many of the artifacts in the dollhouse." I elected not to utter Lord and Lady Morley's names in this room with this wretched interrogator. "A tiny signature plate from Currier and Ives, a chair made from an emerald brooch, the lace canopy over the bed in the main bedroom." I threw up my hands. "Lots of things. I'm not sure I can remember everything. Did you locate Varena's brother, by the way?" I asked, thinking it was worth another shot.

"And in the rest of the room? Did you handle anything other than what was in the dollhouse?"

I didn't expect the detective to acknowledge my question about Varena's brother. I was embarrassed to acknowledge that I merely wanted to annoy her. Tit for tat. Very mature.

"I sat down for a minute. I suppose I touched parts of the chair. The life-size chair."

"Anything else?"

What was the point of nagging me? I wanted to run from the room, find Skip, drag him into a corner, and give him what-for.

Then it dawned on me.

"There's a sword set on the wall and a replica in the dollhouse. I ran my hand over the longest sword in both sets. The life-size one and the mini one." I felt an anxious twinge. Skip had said Varena was struck with a heavy object. "Was one of the swords the murder weapon? Is that why you're asking?"

Detective Rutherford pushed herself away from the table, as if the game were over and she'd finally won.

"Thank you Mrs. Porter. You can go for now."

She was out the door in a flash.

I was right behind her. For now.

I LET the heavy door slam at my heels and took my first deep breath in a long time.

It said something about the awfulness of the interview room that the police station corridor, with its quota of DUIs and other generators of unhealthy odors, seemed like fresh air.

I dusted the back of my pants as if I'd been sitting in the gutter. I searched the noisy, busy area for my nephew, making elaborate plans for when I got my hands on him.

There was no sign of Skip, but I saw Henry off in a corner near a vending machine. A glance at the battered wall clock told me it was well after nine, Rosie's closing time. Henry was engaged in deep conversation with a tall woman in a vibrant, flowing outfit.

My breath caught. Was that Varena Young? Was this all a mistake? A rumor, nothing more, that she'd been murdered?

The interview with Detective Rutherford had robbed me of my good judgment. I saw now that the woman was a much younger version of my friend. She had to be Alicia, Varena Young's daughter.

I could hardly wait to meet her. Except, she'd stood up and appeared ready to leave. I rushed toward the corner, nearly knocking over a female officer and coming perilously close to sending someone's cup of coffee to the floor.

Still I was too late. With great dismay, I saw the blues and purples of Alicia's diaphanous cloak float out of the station. I could have sprinted to cut her off, but I was already slightly out of breath and knew it wouldn't be a pretty sight. Of all times to worry about protocol.

Henry stood and put his arm around my waist, a calming gesture and a gentle message not to run.

"Don't worry. I have it all on tape," he said, with a comforting grin.

I wished he weren't kidding.

MADDIE could be put off for just so long before she forgot her manners. While Henry and I walked to his SUV, I called my home phone line, knowing Maddie would answer.

"Hello?" she said, in that way that translated into a reminder that we'd been gone forever. Away So Long. "We've already had our ice cream. Aunt Kay said we'd better not wait since it's a school night and we need to be in bed soon. And you haven't even seen the dollhouse yet."

The girl knew how to scold. Where had she learned the technique? Looking way into the future, I pitied her children.

"I'm sorry, sweetheart. I'll be there to tuck you in. Everything took longer than we expected."

"What everything?"

Nice try, but Grandma was getting wiser every day, just to keep up. "I'm glad you had your dessert. Put Kay on for a minute, would you?"

Maddie sent a loud, meaningful sigh across the wires. I wasn't too worried since my granddaughter was easy to win back.

I hated to admit that I'd been wrong about my readiness to give up involvement in the case. I couldn't drop it while the police were uninterested in my valuable input. Since when did an argument moments before a murder not count? Since when was a documented reference to a victim's brother dismissed?

I'd find a way for Maddie to use her computer skills in a harmless way in the investigation, maybe to track down Varena's brother.

First I had to find a way to use my own skills. I turned to look back at the police station, its windows still alive with lights. I wondered if Detective Rutherford was writing up a report on me. After my treatment this evening, Skip owed me a place in the investigation.

"We'll be home in about fifteen minutes," I told Kay when she came on the line. "I'm so sorry to hold you up all this time."

"Not a problem," said Henry's daughter who had the calm gene, leading me to believe I'd been misjudging lawyers all these years. "Maddie gave me the greatest present. I'm always complaining about my dry hands, so she gave me this wonderful, buttery hand cream from a specialty store in Monterey."

I didn't remember Maddie's being on a recent trip to Monterey. But it was less than two hours from her Palo Alto home and there certainly could have been a day trip I didn't hear about. "Did I miss your birthday?" I asked Kay.

"No. This was just an unsolicited gift. Very sweet."

I allowed myself a little puff of pride, thinking of the no-occasion miniature earrings Maddie gave me earlier today. I wondered if my son had increased his daughter's allowance.

We'd reached Henry's car. I strapped myself into the SUV. "We have only about ten minutes to get home before Maddie goes into overdrive," I said. "What did you learn from Alicia?"

"She says she has no uncle," Henry said, wasting no time.

My heart sank. No uncle for Alicia meant no brother for Varena. "How about an aunt with a deep voice?" I asked.

We gave ourselves a moment to laugh about the fantasy of a masculine-looking lady who sang baritone.

"Alicia—she's a fashion designer by the way—says there's no family beyond her own brother and their ex-spouses. Varena was the last of her generation."

Henry seemed embarrassed to tell me, but it wasn't his fault.

"I'm stumped," I said.

"Maybe you did—"

I held up my hand. "Please don't say I misunderstood." I relaxed and took a long breath. "Did Alicia leave you with *any* useful tidbit?" My tone was harsher than it should have been.

"Not that I can think of."

I blew out another breath, this one sounding louder. "Well, that's that."

"But I did arrange for you to have lunch with her tomorrow."

I gasped. "Henry!"

California had a strict law against cell phone use while driving, but as far as I knew there was none against smooching.

Chapter 7

I HADN'T BEEN home since my trip to the Rockwell Estate in midafternoon. After a taste of luxury living on Robert Todd Heights, my lowland quarters seemed unworthy of being called a "residence."

Many thought my home was special—an Eichler house built in the sixties by a developer who was ahead of his time, bringing indoors and outdoors together in an efficient design. At the center was a large atrium, topped with a retractable skylight, that served as a living area in any weather. The major rooms of the house opened onto this court, the edges of which were nicely landscaped.

I'd always loved it. Now, after only a few minutes in Varena Young's environment, my home seemed small and unremarkable. Fortunately, the people in my Eichler made up for its lackluster appearance.

Plus, it now held a brand new dollhouse. Actually, a new old dollhouse, since this treasure was obviously a few years old, close to an antique except that it had been repainted in places.

Kay and the girls had managed to set up a card table in the atrium and install the streamlined, cantilevered structure at a level convenient for viewing and working.

"Watch this, Grandma," Maddie said, flicking a switch on the second floor. Lamps, track lighting, and modern sconces came on in the bedrooms, bathroom, and hallway. A tiny reading light attached to a book on a bedside table was the first I'd ever seen.

"Impressive," Henry said.

Taylor got to flick the second switch, squealing at the same

time. I was bowled over when a television set in the living room
clicked on. We stared at a tiny screen that showed a football game.
In action. On a screen less than two inches on the diagonal. With
sound. Obviously a retrofit from the original house. Someone
had been working on this for decades. Varena? It was hard to
imagine she'd have time, in between writing several books a year
and touring the country.

"Beyond impressive," Henry said, and I agreed. Never mind
that I wouldn't have chosen a sports event to showcase such an
amazing piece of dollhouse furniture. The effect was marvelous.

"It's an MP4 player," Maddie said.

"Of course it is," Henry said.

Maddie assured us there were even more astounding features
to our latest acquisition, but thirty-four years married to an architect notwithstanding, I'd had it with houses. First Varena's residence, then Lord and Lady Morley's miniature mansion, now a
completely wired, modern-looking dollhouse that seemed ready
for a biological family to move in.

"I'm buildinged out," I said. "Maybe we can pick this up
tomorrow."

"You've never done that before," Maddie said.

"You mean turned my back on a dollhouse?"

"No. You made up a word, Grandma. You said 'buildinged.'"
She let out her delightful little-girl giggle. "There's no such word,
Grandma. You've never done that before."

"It must be time to go," Kay said, chuckling herself.

"Yeah, maybe tomorrow we can building some more." Maddie laughed, thrilled with her own cleverness, parodying her
grandmother.

What had I started? I never knew with my granddaughter.

While Maddie helped Taylor scoop up articles of clothing
and assorted trinkets, I walked to the door with Kay. "Thanks
again for giving up this evening," I said.

"Oh, it was nothing really. I actually got some work done on
my laptop. Your phone rang just once besides your own call—
Maddie's mom and dad called on her cell, then called back and
left a message for you on your landline. Otherwise it was all quiet."

I guess not everyone was lucky enough to have been trapped at a noisy police station as Detective Rutherford's murder suspect.

MADDIE and I had a long-standing special routine around her bedtime. I knew the ritual was on its last legs as she approached teenhood but for the moment it was thriving.

"Tell me a story about me and Grandpa," she said. She seemed wide awake but I could tell by her drooping eyelids that she wouldn't last long. The only question was who would give in first.

I sat on her bed. "'The Aquarium Trip,'" I began, as if I were reading the title of a book.

I rolled out the familiar story of a trip the three of us had taken to Monterey. I attended a crafts fair for much of the day, so it was bonding time for Maddie with her grandfather and some giant fish.

"You were only about six," I said. "But you could read the letters on the exhibit sign. You saw T-U-N-A"—I tapped out the letters on her freckled nose—"and you sounded out 'tuna.' Grandpa told me how you looked, so upset."

"Then what did I say? What did I say?"

As if she didn't remember. I cleared my throat and aimed for as high a pitch as I could reach. "Are these the same fish that we make sandwiches with, that get squeezed into a can?"

Even as her smile broadened, her eyelids got more and more heavy.

"And I haven't eaten tuna salad for lunch since then," she finished.

I was surprised that Maddie wasn't all over "the case," as she'd learned to call Skip's investigations. I'd expected her to quiz me about my trip to the police station, the fact of which she had surely guessed or wrangled out of Kay. I'd waited for her offer to use her computer skills to solve Varena's murder, but she hadn't mentioned the idea since she tried to wrestle the phone from me during the conversation with Skip that had interrupted our chicken-and-dumplings feast. She'd missed a half dozen opportunities since then to insert herself into the case.

Was it too much to ask that the appearance of a new, spec-
tacular dollhouse had captured her imagination and pushed out
her interest in police work? Either that or Maddie was more tired
than she'd let on.

"Do you like the little earrings I got you, Grandma?" she
asked, just before she nodded off.

"Of course." In my distracted state had I neglected to thank
her properly? I needed to focus more on the important things at
hand. "Why do you ask?"

She opened her mouth to speak, then closed it. Then, "Nothing. Good night, Grandma."

"Are you sure, sweetheart?"

"Did you talk to Mom and Dad tonight?" she asked me.

I'd forgotten about the message Kay mentioned. "Not tonight. I heard you did, though. Is something wrong?"

"Uh-uh. Is everything okay with getting me to school tomorrow? Isn't your car still at Uncle Henry's?"

"He's going to drive it by in the morning." I tucked her still-
favorite baseball afghan, one I originally knitted for her father,
under her chin. "Which is why you need to get to sleep."

One more kiss on her rusty curls and I left the room. I had
the strangest feeling my granddaughter was harboring a concern
or a secret of some kind.

Probably Maddie was simply missing her parents.

I hoped nothing was wrong with my family. Houston was
two hours ahead, so it was too late now to return the call to
Richard and Mary Lou. I assumed if there were some emergency,
they'd have called back. I headed for the answering machine.

I was one hundred percent capable of being too nosy about
my son's and daughter-in-law's lives, but I couldn't stand the
thought that there might be trouble in Palo Alto.

HENRY had made himself comfortable on the living room
couch with a large bowl of ice cream and a paperback—a thriller
judging from the blood-red cover. One day I'd ask Henry how
such a gentle man could have such nasty taste in fiction.

"Just because we were late doesn't mean we don't get dessert," he said, closing the book. He stood and took a step toward the kitchen. "What can I get you?"

"I'll have what you're having," I said. "Only a little less." I pushed the button on my answering machine. "Meanwhile I have a message I need to hear."

"Hi, Mom." My son Richard's voice. "Mary Lou and I need to talk to you. It's important, so call back as soon"—I heard scratchy noises on the line—"Hi, Mom." Mary Lou's voice this time. "It's important but not urgent, so please don't worry, okay? Everyone's fine. We'll catch you tomorrow."

A double phone call. I got them all the time when my son and his family lived in Los Angeles. Sometimes there was singing involved, such as on my birthday and holidays.

But this was different. My daughter-in-law, thankfully, had seen the need to take the edge off my son's message. Their complementary personalities were evident as usual, with Mary Lou bringing an ease to life and the job of parenting that Richard would never achieve.

Mary Lou's reassuring words helped, but didn't take away all my concern. I'd try as soon as I got up in the morning.

Distracted, I picked up around the couch and chairs—detritus of the evening and many days past. An orange sticky note, probably Kay's, with a telephone number on it. A miniature yellow gardener's boot I'd been looking for and a quarter-inch jack of clubs from a mini deck, assorted life-size writing implements, including a souvenir pen from our recent Universal Studios tour. You never knew what scale object you were going to find in my house.

I pulled a piece of paper from under the cushion of an easy chair. Taylor's stationery, with her name across the top in colorful letters. Several butterflies floated down the right side of the page. I saw the greeting, *Dear Maddie*, but kept reading anyway, shrugging off the possible federal offense. It was in my chair, after all, and the girls were minors.

Taylor's large scrawling cursive spelled out a thank-you note. How charming. Maddie hated writing such notes and insisted that emails and texting the letters "TXS" were just as good.

Maybe if I bought her personalized notepaper like Taylor's she'd be won over.

Thanks for the package of markers, Taylor's note read. *I totaly love it. I never had such a BIG set with every singel color I will think of my BFF when ever I use it!!!!!!!! xoxoxoxo Taylor.*

Just as well that it was too late for me to correct spelling and punctuation. And why use only one exclamation point when eight said it so much better? The thought was very sweet.

And it was sweet of Maddie to buy Taylor a present. But the cost of a large set of markers wasn't trivial. What was this spending spree Maddie was on? Three presents—for me, Kay, and Taylor—didn't make a spree, I admitted. And so what if my granddaughter was generous?

Henry, who'd made a detour to the garage with the rubbish, bless him, wandered back with two bowls of vanilla and caramel cashew ice cream. "The girls wiped out the chocolate," he said, knowing my first choice.

I accepted the combo bowl without hesitation. All of Sadie's flavors were delicious. "Did Maddie by any chance give you something recently?" I asked. "Some kind of present, maybe," I clarified, seeing his quizzical look.

Henry snapped his fingers. "Oh, yeah, in all the confusion today, I completely forgot to tell you. She gave me a key ring with a silver *H* on it. It's still in the bag in my car. A thank-you for picking her up all the time—her words. Wasn't that thoughtful?"

I managed a proud smile. I was annoyed with myself that I couldn't stop scrutinizing my granddaughter's every move.

I'd been thinking the worst—maybe she'd somehow learned she was dying and was trying to leave everyone she loved a fond memory. Skip's mother, my own BFF Beverly, contracted scarlet fever at just about Maddie's age. Beverly's heart was weakened as a result, a fact that kept us all on alert whenever she was indisposed or got overtired.

I pushed the thought aside. Richard would have told me, and not through a telephone message. Besides, scarlet fever was so much more treatable now.

What was left? That Maddie thought *we* were dying? Too many years of reading and teaching fiction had taken their toll on my imagination.

Again, our family history came into play in my thoughts—Skip had lost his father when he was Maddie's age. But Maddie had already gone through that crisis of thinking Richard would die when she turned eleven.

Were Richard and Mary Lou's phone call and Maddie's gifts related somehow? I couldn't see how.

One would think I didn't have enough to worry about without inventing scenarios. I brought my focus back to the present realities, deciding not to drag Henry into another drama of my creation. Once I talked to Maddie's parents, it would all be cleared up anyway.

"Let's talk about tomorrow's lunch," I said to Henry. "I still haven't heard how you managed to set it up for me to meet Alicia. I feel like I should rehearse. You did say it's just going to be bagels at Willie's, nothing formal?"

"I did."

"Good, because otherwise I'd be spending a lot of time worrying about what to wear or what to order."

Henry cleared his throat. "I might have misled Alicia."

"Uh-oh. Is there something more important that I should be worried about?"

"It's possible I left her with the impression that you and her mother were closer than you actually were."

I crossed my index and middle fingers. "We were like this," I said.

"Good," Henry said. "And I did indicate some potential added value if she chose to meet you."

Now I was nervous. "Such as?"

"I pointed out that you were at that very moment in a room with a detective working on her mother's case, and that you had a nephew—"

"Henry," I interrupted. "I was being interviewed as a suspect. Well, at least a material witness. Or something like that. And Skip—"

"She doesn't know any of that. All she knows is you're the favorite aunt of an LPPD homicide detective and that you were on the scene helping out."

"You've really pushed things here, Henry. Exaggerating, worming your way into a homicide investigation, misrepresenting me."

"Yeah."

I leaned over and kissed him. "I can't thank you enough."

Henry drew me close. "You know, it really did seem like she wanted to meet you."

"Really?"

"Well, who wouldn't?"

I moved closer.

Buzzz. Buzzz.

Heavy sighs from both of us.

I knew my nephew would be coming around tonight as he always did at the start of a new case. Ordinarily, I'd be eager for an update, especially tonight considering my interview with Detective Rutherford.

But I'd have been perfectly happy waiting another hour or so.

"Skip?" Henry asked, getting up to answer the door, straightening his shirt on the way.

"I'm afraid so."

Henry grinned. "I was ready to leave anyway."

I doubted it.

ONCE Henry left, the scene in my living room morphed quickly from a cozy make-out session between consenting adults to a formal inquiry with a member of law enforcement.

I said as much to my nephew, skipping the making-out part.

"It's not as bad as all that," Skip said, handing me a folder with four typed sheets. "I figured I'd help you out by bringing you your statement, saving you another trip downtown."

"I didn't know I was giving a statement," I said, with a touch of huffiness in my tone.

I'd mellowed a bit since my encounter with Detective–Nurse Ratched, but Skip didn't need to know that.

"Just routine," Skip said. He pointed to the new dollhouse in my atrium. "That from Varena Young? Pretty fast work."

I explained how the dollhouse appeared on my doorstep this evening. "I suppose Detective Rutherford will think I killed Varena to get the dollhouse."

Skip made a *pshaw* sound.

I looked at the sheets he'd handed me. The first thing that struck me was Detective Rutherford's first name.

"Blythe?" I said.

Skip shrugged and mumbled awkwardly. Apparently he also felt that such a lovely name should have been reserved for a less brash persona. I thought it perfect for one of Varena Young's romance heroines. I pictured a nymphlike Blythe wearing a billowing ball gown, laughing sweetly—not sporting a suit bulging with a weapon and topped off with an attitude.

More annoying than Detective Rutherford's first name was the notation in the box below the case number: GERALDINE PORTER—INVOLVED PERSON.

I felt my jaw tighten. "Involved?"

"It's nothing. It just means you were there shortly before the murder, likely the last person to see the victim alive."

"Alexandra Rockwell was her name. Or Varena Young, another perfectly good name." Why did I have to keep reminding people of that? "And I probably was *one* of the last people to see her."

Skip nodded vigorously. "Right. Right." He scratched his head, covered with the same thicket of red hair as Maddie's, but not as curly. I could almost read his thoughts—*Why is my usually kindly aunt so grouchy tonight?* "Look, I'm going to grab a cup of coffee while you read that over and sign it at the end. Oh, and initial any corrections."

"Yes, sir." I saluted.

"Didn't I say 'please'?" Skip grimaced. "Please."

He turned and walked out of the room.

On a good night I would have sprung up and prepared his mug of coffee and a plate of cookies, but I wasn't completely over the Corazón Cruz incident, let alone the Blythe Rutherford incident, let alone this involved person incident.

Skip rumbled in the kitchen, still dressed in his professional detective outfit—navy pants and tweed sport coat. I resigned myself to reading the report he'd thrust upon me.

From the first page, I felt renewed tension in my shoulders and limbs as I recalled the unpleasant interview in the run-down, offensive room.

"Look at this," I called to Skip, who'd managed to find the jar of ginger cookies in spite of my lack of hospitality. "There's at least one typo on each page. I've corrected them. Why do I have to initial crossed-out words?"

"It's…uh…a way to be sure you read it all."

I looked at him over my reading glasses. "You mean you do this deliberately? Make errors?"

"Something like that." Skip came into the living room and sat on the chair across from me. He shifted until he was perched on the edge. Getting up close, assuming a trustworthy posture. "I'll let you in on a little trick of the trade. The typos are there for a reason. If we go to court, you can't say you weren't given time to read the statement. Also, your initials are all over it, so you can't claim that the cops just showed you where to sign at the bottom."

"Someone thinks I'd lie in court?"

Skip held up his hand. "Of course not, Aunt Gerry. But, you know, the whole purpose of a statement is to lock down a person, so when we get them in court—not that you're going to court, but procedure is procedure—then we can impeach them if they try and say something different. It's just routine."

"I'm beginning to like your 'just routine' less and less."

Skip finally popped a cookie into his mouth. Sensing my mood, he'd shown great restraint. "I take it you weren't impressed with Detective Blythe's bedside manner," he said.

"She treated me like a suspect." Silence. I waited a few more seconds. "Here's where you're supposed to say, 'Oh, no, Aunt Gerry, you wouldn't be a suspect, not in a million years.'"

Skip took another cookie, managing to say, "These are great," before stuffing his mouth again.

I squirmed. "Skip?"

"It's just—"

I folded my arms and broke in. "Do not say 'routine.'"

"Procedure," Skip said. No better than "routine," but at least I got him to exercise his synonym-finding skills. "You have to let the LPPD follow its procedures. People have to be eliminated. As suspects, I mean. That's how it works. Of course no one in his right mind thinks you killed the woman."

"Fine. Then let's talk about suspects. How about Varena Young's brother? You know, I forgot to tell you, but I heard them arguing upstairs as I was leaving the house. I think there was a third person there also. Another man."

Poor Skip. He brushed crumbs from his jacket and blew out another agonized breath.

"We've been over this, Aunt Gerry."

"Yes, and what a coincidence that the person who told me about Varena's brother is nowhere to be found."

"She doesn't work there anymore. That doesn't mean she's MIA."

"I guess I'll have to find her, or him, myself."

Skip stood and picked up the folder containing my brilliant statement. "This all done?"

I nodded. "You're leaving?" I asked. I wasn't nearly finished with my own interrogation.

"Good night, Aunt Gerry." He turned his back and waved good-bye over his shoulder as he walked to the door.

I couldn't remember the last time my nephew left my house without a bag of cookies and without giving me a hug.

It also occurred to me that he never did confirm that I wasn't a suspect. He'd said no one in his right mind... But what about those in the LPPD who were not in their right minds?

It was going to be a long night.

I SAT in front of my computer, shiny and new on my dining room table. Richard and Mary Lou had given me a laptop for my birthday, one that finally met Maddie's criterion of being "not lame." I had half a thought to wake her up, school night or not, and ask for help. Even a new, smarter machine required some skill at research and she was the queen of browsing.

Before I assumed the role of bad grandmother, I gave myself a pep talk. I could do this. I'd seen Maddie do searches enough times. I had a master's degree, for heaven's sake, and I'd done some online shopping. How much harder could finding a family tree be than ordering Christmas presents?

I took a sip of tea and typed in Varena's name. Up came a page of links, most of which were related to her Regency romance novels, giving synopses, book tour schedules, and an impressive number of awards. I scrolled through a list of her book covers until I got tired of looking at impossibly high waistlines and more-than-puffy sleeves. Did every woman in those days wear her hair the same way—with wispy curls framing her face and the rest of her locks tucked into a frilly cap or piled high on her head?

I needed something more personal about Varena, not about her heroines.

One site claimed to have an exhaustive list of Regency romance authors' biographies. Each bio was written up in the same format, with sections labeled LIFE, WRITING CAREER, AWARDS, BIBLIOGRAPHY, FUTURE WORKS, and REFERENCES.

I stopped to read the entry for a Carly Aaronson to get an idea of what kind of information was available. The LIFE section was only a couple of paragraphs and ended with the standard line for authors of any genre: Lives in such-and-such a city with her husband, *x* number of children, and *x* number of dogs (or cats). Not very useful for tracking alleged siblings.

The list of books in print for Ms. Aaronson was astounding. I knew from my volunteer library work that romance publishers put out many titles each month and that their authors often wrote up to three or four books a year.

By contrast, Jane Austen, also included on the site, was credited with only six novels, total, for her career. Not very productive, but I doubted that Ms. Aaronson's twenty-five novels to date would be studied two hundred years from now. Though it pained me to admit it, I didn't think my friend Varena's body of work would be the subject of future book groups either.

I wondered if Varena, at her age, had been able to keep up with that schedule herself, or if she had help. Skip had mentioned a research assistant, Paige Taggart, who'd been at the Rockwell home all afternoon while I was there. I made a note to pay her a visit, hoping she might still be around to collect her things, if nothing else. With a name like Paige, there was a good chance she spoke unaccented English and might be able to enlighten me as to the whereabouts of Corazón and Varena's brother.

Searching the romance site, I was proud of myself for finding a not very clearly marked pathway to clicking on a particular letter of the alphabet for authors. I headed over to the Ys.

A small, postage stamp-size image of Varena popped up, startling me for a moment. I choked up. Yesterday, I'd been in the presence of a vibrant woman; today I was left with a tiny, posed photograph of her.

I cleared my eyes and nose and read:

Varena Young is the pseudonym of Mildred Swingle. Born between the two world wars on a farm in the Central Valley of California, she eventually obtained a GED and left the West Coast for Chicago. She was hired by a publisher, who…

Wait. There was too much wrong with this picture.

Mildred Swingle? I couldn't think of a less romantic-sounding name. Varena Young was a perfect pseudonym, and the world assumed Alexandra Rockwell was her birth name.

Varena Young had dropped out of high school? I had great respect for the GED program, and even tutored students on the way to earn the certificate, but I'd imagined Varena an insatiable scholar from her first day of school at a private boarding school in England, not a late bloomer.

And what was this about her being born in California's Central Valley, which meant a place like Merced or the farmlands of Stanislaus County, not exactly a breeding ground for duchesses.

I read a few more lines:

She wrote for nearly twenty years before entering the Regency romance genre and her career took off.

Reason told me there couldn't be two Varena Youngs of the same age writing in the same genre. But, as indispensable as the

Internet had become, errors abounded and mix-ups like this were bound to happen.

And how appropriate. Mistaken identity was one of the tropes of Varena's genre, Regency romance novels—and of Shakespeare's plays, I recalled with a smile.

I remembered trying desperately to nudge adolescents toward an appreciation of the humor of twins being mistaken for each other, or of girls and boys disguising themselves as the opposite gender. Much to my dismay, very little of Shakespeare had amused the teenagers of Abraham Lincoln High School. I wondered if I'd have fared better teaching the complete works of Varena Young. To the girls, anyway.

Mildred Swingle, indeed. To me it was a hilarious comedy of errors featuring a duchess and a farmer's daughter.

I realized it was well into Tuesday morning. I had no business sitting at my desk at this hour. Computers baffled me in the light of day. Why did I think I could get anything useful done after midnight?

"Time to pack it in," Ken would have said.

And I did.

It must have been a rough, confusing day for me to go to bed without another glance at the brand new dollhouse in my atrium. I did give some thought to its miniature television set, however. An incongruous addition to an old dollhouse.

I fell asleep wondering where I could get a TV for one of my own dollhouses, and if I could buy tapes—or was it chips?—of "The Ed Sullivan Show."

Chapter 8

MADDIE JUMPED ON my bed, landing on my legs, as she hadn't done for many years. The effect on my body was much greater now that she was a tall, bony eleven-year-old. She was dressed for school, fortunately without her backpack, or I'd never have been able to get up.

Maddie's voice was urgent. "Grandma, Grandma. You have to come and see what I found."

I blinked a few times and put my pillow over my head, only partly teasing. "I'm sound asleep," I said in a genuinely groggy voice.

Maddie laughed like a toddler, bringing back happy memories. "Come on, Grandma. Wait till you see what I found this morning. Did you know our new dollhouse has a secret room?"

"It's not exactly ours, sweetheart, and no, I didn't know. Have you been working on the house already?"

"Yes, yes." Maddie had grabbed my old bathrobe from a chair in my bedroom and now she held it open, looking like a bullfighter who'd been stuck with ragged blue chenille instead of a snappy red cloak. "Come on, come on."

"You went to the dollhouse instead of the computer?"

She gave a slight nod. "When are you ever going to wear that new robe we gave you last Christmas?"

"It's my backup." My head was still in my computer search for Varena Young. "I could have used your help last night," I said, sticking my arms into the comfortable robe. "I was trying to do a search, and I didn't get anywhere. It's about the lady who died yesterday. I don't think she has a website of her own, and I'm not sure I can trust what's on the generic sites."

"Huh," Maddie said, hardly pausing before telling me, "your slippers are right here."

I'd told her about a case, invited her help, and her response was another "Huh"?

No screaming, "Let me do it! Let me do it!" I hoped my granddaughter wasn't ill.

I'd been hoping to ask Maddie about genealogy sites or blogs or other ways to find out about the personal life of a celebrity. Surely having or not having a brother wasn't too intimate a detail to be public. I'd gone through the standard hoops, plugging in "Alexandra Rockwell," but the name was more common than I thought. I'd been bleary-eyed by the time I learned of the possible Mildred Swingle connection and hoped Maddie would come to my aid.

I'd also been surprised last night when Maddie didn't shuffle into the living room when Skip arrived. Her room fronted on the driveway and she invariably heard his car. She'd typically make her sleepy way to wherever we were, and offer to help solve his case.

Not today, though. No "Please, please, please." I was tempted to feel her forehead for signs of a fever, but I didn't want to frighten her. I needed to call my son before breakfast and clarify the state of her health.

"Uncle Skip came by. I guess you didn't hear him," I said, pushing my feet into my slippers, which were older than my robe.

"I must have been very tired, probably from waiting so long for you to come home for ice cream."

At least she hadn't lost that edge. "Because I was Away So Long," I said, reaching out to her most ticklish parts. "Aren't you smart, getting that little dig in so early in the morning."

Also, another bit of avoidance, I mused.

I thought of all the times I wished Maddie would not get involved in law enforcement, even from the safety of her computer.

I should be relieved about that now, not focusing on the needs of my little unsanctioned investigation.

But this was a sudden and unexplained reversal of roles. It had taken me a long time to get my granddaughter away from computers and interested in dollhouses. Now here I was trying to woo her away from a new house back to cyberspace.

Maddie took my hand and pretended to tow me into the atrium where the dollhouse awaited. We arrived at the threshold, the moment she'd been waiting for.

"*Ta da!* Isn't it great, Grandma?"

It was early enough in the morning that no sunlight crept in to spoil the effect. Maddie had turned on a tiny light here and there in the dollhouse and a magic world awaited. I saw that she'd added little touches with items from my own crafts drawers. A box of cereal, bowls, a loaf of bread, and a pot of jam sat on the kitchen table, ready for the dollhouse family's breakfast. Upstairs, she'd placed clothes and toys strategically on beds and chairs. One tiny sneaker was on the dresser next to a lamp in the child's room, the other upside down on the floor. I had the impression she was reproducing her own décor.

"You've done a wonderful job, sweetheart."

"Now watch this, Grandma. This is the main thing I was telling you about."

Maddie had me sit on a stool so that I was at eye level with the second floor of the dollhouse. When I was settled, she pressed her finger on the back wall of one of the bedrooms, about fifteen inches by twelve inches (fifteen feet by twelve feet if scaled to life-size), with a play area in one corner.

"Watch, watch."

I was ready for fireworks, but saw nothing. "What should I be looking for?"

Maddie frowned and pressed harder on the same spot, then moved her hand around the area. The wall was nicely painted in an abstract design, geometric shapes in primary colors, but I saw nothing unusual.

"I don't see anything, sweetheart."

Maddie growled and clenched her fists. "There's a secret room right here behind this wall. I saw it this morning." She slammed her arms against where her hips would be if she had any to speak of.

I got up and looked more closely. "Where was it?"

She pushed so hard I thought the house would topple. "Right here, right here. I just touched this spot"—her finger tapped a bright red circle—"to see if it was thick paint or paper or what, and this wall slid across, like, *zoom*"—another gesture punctuated this highly animated presentation—"and there was another wall and there was a space." Maddie held her thumb and index finger about two inches apart. "It was like a hallway or something."

"The wall slid automatically? So it's wired up somehow?"

"Yeah, I guess."

"So we should be able to see some electrical...stuff."

"Yeah, there must be a little motor and a battery," she said, feeling along the edges of the wall.

I placed my finger on a yellow rectangle next to the circle. "Maybe you were pressing here." *Tap tap.*

Nothing.

"Nuts. Nuts. Nuts," Maddie said, pouting between words, as her father had done before her whenever he was stressed. "I should have taken the letter while I had the door open."

My ears perked up. "Letter?"

"There was a letter in the hallway. The secret hallway."

"You mean a miniature letter?" I'd fashioned tiny letters for many a room box myself.

"No, a real letter. A full-size letter." Maddie held her hands out to roughly the size of a typical envelope that comes in a stationery set, about four-by-six inches. "Like the kind you used to send when we lived in L.A."

As if a secret room weren't enough to intrigue me, the chances of finding a letter—I heard "clue"—in the dollhouse motivated me even more strongly to locate the magic spot.

Now both our heads and one hand each were battling for

space in the bedroom. We moved the furniture out and checked again, including the outside wall, and came up with nothing.

"It was there, Grandma, really."

"I'm sure it was."

"You don't believe me."

I put my arm around my distressed granddaughter. "Let's have breakfast and get you to school. We'll try again this afternoon."

I heard her soft, frustrated "Okay."

I couldn't help thinking—this was how I'd felt when I was told there was no brother.

FINALLY the time was right. I was free to talk to Richard and Mary Lou, who would surely be up, while Maddie started break-fast, this time on a real-life scale. I headed for the phone.

"I'll be back in a minute," I told her. "I'm going to call your parents."

Thud. Plop. Maddie dropped the wooden-handled spoon, sending sticky globs of oatmeal to the tile floor.

She gasped.

In fact, I thought I heard the gasp before the spoon fell.

"No, no, don't call them yet," she said.

"I'll be done before the oatmeal is ready," I said, confused by her pleading tone. She'd never cared this much for punctuality at breakfast.

I pulled a paper towel off the roll and wet it, ready to kneel down and help clean up the spill.

"Please, please, please, Grandma."

Maddie, hiding tears, I felt, buried her head in my chest. My first thought was how incredibly tall she'd gotten and how increasingly inadequate a counselor I'd be as she got older. But that wasn't the immediate problem.

"Maddie, please tell me what's wrong. I know something is bothering you. Maybe I can help."

She sniffed a few more times, then broke away. "Grandma, I promise I'll tell you, but can we please just wait until after school?"

It was a step in the right direction, if not great progress. Maddie had at least owned up to a problem. It broke my heart to think she'd been suffering with it for even a day.

"I'll wait, but only if you answer a couple of questions," I said. I heard her weak "Okay."

I took a breath. "Is anyone sick? You, your mom, your dad?" I thought a minute and threw in Beverly just in case.

"Uh-uh. No one in our family is sick."

Maddie crossed her heart and held her right hand in the air.

"Is anyone in trouble?" I didn't have any idea how to make the question specific. Trouble with the law? Richard was about the straightest arrow I knew. Skip teased him about it when they were kids, and he teased him about it now. Mary Lou was a little more adventuresome, but not in the gamble-away-your-house or lose-your-family kind of way.

Dum, ta da dum, ta da dum, ta da dum.

My cell phone-cum-marching band, wired to the wall through its charger.

Maddie pounced on it. "Don't take it, okay? Let it go to voicemail."

"Your mom?"

Maddie nodded, her eyes more soulful than when she'd sat on Santa's lap, barely able to talk, and earnestly pleaded for a tricycle.

I gave her a silent "Okay." I'd made a promise. I hoped I wouldn't regret keeping it.

Buzzz. Buzzz.

Maddie's face collapsed into relief. "Grandma, can you get the door? I don't want the oatmeal to burn."

She returned to the stove and stirred the oatmeal with a clean spoon. She knew I wouldn't continue my probing in Henry's presence, though I hadn't ruled it out. I needed advice from an adult and Maddie's parents were off limits, thanks to my rash promise.

"We're going to continue this as soon as you get home," I said in my firmest voice. I hoped the hug that accompanied my admonishment didn't detract from my position of authority.

"Okay, okay, okay."

I opened the door to a smiling Henry, who bent down and gave me a kiss.

"Nice," I said. "Have you had breakfast?"

"Not yet. I smell oatmeal, but I had something less healthy in mind, after we drop Maddie off."

"I like a man with a plan."

Henry sat and drank coffee while Maddie ate oatmeal and I pretended to be too full from dinner to have any.

For Henry's benefit, and as another chance to entice Maddie to action, I summarized my needs and failure at the computer. It still wasn't clear to me why Maddie hadn't been bombarding me with a million different things she could do for me on the computer, if I'd only let her skip school today.

"I'm trying to find out if Varena Young put out a newsletter or something like that," I said. "She's listed on her publisher's page, but there's no information of a personal nature."

"Did Taylor finish the puzzle we started yesterday? The one with no straight edges?" Maddie asked Henry. A conversation ensued about the pros and cons of jigsaw puzzles online and in a box.

I was free to go off mentally on my own, and I took the opportunity. I was sure Varena's personal assistant, the stiff Ms. Overbee, knew her employer's personal details. I made a note to ask her, but I didn't hold out much hope of her cooperation. I needed a way to meet with her and Paige, the research assistant. Or if my lunch with Alicia went well, maybe all mysteries surrounding her mother's death would be solved.

"How's your uncle?" I might ask Alicia, catching her off-guard, in case she was prepared to lie. She'd told Henry that she didn't have an uncle, but she didn't know that he'd passed the information on to me. As usual, my head hurt from the complicated planning necessary for a good strategy.

I couldn't help thinking also of the envelope, the full-size envelope that was in the secret room in the dollhouse. If there was a secret room. The dollhouse had come to me unexpectedly, and it was decidedly not the one Varena had offered me. If someone wanted to send me a message, a letter in a secret room would be the perfect vehicle. If the someone was Varena, why wouldn't she have sent the Tudor that I was expecting? Did Varena have time to do that before she—

"I have an idea," Henry began, jogging me back. "This is a job for our resident computer guru." He turned to Maddie. "Maybe when you get home this afternoon, you can work with your grandmother to find the information she needs to help your uncle solve the case."

Henry couldn't have put more tempting words into the plea. *Computer, information, uncle, solve, case.*

"Maybe, but I have lots of homework this week."

I put my cup down and laughed, but Maddie showed no sign that she'd made a joke.

Where was my real granddaughter?

"IS it too soon for boy trouble?" Henry asked as we drove back from Maddie's Palo Alto school. "Strange that she doesn't want to hop right into this investigation."

I'd decided not to share the yet-to-be-determined problem Maddie was dealing with, but Henry had picked up on a change in the atmosphere around my granddaughter anyway. I also had no idea whether the three things were related—her sudden avoidance of computer projects, her lack of interest in the case, and the mysterious call from Richard and Mary Lou.

"I hope it's too soon for boys," I said. "How about Taylor? Any significant changes?"

Henry laughed. "Not yet. Her mother says she'll start to worry when Taylor takes a shower and changes her socks without being told."

"Maybe it's a phase Maddie's going through. I don't remember Richard's moods that well. I don't think he had many, and anyway it would be different for a boy."

"My life has been full of girls," said Henry, whose offspring comprised one daughter and one granddaughter. "And as for me, well, kids weren't allowed to have moods in the old days."

I knew what he meant. I couldn't even imagine looking at

my mother cross-eyed, as she would have said, let alone frown at her or talk back, or claim I just wasn't in the mood.

"I guess I'm no help," Henry continued.

"Maybe not that way. But there's something else you could do, if you choose to accept the mission."

"Bring it on."

I told Henry about the secret room and Maddie's inability to reproduce the action that had brought it to light. "I'm sure some wires and batteries are the key, if it does exist, and I hope it does, since there may be a clue in it," I said.

"Aha."

"But the only dollhouse wiring I've done is with a kit, where you run electrical tape along the floor and hope it doesn't show too much. Don't tell Linda Reed."

"Promise. Let's look at it right after breakfast," Henry said, parking my car.

I hadn't noticed until now that Henry had pulled in behind the row of shops on Springfield Boulevard. A new strip mall had sprung up about a year ago and now, to my surprise and delight, there was a French bakery wedged between a Mexican restaurant and a bank.

Our small town was already home to gourmet bagels at Willie's, homemade ice cream at Sadie's, a hardware store, a card shop, a produce market, and a butcher shop. With a new bakery, I felt Lincoln Point was now complete.

Except for the lack of a miniatures store, of course, but I knew that was too much to ask even of the major cities in the Bay Area. Besides, I enjoyed outings with my crafter friends to the dollhouse stores in the neighboring towns, and who knows what my financial health would be if there were a store full of adorable, tiny things within walking distance?

"How did you find out about this?" I asked Henry.

"I live here," he said, a running joke between us, since Henry was a California native and I still held onto my roots in the Bronx by reading only New York newspapers.

"Why should I read a local paper as long as you can give me the highlights, like bakery openings?" I asked.

"And I'm not going anywhere," he said.

I liked the sound of that.

WE sat at a table in the new La Cabane en Rondins, which was small, red-and-white, and smelling like there were only delicious selections in the display case. At last I learned what Henry had meant by "less healthy" choices for breakfast.

"The name's a mouthful," Henry said, working on an apple turnover.

"I think *cabane* is 'cabin' in French," I said. "What do you bet the rest means 'logs'?"

"Log cabin." Henry laughed. "Honest Abe rules. I'm sure it was a condition of setting up business in Lincoln Point. It's probably on the permit form."

I stripped a layer from an enormous morning bun, sending sugar everywhere. "I think you're right. The form probably says, 'State your establishment's connection to Abraham Lincoln.'"

The regulations didn't matter, as long as the éclairs, which we'd already decided to take home, were fresh.

I was glad to see a bustling business as a stream of people picked up orders or lingered to chat and eat, but my mind was on romance. Not romance with Henry, as nicely as that was shaping up, but on the romance writer who had so swiftly become my friend, and just as swiftly, been murdered.

I wasn't sure why I felt oddly connected, almost responsible for her murder. Survivor's guilt because I'd been there so close to the hour of her demise? Would the killer have had the opportunity if I'd waited until after her meeting instead of slipping out without saying good-bye? Would Varena have been home at all if she weren't meeting me?

One factor in my sorrow was surely the loss of someone with a mutual love of all things miniature. Perhaps we would have started room box projects together. We might have refurbished a dollhouse in her collection for a charitable organization. My crafters group worked with one that gave dollhouses to children with life-threatening diseases. I knew Varena would have been amenable to that.

I'd felt an immediate, strong connection to Varena Young. Though I'd just met her, I'd been ready to become a member of her adoring fan club.

"I want to help with this investigation," I told Henry, who was dusting small flakes of pastry from his shirt. "But I'm stuck with no resources. I'm going to need her daughter's cooperation. What if Alicia doesn't want me to get involved, or doesn't like me, or—"

"Why don't you just ask her?" Henry said, nodding and smiling to someone behind me.

I felt my face flush.

It seemed the Meet Alicia Rockwell show was starting without benefit of rehearsal.

Chapter 9

FROM THE LOOK on Henry's face, he was as surprised as I was to see Alicia Rockwell, several hours before our scheduled lunch date. I ruled out "setup."

The question was, how long had Alicia been standing behind me? Had I said anything compromising? The second question was, could I please have a minute to go home and change out of my casual run-Maddie-to-school attire? And another minute to draw up a list with the rest of the questions.

Too late now to worry about any of that.

I stood and turned on my best smile. "Good morning," I said, annoyed with myself for not having done research on her name at least. Should I address her as Ms. Rockwell? Mrs. Something Else? I remembered Skip's mentioning that both the Rockwell— oh, dear, Swingle?—children were divorced. And that Alicia was a fashion designer in San Francisco.

She looked so much like her mother, with the same prominent cheekbones and high forehead, I almost called her Ms. Young. Alicia also wore her light brown hair swept back the same way and had dressed in a flowing bright blue outfit Varena might have worn, but without the multitude of beads and chains Varena would have added.

"This is a nice surprise," she said, holding a cup and saucer in one hand and an oversize purse in the other. "I prefer breakfast meetings, anyway. Shall we just do it now?"

I gave an enthusiastic nod though I wasn't sure what "it" was, except that for Alicia it didn't involve a pastry, but only a foaming drink topped with sharp-smelling cinnamon. The European way, whereas I chose the American way and dumped a load of chocolate powder on my coffee drinks.

Once he was assured he was welcome to stay, Henry moved stubby wooden chairs around to make a place for a third at our small table. He and Alicia seemed like old friends and exchanged a double cheek kiss. Maybe it was the buttery aroma filling the air that inspired the camaraderie.

Alicia seemed unnaturally cheery as we all sang the praises of this new venue in town, the walls of which were faux-painted to look like a room in the Louvre. So much for log cabin décor. We were all so amused by the mismatch, I briefly forgot the reason for our meeting.

"I can't tell you how sorry I am about your mother's death," I offered finally. "I feel as if I knew her a long time."

Alicia's face collapsed, as if a network of strings had let loose under her skin. I almost regretted my sympathetic offering, as if I'd been the bearer of bad news. I was usually sensitive to the choices of grieving families, some of whom preferred not to display or discuss their sorrow.

I, who'd captured any willing listener and pummeled her with stories and tears after Ken's death, turned away to give Alicia some belated privacy. Henry put his hand on hers. She gave him a tiny smile and covered his hand with hers for a moment, then took out tissues and dabbed at her face.

She turned her attention back to me and gave me a gracious, composed smile. "Yes, everyone says that, Geraldine. My mother's readers felt she was a lifelong friend. Her books had that effect," Alicia said.

Uh-oh. I decided to let the assumption stand. This was not the time to lay bare my reading preferences, which didn't include romances of any period, unless you counted Jane Austen. What did it matter how I came to feel close to Varena Young? I wondered if Alicia shared her mother's love of miniatures. I wondered if she read her mother's books. As long as she didn't ask to inspect my bookcases, check my library card, or quiz me on her mother's titles, my secret was safe.

"Mr. Baker—Henry—has told me so much about you." Alicia gave him another pleasant smile. "I hope you don't mind if I insinuate myself and ask for your help." I started to speak, but Alicia wasn't through. "First, I have absolutely nothing but the highest regard for the Lincoln Point Police Department. I'm sure your nephew is a stellar detective, but I want to leave no stone unturned to find who did this terrible thing."

"I understand," I said. I had the feeling Alicia had spent a long, emotionally difficult night and was now ready to take care of business. "It's every Lincoln Point detective's priority right now," I added, still struggling to contribute something meaningful to the ad hoc meeting.

"I'm sure that's true." Alicia paused to sip from her cup. "But I've given this a lot of thought. All night, as a matter of fact. And the reality is, the police have too much to do to give my mother's case the attention it needs."

Not really. The crime rate was pretty low in Lincoln Point. And I couldn't remember a time when Skip or the squad was dealing with more than one murder at a time.

"The police are extremely busy," I lied.

Alicia nodded as if I were the first to make the observation. She fingered the single elaborate pendant that perfectly complemented her outfit. I supposed fashion designers had their own jewelers on staff. The most I could claim this morning was that my sweatshirt wasn't stained and didn't have a silly logo, as some of mine did, like my favorite one with MINIATURISTS WORK AS LITTLE AS THEY CAN.

"That's why I'd like to hire you," she said.

I started. I knew she wasn't referring to my fashion sense. "No, no. I have no official standing at all." I looked around to be sure no genuine officer of the law was nearby.

Alicia's face, seeming fully recovered from its breakdown, took on an amused look. "I've heard about you, Geraldine, and not just from Henry here. I know you're good and I trust you."

I blushed. "I don't want to mislead you about what I can do, but I would love to look into things on my own."

"That's what I wanted to hear."

"I hope you'll be able to fill in some gaps in my knowledge."

"Of course, whatever you need. But I insist on giving you some kind of compensation."

I shook my head and held up my hand. "Really, Alicia, it's not—"

Alicia cut in with an idea. "Perhaps I can give you a dollhouse or two from my mother's collection."

Be still my heart. She spoke of a "dollhouse or two" the way I might say, "a batch of cookies or two." But I couldn't be greedy. "The one you sent for the bookmobile auction is exquisite," I said. "That certainly is sufficient." Though it wasn't for me. Was I actually refusing a dollhouse for me, myself, and I? I needed to rephrase. "However—"

Once again, Alicia interrupted, giving me a quizzical look. "I didn't send you a dollhouse."

I glanced at Henry, back from picking up three small fruit tarts to share. He shrugged.

Though I'd played the innocent with Detective Rutherford, I'd been all but certain the dollhouse had come from the Rockwell Estate. I tried to trace the origin of that assumption. According to Kay and the girls, there had been no packaging or return address. But it had seemed too coincidental that it arrived right after my visit, brief as it was. And who else had a dollhouse to spare?

I thought of the secret room Maddie found, and the letter it held. Now, with Alicia's denial, the very provenance of the house was in question.

There was more than one secret about this dollhouse.

"I forgot to tell you about that, Gerry," Henry said, pausing in the consumption of a tart covered with blueberries and strawberries. "There was a mix-up about the house. I'll explain later." He waved his hands, mixing up the air. More like a cover-up, and I was grateful.

I felt the need to bring this meeting to a focus. No time to fret about the proper wording. "Ms. Rockwell, do you—"

"Alicia, please."

I was glad Maddie wasn't present. She might be inclined to think that it was okay for grown-ups to consistently interrupt as long as they were wealthy and/or successful professionals.

"Alicia, do you have an uncle on your mother's side?"

Without hesitation, which would have given me hope, Alicia shook her head. "No uncles on either side. My mother did have a brother, but he died when I was a child."

So now I was dealing with a ghost.

It seemed rude and ignorant to ask if she were sure about her family tree. I followed up for the sake of politeness. "That must have been hard on the family. What happened to him?"

"He was in a car accident. I was only about two years old, so I barely remember Uncle Caleb. He was a couple of years older than Mother. Adam was five, so he has a little more recollection of him. Mother kept a photo of him on the piano for a while, then eventually it disappeared."

The three of us simultaneously took sips of our drinks. It wasn't clear to me whether condolences for a deceased uncle were appropriate decades later.

Alicia broke the silence. "My own living brother is useless at the moment. Adam has just been sued for divorce and frankly, that seems to matter to him more than our mother's death."

"I'm sorry to hear all this," I said.

Alicia nodded, slightly teary again, and checked her watch. "I'm due at the studio, so I'll be off. I'm assuming you'll do what you do best, Geraldine. I've already taken the liberty of inform-ing all the family and household staff that they should cooperate with you one hundred-and-ten percent." She handed me a card. "Please, call me directly if you need anything, anything at all."

I needed everything. I needed to know about Varena's per-sonal assistant, Laura Overbee; her research assistant, Paige Tag-gart; her financial advisor, Charles Quentin. I still hadn't met Adam. What about the Mildred Swingle reference? And there was still the Corazón Cruz mystery.

But Alicia was gone, as quickly as her mother had left me yesterday. Hopefully, she wouldn't come to the same end before I could catch her again.

"HOW do you think that went?" Henry asked, once we were alone again at the table.

I shot him a look. How could he even ask? "I've never been so unprepared for a meeting." I ran through the list of questions I'd just reviewed mentally.

"I was going to say 'very well.' I hope you're not sorry I suggested coming here. Maybe we should have hidden out and practiced interview techniques until lunch time."

I waved away his apologetic look. "No, no. It's just as well that it's over. I probably would have stewed all morning and wouldn't have done any better. The answer to the brother question would have been the same. Plus, we have a new question."

"Who sent the dollhouse?" Henry said.

"I feel like I've taken two steps backwards. And now Alicia is counting on me. I have to find a way to meet the other people in Varena's life."

"Are you thinking they're all suspects?"

"No, not exactly. But I do need to find out what each one would gain from Varena's death, what conflicts there might have been in the family and household, where everyone was at the time—" I thought fleetingly of mentioning that it would be good to find out if the Rockwell Estate had a butler.

"So, they're all suspects," Henry said.

I grimaced. "I guess so."

I raised my cup to finish off my cappuccino and looked beyond the next grouping of tables, at the counter. Where the barista was handing over a tall iced drink to a stiff-looking young woman with clothes too formal for a morning in a bakery. Could it be?

I poked Henry. "Coming here was the best idea you've had. The lady in the tweed jacket?"—Henry sneaked a look—"That's Laura Overbee."

"The now-unemployed personal assistant?"

I hadn't thought of it that way.

We barely returned our expressions to normal before Ms. Overbee looked our way and gave a discreet wave. She picked up some napkins and marched over to our table. I caught a whiff of rosewater cologne.

"Mrs. Porter, isn't it? What a surprise."

I doubted it.

Henry stood and introduced himself. "Please join us," he said, pulling out the chair Alicia had abandoned moments ago.

"I'm glad to run into you, Mrs. Porter. I wanted to apologize for being so short with you yesterday," Ms. Overbee said. "You know, it was such an upsetting time for all of us." She fanned herself with a floppy Cabane en Rondins napkin. "You can't imagine the drama. I'm sorry I took it out on you."

"Think nothing of it," I said.

"Poor Varena," she said. "I feel so awful."

My assessment of her sincerity might have been clouded by the sting of her treatment of me yesterday, but, again, I doubted it. I noticed that under her jacket she wore yet another sweater set, this one pale green. It might have been the one thing about her that I related to—having a standard outfit, almost a uniform, to eliminate wardrobe stress and decision-making before coffee.

"How is everyone doing?" I asked.

Henry gave me a grin. "Why don't I get you another coffee?" he said, and left for the counter.

"Well, things are upside down, of course," Ms. Overbee said. She shuddered and took a long pull on what was probably the advertised special drink today—strawberry frappuccino. "It was quite a shock. I mean, Varena was old, but to go that way…everyone was in a state yesterday. Especially Paige, of course."

It hadn't dawned on me to ask Skip or Alicia who had discovered Varena's body. It seemed I'd just found out.

"Paige Taggart was the one who—?"

Ms. Overbee nodded solemnly. "She's crushed with guilt, too." Ms. Overbee put aside her drink and leaned in, chummy and secretive. "She and Varena had been so at odds lately."

"Is that right?" I asked, also leaning toward her, in a do-tell kind of way.

Henry was back. I thanked him for the fresh cappuccino but avoided his eyes, knowing I'd burst into laughter if we connected.

Ms. Overbee was in a telling mood. "Well, Paige has always wanted more credit than she was getting. Let's face it, Varena had lost it as far as her writing was concerned. She had no trouble coming up with new ideas, but it's another thing to turn an idea into a two-hundred-fifty-page novel and keep up the pace publishers demand these days."

I wasn't sure I wanted to hear this. I wanted to maintain the image I had of Varena Young as a creative and energetic woman, not a has-been, too old to back up her own name. But Ms. Overbee had an agenda and I needed to pay attention.

"Are you saying that Paige actually wrote the novels?"

Ms. Overbee raised her eyebrows, pushed her chin out, and shrugged her shoulders suggestively. She pointed at me, as if declaring me the winner in a guessing game. Where was the rigid assistant-not-servant of yesterday? Apparently Varena's death had set her free.

"All Paige got was an acknowledgment, her name buried in a list of other resource people at the beginning of the books. She was not a happy worker, let me tell you."

"Did Paige and Varena argue in front of you?" I asked.

"Constantly."

"That must have made for an unpleasant work environment," Henry said, giving Ms. Overbee a sympathetic look.

"Beyond unpleasant." Ms. Overbee rolled her eyes. "Varena insisted that it was her fan base that sold books, her name, not Paige's, and Paige's name on a book would mean nothing."

I wondered whether those were Varena's sentiments or Ms. Overbee's. If they were Varena's feelings, I doubted she'd have expressed them with a screwed-up face, as Laura did.

"I don't know much about the publishing industry, but I'm sure you do. Do you think Paige had a point?" I asked. "If she actually wrote the books, shouldn't she receive credit?"

"I suppose if I were in her shoes, I'd feel more than a little frustrated, leaving the lap of luxury on the Heights every night for a dorm room." Ms. Overbee rolled her eyes. "A flowery comforter doesn't hide the fact that all you have is a bunk bed and a plywood-and-cinderblock bookcase."

I wished I knew how Laura's lifestyle compared—did she have an expensive duvet-and-dust-ruffle set and a Chippendale case for her books?

Laura hadn't finished her rant against Paige. "If you ask me,
Varena hired her more because of her interest in miniatures than
any particular literary talent. I'm the one who's been around
awhile, managing Varena's fans, and believe me, their devotion
was to *the* Varena Young. They certainly would not accept some
college-student wannabe."

"So Paige wanted credit as co-author?" I asked, still trying
to fathom what the disagreement was about between Paige and
Varena.

"Well, preferably her own contract, of course, but Paige would
have settled for a *with*." Our turn for raised eyebrows. "Like 'by
Varena Young with Paige Taggart.' Then she could eventually get
her own deals when Varena retired."

"Or died," I said, surprising myself.

"Or died," Ms. Overbee said, and took another long pink
sip.

Act One had ended. Ms. Overbee had established Paige Taggart as a suspect in Varena Young's murder. Her performance was
almost good enough for me to eliminate Paige then and there,
but I tried to keep an open mind.

The three of us took deep breaths and sat back.

To start Act Two, I brought up an item from my own agenda.
"I wonder if you could help with another matter, Ms. Overbee?"

She waved her hands, as if trying to clap but missing the
mark. "Call me Laura, please."

I loved being on a first-name basis with a host of people who
lived and worked on Robert Todd Heights. "I have some questions about Corazón Cruz," I said.

"The former housekeeper." Laura seemed unruffled, which
surprised me. I'd hoped there was some controversy to exploit in
their relationship.

"Yes. First, how long was she with the family?"

Laura pursed her lips and rocked her head from side to side.
Making an estimate. "Not very long. About three months, I'd say.
The household manager who'd been with Varena forever died last
summer. If it's really important, I can check the records and get
back to you."

Cooperation above and beyond. Stunning for a woman who tried hard to close the door in my face less than twenty-four hours ago. I was impressed by Alicia Rockwell's reach. I wondered if Laura Overbee was jockeying for a way to be kept on at the estate. As Alicia's assistant? I guessed the whole question of who would live or work there, if anyone, was up for grabs.

"And Corazón was let go because…?"

"Beats me. All I know is that Charles sent her packing without a word to the rest of us."

"He could do that?"

"He does it all the time. No one asks if he has the right. We all just assumed Varena put him in charge. Most of the time, the decisions haven't had much effect on the rest of us anyway."

"He fired Corazón after Varena's body was found?"

Henry had disappeared again. I wished we'd had time to strategize about the two French log cabin interviews. I hoped he didn't think I wanted him gone from the table.

"Yes." Laura answered my question emphatically. "I know for a fact that Charles immediately offered her a handsome severance package and a one-way ticket to Mexico."

"Did that seem strange to anyone?"

"Not more than usual. Charles has some strange ways."

"Had he been at the estate all afternoon?"

"He'd arrived early, around three-thirty, for a dinner meeting. Varena often did that. She'd combine things, arranging a lunch or dinner with one or all of us."

"Were you invited to last evening's dinner?"

"No. Just Charles. I was all packed to leave for the day when…"

I was struck by Laura's tearing up. It seemed to stem from genuine sorrow this time and I chided myself for thinking ill of her.

I put my hand on her arm, hoping I'd wiped all the sugar granules from my morning bun off my fingers. "I'm sorry to upset you all over again, Laura." I spotted Henry at the newspaper rack in a corner and waved him over. "We're leaving now anyway. You take a minute to feel better."

"Thanks, Geraldine. It really is a shock."

"I know."

She pulled a card out of her purse and handed it to me. "Give me a call, okay? If you have any more questions or anything." I took it and filed it in my purse next to Alicia Rockwell's card.

I was feeling more and more like an investigator.

I WONDERED if it would look silly if I were to take out my notebook and pen and write while I walked to my car. I wanted desperately to jot down important phrases from this morning's meetings before I forgot them. I recited a few to myself. Uncle Caleb died many years ago. Paige found Varena's body. Alicia knows of no dollhouse delivery. Laura blames Paige, is really upset. Charles is in charge, fired Corazón. Adam distracted by divorce.

"Should we stay around awhile and see who happens to drop in next?" Henry asked.

"Thanks, but if I eat one more French pastry or sip another fancy espresso drink, I won't be able to get the seat belt around me." I buckled myself into my car on the passenger side, glad I didn't have to shift my concentration to driving.

My mind then took its usual wild trip, free associating. I thought of my chubby friend Linda's woeful complaint that I could eat a dozen French pastries a day and not gain an ounce, while all she had to do was look into the tubs of ice cream at Sadie's and she'd feel her stomach expand.

We'd never tested her theory, but it was true that I had the skinny gene and had passed it not to my son, Richard, but to Maddie.

Maddie, who still owed me an explanation about her parents' phone call, I remembered.

This day's work had hardly begun. It was a good thing I'd had a hearty breakfast.

Chapter 10

AS HENRY DROVE north on Springfield Boulevard toward my Eichler neighborhood, I strained to get a glimpse of Joshua Speed Woods to our left. I was hoping for a fall palette, but it was well past prime time for autumn colors, which even at their peak were dim here in the lowlands south of San Francisco. Things were better at higher altitudes, where there were spots that could pass for fall, but it had been a while since I'd visited any of those locations. Not for want of Henry's attempts to drag me away from Lincoln Point, but there was always a crafts show, a tutoring schedule, a volunteer shift at the library, a commitment to take care of Maddie—something to keep me home.

And now a murder to investigate.

Henry maneuvered expertly around the construction site at the Gettysburg–Springfield intersection.

"Do you think Laura Overbee followed Alicia? Or me?" I asked.

"She certainly came with an agenda."

I nodded. "To throw suspicion on Paige."

"Remember, Alicia admitted she'd already told the staff she was going to hire you."

"Don't say hire. I don't think I've ever been"—I stumbled—"well, hired, sight-unseen before. Certainly not to do anything like police work."

"Your reputation precedes you. It's conceivable that Laura Overbee followed you and then saw Alicia and decided she'd like to get in on the action at an early stage of your investigation."

"Don't say my investigation," I said, poking the driver. "It makes me even more nervous that one of the suspects is following me, though I know nothing that should worry anyone."

"You have enviable skills," Henry said.

"How's this for a skilled investigation? I just realized I didn't even ask Laura about Varena's brother, dead or alive, or if she had a forwarding address for Corazón. She, or Charles, must know where to send a final check, don't you think?" I covered my eyes, as unhappy as if I'd just gotten word of my students' poor SAT results. "I'm not good at ad hoc anything."

"You have Laura's card, and Alicia's. I know you. You'll sit down and get all organized with a list of questions for each of them and before you know it, you'll have an *aha* moment and figure out who killed your friend."

I liked it that Henry was so confident of my skills.

One of us had to be.

To prove Henry's point I took out my cell phone. "You're right," I said. "It's time to get organized."

"I didn't necessarily mean right now."

"Since you're such a willing chauffeur, I might as well do something useful from this seat. I'm going to call my neighbors and see if anyone was around when the dollhouse was delivered."

"Wouldn't they have called you if they saw something like that?

"A dollhouse arriving at my front door? No one would blink an eye."

"What was I thinking?"

I needed to work out the timeline before I made the calls. I reviewed Monday's events out loud, so I could have Henry's input.

"I left my house about two-thirty yesterday to go to a three o'clock meeting at the estate."

"It's hard to believe it all started such a short time ago," Henry said, echoing my own thought.

I paused, allowing myself a moment to remember what seemed like a whirlwind hour behind the gates of Robert Todd Heights on what turned out to be the last afternoon of Varena's life.

"Afterwards, I went directly to your house. Then Kay and the girls went for ice cream—what time would you say?"

"After Skip's call."

"Which was at six-fifteen. Now I remember looking at the clock to check how long it had been since I'd left Varena's home. I wish I'd known how handy it would have been if I'd taken a log book with me."

Henry smiled. "We're figuring it out. Kay and the girls would have landed at your house around seven-fifteen, seven-thirty, and found the dollhouse."

"Five hours. It's a long window of opportunity for a delivery."

"It includes the dinner hour; someone must have been home," Henry said.

"We'll see," I said, with as much optimism as I could muster.

I started with June Chinn, my neighbor to the right, facing my house from the street. June was a tech editor and Skip's current and longest-running girlfriend. Her Eichler was pale green with dark green trim, a nice complement to my two-tone blue version. There was a good chance June would be around now and also last evening since she often worked from her well-equipped home office.

I was delighted to hear her voice. Success on my first call. Then she launched into what was on her mind. "Hey, Gerry. What's up with that woman who was murdered in the rich part of town? You usually have the skinny on such things."

"It turns out, she was a friend of mine."

The long pause told me I should have led up to the announcement more slowly. I hadn't meant to sound abrupt.

"Oh, Gerry, I'm so sorry. Me and my big mouth. I haven't talked to Skip or I would have known. We're kind of on the outs."

Uh-oh. I didn't want to hear more bad news. "What's wrong?"

"Oh, never mind. It's the usual. Taking our relationship to the next level and so on."

"Do you want to talk about it?" I hoped not right now.

"No, no. I'm sorry about your friend. On the news this

morning, they said she was a famous writer and I'd never heard
you talk about her."

"It's my fault, June. I shouldn't have dropped that so uncer-
emoniously. You couldn't have known, and actually I'd just met
her. But we clicked right away and I feel more of a loss than I
expected."

"I totally get it. Wow."

I pictured the totally cute June, sitting in her sweats, with her
straight black hair pulled into a ponytail. Skip's mother and I were
big fans of June, and apparently more eager than the two of them
to seal the relationship with a marriage license. I wondered if that
was the "next level" disagreement now in effect between them. I
wondered which one wanted to go up a step.

"Do they know anything about who killed her?" June asked.

"Not yet."

"That's really tough, not even knowing." A pause and a
breath. "Oh, wait, are you working on it, helping Skip?"

"Not really."

"You are. Great. All is well."

Another vote of confidence for my detecting skills.

"I have a question for you that's not connected to the investigation." Not so far, anyway.

"Shoot."

I heard the sounds of June taking a long drink from her ever-
present water bottle.

"Were you around your house yesterday afternoon?"

"Yeah, I was here all afternoon with my head in my keyboard. We're working on a new version of a GUI—a graphical
user interface—that's supposed to be delivered by the end of the
week. That's why I wasn't even thinking that the victim could
have been someone you knew."

"Don't worry about it, June."

"Now I got you off track. Shoot with your question. Oh, bad
choice. I hope your friend wasn't shot?"

June seemed more hyper than usual; I wondered about the
amount of caffeine she'd imbibed this morning.

"No, she wasn't shot."

"Whew."

"There was a delivery to my house yesterday, some time between two-thirty and"—I looked over at Henry, who held up five fingers, then two, then a bent index finger; I smiled—"about seven-thirty in the evening. Did you happen to notice?"

"Gee, you mean like a UPS truck or something?"

"I'm not sure. It's a very large dollhouse."

"Hmmm."

I took that as a "no," but I persisted. "It wasn't in a box. So, I'm assuming it probably wasn't an official delivery service like UPS or FedEx. Maybe just a small truck or an SUV. But it would have taken two people a few minutes to carry it to the front door."

"Hmmm. Sorry. I didn't hear any noise or anything. I'm on the other side of the house, though. Did they send the wrong one?"

"Yes." Close enough.

"Let's see. Who might have seen something? Mari and Jeremy just got back from vacation this weekend and I know they were planning to take one more day at home. They might have seen something. They're probably more observant than I am. Do you have their number?"

"Yes, but I'm not at home. Can you give it to me?"

I wrote down that number and those of several other neighbors and thanked June.

"No problem," she said. "If I think of anything else, I'll buzz you. And, again, Gerry, I'm—"

I couldn't take another apology. "You've been a big help, June. I hope you can get back to work on your GIU."

June chuckled and I figured I'd mixed up the letters. I didn't flub on purpose, but I was glad she'd have a good laugh once I hung up. If she and Skip were on the outs, she might need one. I know I did.

I repeated my story to Mari, who lived on the other side of me.

"Don't you know where you bought it?" she asked.

"It's a gift. I think my son is trying to surprise me, but I don't want to thank him if it was someone else."

Henry gave me a thumbs-up, apparently not concerned about the easy lie he'd heard from my lips.

I left a message for Shelley and Joel across the street. Next to them were Yvette and Andrea, both of whom worked from home but weren't aware of a dollhouse delivery.

"I could come by if you need help getting it in the house," Yvette said, a nice gesture.

After five calls, I had no more information, but I did catch up on what my neighbors had been doing lately and acquired an insight into who was paying attention and how people responded to an off-the-wall question.

I felt like a reporter interviewing for a "man on the street" column. Or a police detective investigating a crime. Neither of which I had credentials for.

My last hope was Esther Willoughby, a nonagenarian who lived by herself in a beige Eichler with brown trim at the corner of the cross street near my home.

It took a few minutes for Esther to come around to my question. First, I heard about her club's project to knit fifty baby blankets for the firemen's holiday drive. In a burst of altruistic feelings, I offered to contribute one though it had been years since I'd knit anything bigger than six inches square. Then we reviewed the status of her four children, all older than me, an update from just last week. They were all doing so, so well, but none of them visited as often as she'd like.

Finally, she said, "I was in the front yard tending to my heather and azaleas—some have already turned brown, sorry to say—and I happened to see two men leave your door, Geraldine. It was around five, right after all the four o'clock shows. I switch back and forth, you know."

I didn't know, and tried to picture Esther wielding a remote, following several talk shows at once. "Were the men carrying the dollhouse?" I asked, cautiously excited.

"No, no. And I can't even tell you for sure that they left anything at your house, because I didn't see them walking to your door, just away from it, empty-handed. They got in a red truck, kind of old and dusty, like the kind George and I had when Lincoln Point was all farm land. Nowadays families have those large types, those SVUs."

I smiled and empathized with Esther's mixing up the common letters as I was sure I'd mixed up the acronym for June's work. The smile was also in honor of the first bit of information I'd had since starting my polling of my neighbors.

I let Esther go on. "I'll bet these young mothers wouldn't know what to do if they had to load their kids onto a bus, like I did with my four. We never even owned a car, you know, until my youngest was in high school."

It was time to cut in before Esther could launch into a discussion of families these days versus those in the good old days.

"Can you describe the men?"

"Oh, dear, they were too far away for me to see any details. I'm sorry. They were husky, though, and white, and walked like they were kinda young, but everyone's young to me."

"I know what you mean," I said, joining her in a laugh.

"They had those baseball caps that all the men wear."

"Did you happen to see a logo on the cap or anything that would distinguish them?"

"No, sorry, dear. They drove right by me, but with these eyes I have now I couldn't see inside. I tried, too. Not that I'm nosy, but I do keep watch for strangers in the neighborhood."

Burglars, beware, with Esther on the job. "You've been a big help," I said, for the second time in several minutes.

It was true. Esther had given me more than anyone else in the neighborhood. I knew from experience that when an older person gave you television shows as time markers, they were usually correct.

"There might be one other thing that could help you," Esther said.

"What is it?" It always took awhile to leave Esther, whether in person or on the phone. I didn't have a lot of hope for more information during the long good-bye.

"It probably doesn't matter, but I did notice an Arizona license plate on the truck those two men were driving. I couldn't see any numbers though. They weren't sticking to the speed limit, if you know what I mean."

"Arizona? You're sure?"

"You can't miss Arizona plates. They have a big cactus on the lefthand side. My granddaughter lives there, is how I know, and Terry's the only one who comes to visit me, even though her parents live right across the bay in Union City. Terry goes to school in Tucson."

I couldn't wait to get off the phone and mull over this new information. It was more than I'd gotten all day. However, I couldn't get away from Esther without a promise to stop in for tea very soon. "And bring that handsome new friend of yours," Esther said. I knew there was a twinkle in her eyes at that point.

Maybe Alicia Rockwell should have hired Esther for this job.

"IT'S something," Henry said after I filled him in on Esther's end of the conversation. He'd pulled over while I finished talking.

"And since nothing else was left on my doorstep yesterday, it's a good bet that we're looking for an old red pickup with Arizona plates."

I envisioned our riding around all day scanning every truck's license plate we passed. I hoped we'd come up with a better idea.

"How old did you say this lady is?" Henry asked.

"I went to her ninetieth birthday party within the last couple of years."

Henry frowned. "Do you think her eyesight is reliable?"

"It's not that good, but I think she would know her grand-daughter's license plate. She's very sharp, writing her memoirs. June helps her with the computer."

"She has a computer?"

I guessed Henry was feeling left out. He still refused to participate even in email, let alone online shopping or other activities. I didn't blame him. If Richard and his family hadn't lived in Los Angeles for many years, I probably wouldn't have been as agreeable to learning how to email. I managed to retire from ALHS before it was a requirement for teachers. Now, even Maddie's sixth-grade class accessed homework online.

But once you have a computer, I learned, you can find a myriad of uses, from keeping bank records to creating a calendar that can be shared with anyone you choose (very handy for scheduling Maddie-care), to making mailing labels from your address book.

"Esther has trouble locating her files now and then, but so do I," I said. "Otherwise, June's very impressed with what Esther can do."

"A motley crew of neighbors," Henry said. "Is that about it for calls?"

"For now," I said. "What do you think about searching for that pickup? What if it's back in Arizona?"

"We could alert Skip."

I grunted. "Maybe not right now."

"You're telling me you're not on good terms with the one person who can help us out?"

"I'm afraid not. He might be mad at me."

"Well, he's not mad at me," Henry said.

"Get on it then," I said, giving him a playful jab in the ribs.

I loved it that Henry brought out a side of me that was dormant most of the time.

WE pulled up in front of my house after a morning that was more eventful than I'd expected. I scanned the rows of Eichlers on both sides of my street, in different colors and trims, and pictured the neighbors I'd just spoken to, going about their business.

All was quiet.

I glanced at my blue doorway with some trepidation. *Whew.* No deliveries this morning.

On the other hand, I felt a twinge of disappointment that a midsize Tudor hadn't been set on my front step. It also would have been nice if a red pickup with Arizona plates had been parked at my curb.

This detecting work was harder than I'd thought.

Chapter 11

I WAS A firm believer that often inspiration for one project comes when you're working on another. (In other words, I was the world's best procrastinator.) I decided to take stock of my dollhouse inventory before digging further into the secrets of the new house in my atrium. My visit to Varena's home and my short-lived friendship with her had inspired me to get myself organized.

Besides, Henry had offered to take a shot at unlocking the secret room Maddie had found.

While he rummaged around my garage and crafts room for tools, I surveyed my collection of finished and half-finished doll-houses and room boxes. The midsize-Tudor-turned-large-modern dwarfed my own projects and highlighted their deficiencies.

Most of my pre–special-delivery houses were squeezed into my crafts room. I saw my holdings in a new light. Stuff—there was no other word for it—was crammed into miniature bedrooms, living rooms, and playrooms. Using found objects was my forte, and much of the so-called furniture was made from bottle tops and plastic throwaway items.

Not for the first time, I considered my friend Linda's perfectionist approach to crafts. I wondered, if I'd put my investment of time and energy into one really well made and beautifully furnished dollhouse, like ones Linda crafted, it would have been a better use of my time.

That was Linda talking, I decided. There was more than one way to approach a hobby, and as long as it gave me pleasure, no further judgment was called for.

I checked out my street of stores—replicas of the bookstore, ice cream parlor, and bagel shop in town. I mused about adding a French bakery. How hard would I have to work to get Maddie to help with that one? Not at all.

All day I'd been avoiding thoughts of Maddie and what she had to tell me. She'd be home in a few hours and my nail-biting would be over. Or just starting.

Skip was right, though. I had to get rid of a couple of houses. One was already earmarked as a donation to our Lincoln Point Library playroom. I'd talked to our chief librarian, Doris Ann Hartley, about fixing it up so that each room was decorated as a scene in a different children's story. I planned to introduce the idea at the regular meeting of my crafts group tomorrow evening. My goal was to persuade each lady to sign up for a story.

I'd already decided I'd take on *Snow White*. Nothing was more fun to craft than the seven dwarves. Except I wouldn't actually make the characters, I'd make something to remind the children of them. A few crumpled tissues for Sneezy; a pillow for Sleepy. A—

Rrring. Rrring.

Someone was calling an end to my escapism into the land of little things. I checked the screen on my landline phone. Doris Ann Hartley herself. I realized I'd been hoping for a call from Skip all morning. I wasn't used to our being at odds and wondered who'd give in first.

"Gerry? I heard about Varena Young. What happened?"

"I wish I knew."

Our librarian since as far back as our family had a Lincoln Point Public Library card, Doris Ann called herself the Two-Thousand-Year-Old Librarian. She certainly seemed to know everything that had gone on during that period of human history and beyond. She was such a willing and knowledgeable resource for school children, they probably thought she'd done live interviews with the cave men.

"Everyone here's talking about it," Doris Ann said. "She has so many fans in town, I have a hard time keeping enough of her books on the shelves. I can't believe it. First you say you'll be in contact with her about a donation for the bookmobile auction, and the next thing I know she's murdered?"

I hoped I didn't need to remind Doris Ann that the two events weren't connected, Detective Blythe Rutherford's opinion notwithstanding.

"It's a great loss to everyone," I said, not meaning to sound like a graveside preacher.

"I hate to ask at a time like this, Gerry, but I'm working on the publicity for the auction as we speak. Do we have a dollhouse?"

I hesitated. How could I be sure the modern dollhouse was available to donate if I didn't know who left it on my doorstep? Maybe there was a midsize Tudor on the way to my house now, as promised. Maybe not. I should have asked Alicia when I had the chance, or even Laura Overbee. Alicia had offered to compensate me with a couple of dollhouses. I liked the sound of that, but we never closed the deal. At the time it seemed the thing to do was to cut off the discussion until I knew more about the modern house that had been delivered, apparently without her knowledge.

"I think I have a house," I told Doris Ann.

"You think?"

I pictured her in her library office in the Civic Center, overflowing with books and papers. Her white hair would be beautifully coiffed, but her perpetual smile, telling everyone she had the cushiest job in the world, was the big attraction.

"It's complicated," I said.

She groaned. "Not you, too."

"What do you mean?"

"Just that everyone is using that phrase now, indiscriminately. My student aide was late and when I asked what kept her she said, 'It's complicated.' When I asked my daughter why she and her husband had decided to separate, she said…Well, you see what I mean. It tells me the person doesn't want to bother helping me understand. Or they think I'm too stupid to get it." She paused. Reconsidering? "Not you, of course, Gerry."

"Yes, me, too, I guess. Let me just say that I'll have everything cleared up in plenty of time for the auction."

"Good. I'll take you at your word."

I hung up hoping I could deliver. There was no denying it would be complicated.

I LET out a little gasp when I saw Henry, hammer high over his head, ready to swing at—and hit—the mystery dollhouse in my atrium.

He stopped in midair and smiled. "Scared?" he asked.

I cleared my throat. "Of course not," I said, pretending to have known all along that he was teasing.

He followed through the swing, ending with a set of light taps on a miniature white bookcase in the bedroom. The books seemed to be glued in place, not budging from the shelves when the hammer landed.

"Nothing's happening," he said. "I guess that would be too obvious, a secret room behind a bookcase. It's there, though. I made some measurements and I figure there's a two-inch gap that must be what Maddie discovered."

I admired the patience with which Henry accepted the results of his efforts. I knew he'd try again, but in the meantime, there was no panic or even frustration as there might be for me, and certainly would be for Maddie.

"I have an idea," I said.

"Bring it on."

I picked up the phone in the atrium. "I should have thought of this earlier. Linda Reed. She's seen everything there is to see in tricks of the dollhouse trade. She might have a clue as to how to locate the secret room, even from a distance. If I can just be patient while she goes through the trials of the day."

Henry already knew all sides of Linda Reed—the whiny perfectionist, complaining about the smallest inconvenience; the concerned, adoptive single mother of a troublesome teenager; the creative and generous friend. Linda could be counted on to ply you with complaints about the worst moments of her day, but also to show up with her nursing skills at the drop of a hat when someone she cared about was in need.

Linda picked up after a couple of rings. I let her go through her opening routine.

"Gerry, I was just going to call you. That new supposedly extra-hold glue I bought? Well, guess what? It won't even hold paper to paper. Don't buy it, no matter what it says on the package."

"Thanks for the tip. I won't go near it."

"Did I tell you? Jason got hold of my credit card again and went crazy on eBay. He's grounded. But then he sprained his ankle and you know what a soft touch I am"—I was about to break in and agree when Linda wound down—"So what did you call about, Ger? Anything special?"

Very special. "Have you ever seen a dollhouse with a secret room?"

"Sure. Lots. Remember, I showed you a photo of that one at the dollhouse museum in Carmel, Indiana? There was this beautiful flowered wallpaper in an upstairs bedroom, and you had to look really closely to see that part of the wall was a door to a little passageway. When you pulled on a little knob, the wall slid open and there was a hallway kind of thing. Very nicely done."

Interesting, but there was no door or doorknob on my Frank Lord Wright, as Maddie had called it. "Any other mechanisms that you've seen?"

"Let me think." A pause, then a slight gasp. "Oh, no. Gerry, are you building a secret room?" She lowered the pitch of her voice and I pictured her mouth screwed up in distaste. "Don't tell me you found a kit?"

"No, I wouldn't do that to you, Linda. What other ways can you rig a secret room or hallway?"

"Let's see, I saw an idea in a book where they used a two-way mirror on a wall, one of those mirrors like when the police interview their suspects."

How well I knew. "How does that work?" I asked. Though there wasn't a mirror where Maddie had seen the passage, there was one on the side wall over a vanity. Maybe they were connected.

"The mirror looks ordinary until somehow the room behind it gets lit up. I always thought it would be fun to put a really creepy staircase behind the mirror in a narrow room and you could use a remote control to operate the lights. It would be cool for Halloween, don't you think?"

"I'll think about it. Anything else? Maybe something simpler?"

"Well, unless you want to do the old standby of pushing on a bookcase, but how boring is that?"

"Wouldn't think of it."

I heard an intake of breath; Linda had thought of something else. "Oh, there was this stairway I saw, but it was in a real house, not a dollhouse. The lady had a remote and when she pushed it, this half flight of stairs leading up to the next floor swiveled up on hinges. Then you saw this other half staircase leading down to a lower level. I can draw a picture if you want."

"Never mind," I said, losing interest by now. There were only full staircases in the house in my atrium. They were open on both sides, the levels clearly distinguishable from the open side of the house. I didn't see how there could have been anything hidden under them.

"So are you going to tell me what you're going to use, Gerry? Are you really building from scratch?"

Linda was still under the impression that I was building, not unbuilding, a secret room. Rather than explain that it was complicated and perhaps annoy her, I let her misconception stand and thanked her for her ideas. Nothing Linda said helped a lot. It was going to take brute force to find the room and that intriguing letter, searching splinter by splinter if need be.

I promised Linda I'd explain everything at our next crafts meeting tomorrow evening, and we hung up. If I hadn't solved the problem by then, I might just make finding the secret room a group project. Or I might encourage Henry to complete that hammer swing with full force.

NOISES from the kitchen led me to Henry, taking a break. He rummaged through my refrigerator, looking for something to call lunch. I liked it that he felt free to make himself at home. I didn't like it that I'd neglected my larder lately and the pickings were slim.

"Back to the bakery?" he asked.

"I don't think I can take another pastry for a while. I'm sure I can whip up something."

It was over basic tuna melts that I had a brainstorm. Not about the secret room, but about Maddie and her secret. Something Linda had revealed about Jason's most recent offense had been nagging at me.

"I think I know what's wrong with Maddie," I said, refilling our cups of tea. "You know those presents Maddie has been buying?"

"Like my keychain?" Henry asked.

"That, and did you know that she bought Taylor an elaborate set of markers?"

He scratched his head. "Yeah, now that you mention it. Where are you going with this?"

I counted off two other presents that I knew of. Miniature earrings for the dresser in my latest room box project, and a specialty lotion for Kay. I was fairly sure there were gifts I didn't know about, for her Palo Alto friends, or for Skip and Beverly.

I told Henry what Jason had done with Linda's credit card, and how Maddie didn't want me to return Mary Lou's phone call, and how two and two might add up to a huge misdemeanor for my granddaughter.

Henry shook his head. "I just don't see her doing anything like that."

"I don't like it, either. But think about it. She was home alone, bored, for several days, with a bug, not so bad that she was in bed, or Mary Lou would never have left her. She had neighbors checking on her regularly, and of course, her parents and I called her often, but essentially she was on her own with not a lot to occupy her."

"I'm with you."

"I wasn't feeling that well myself or I would have gone to stay with her. Now I wish I had. Maybe if I—"

"You don't need to go there. And I don't mean to Palo Alto."

"You're right, and thank you. But there was my poor granddaughter with access to her parents' room and their desks and she must've known where there might be a credit card lying around."

"Kay leaves one by her computer. I never understood that."

"I'll bet Mary Lou does that, too. She makes a lot of online purchases and I'm sure it's just more convenient. Now, suddenly all of Maddie's relatives and friends are getting presents. Then, her parents call me, and Maddie makes me promise not to return the call until she can talk to me."

"And, also, suddenly she's not interested in using the computer."

We looked at each other, neither of us wanting to say it out loud.

Henry broke the silence. "She's been busted," he said.

"And grounded, as far as computer use. I'm sure that's what Richard and Mary Lou want to tell me."

We both went back to tuna and tea and deep breaths.

"I don't want to believe this," Henry said.

"It breaks my heart."

"It's a different world, isn't it?" Henry mused. "The most trouble we could get into was skipping school for a day at the lake."

"Or sneaking some cookies from the pantry."

"I guess it would be easy to match the crime with the kid as far as the two of us are concerned."

"Not to excuse Maddie, but you're right that the world has changed dramatically," I said. "There are temptations you and I couldn't have dreamed up, let alone faced every day."

"What are you going to do next?" Henry asked me.

A tough question. "I promised I'd wait until she got home before returning her parents' call. She said she'd tell me this afternoon what this is all about. I'm anxious, but I guess I'll keep my promise."

"Maybe it's something else entirely," Henry said.

I looked at him. We both knew that wasn't likely.

Chapter 12

BUZZZ. BUZZZ.

We thought we'd have an hour or so to ourselves. No investigations of any kind. No inquiries into Varena's murder. No poking around the dollhouse. No speculation about a blossoming life of crime for my granddaughter. No impossible task of locating a battered red truck with Arizona plates.

Buzzz. Buzzz.

No alone time either, it turned out.

I opened the front door, secretly hoping for another dollhouse delivery, preferably a midsize Tudor, with a clearly written TO/FROM gift tag, and unencumbered by secrets.

"I'm so glad you're home, Mrs. Porter," said the young woman on my doorstep. "I'm Paige Taggart."

Paige Taggart, college student, research assistant to a bestselling novelist, discoverer of said novelist's murdered body, possible author of said novelist's recent works.

Another unexpected interview coming up. Did people just walk up to police detectives and ask to be interrogated, I wondered. If I were ever on speaking terms with my nephew again, I'd ask him.

"Welcome, Paige," I said.

"Thanks. I was heading downtown and just took a chance that you might be home."

I was glad the "I happened to be in the neighborhood" ploy was alive and well with the younger set.

I really should have guessed that Paige would pay me a visit. Hadn't her late boss's daughter told her that she should cooperate with me? Alicia had confessed to spreading the word even before I agreed to be hired, though I still wasn't comfortable with the word.

Paige wore an expression that cleverly combined sadness at her old boss's death and compliance with her new boss's request. I wondered if she knew that her co-worker, Laura Overbee, had pointed in her direction as a highly motivated suspect.

She stepped over the threshold, pulling close a blue-and-gold football sweater, the likes of which I hadn't seen since my own college days. In fact, I hadn't seen that much clothing on a woman her age in many years, in any weather. I'd become used to the fashions of June Chinn and her friends, who often wore what I considered undergarments on the outside and left little to the imagination as far as exposed body parts.

"Mrs. Porter, I…"

In a flash, her smile collapsed and her face turned white.

I turned to see what had caused her consternation. Surely not the benign presence of Henry Baker, retired shop teacher and my BFF. And not my peaceful ficus either.

It was the dollhouse.

Sitting on a card table, its edges barely fitting on the forty-inch-square surface, the modern-style dollhouse dominated the atrium, crying out for attention.

"Is something wrong?" I asked.

With much stuttering the petite Paige said, "No, I…uh… have allergies this time of year."

I decided to push a little. "Isn't this a grand dollhouse?" I asked, drawing Paige into the atrium.

She slipped around behind me as if the streamlined rooms and angular staircases of the dollhouse gave off an unpleasant odor or a frightening aura.

"Grand," Paige managed, after two significant throat clearings. I began to think she might be telling the truth about allergies.

"Have you ever seen a dollhouse this big?" Henry asked, backing me up. Not to be too subtle.

"I don't think I have," Paige said. "Well, except for the

Morley Mansion." She chuckled, seeming to have recovered her
mental balance.

"What brings you here?" I asked, though I knew the answer.

"Alicia said you'd be wanting to talk to all of us. I can't imagine what help I'll be. I've already told the police everything I
know."

Not quite, I decided, since she was clearly holding something
back vis-à-vis the dollhouse. I wanted to ask if she had any ties
to a pickup with Arizona plates, but realized Paige wasn't behaving like one who'd been responsible in any way for the delivery.
On the contrary, she seemed to be holding back great surprise at
finding the dollhouse in my home.

"It must have been a terrifying experience, to come upon
your boss—your mentor, really—that way," I said. I led her past
the dollhouse, into the living room, watching her reaction, which
was to treat the dollhouse as if it were one more dead body that
she had to suffer.

Her hands disappeared into the long sleeves of her sweater,
meant for a much larger person, most likely a male. Her face took
on a tragic look as she settled into a chair.

"Can I get you some tea or coffee?" Henry asked.

"I'm good," Paige said. The current synonymous expression
for "No, thank you." I wondered if she was wishing something
stronger was on the menu.

I needed to quickly decide which role I would assume, since
Henry had drifted into and out of the room and into the role of
host. I could play mother and try to soothe Paige after the terrible ordeal she'd been through. Or I could take on the persona
of homicide detective. I'd had a good model of how intimidating
it could be as I sat across from Detective Blythe Rutherford.

I'd always had the most success with the teacher role, however. One look, arms across my chest, and freshmen and seniors
alike withered and confessed to the real reason their homework
was late. Though Paige hadn't passed through ALHS, she fit the
universal type.

"What year are you in, Paige?" I asked, establishing her status
as a student, and thus an underling.

Paige sat erect and folded her hands in her lap. "I'm a junior English major at San Jose State."

"Wonderful. That was my field, too, so of course I'm happy it's still popular. I taught English for many years at Abraham Lincoln High School. I'd love to talk to you about your reading list some time."

"My concentration is in creative writing, so this semester, I have a bunch of workshops and a class in the American novel."

Suddenly, I wanted to go back to college. I knew the feeling wouldn't last.

"It's quite a coup that you got to work with a bestselling author."

"Varena was like a mother to me. I couldn't believe my luck that she chose me. There are seniors I know who would have killed for the job." Paige gasped. "Oh, my God, I can't believe I said that."

I let her stew for a while, mean person that I am, while Henry announced that coffee was ready, in case she'd changed her mind. I was impressed that he'd found just the right small platter for the cookies. There were only two cups on the tray.

"I'll be in the garage," he said.

I gave him a grateful smile. "Why do think Varena chose you, Paige? Had you published your own work by then?"

"I wouldn't say published, but I'd already written a couple of romances. I've always loved them, and I submitted a few chapters with my application to work for her. During my interview she told me I had great promise." Paige broke down in tears. "She was like the mother I never had. My parents were both alcoholics. That's probably why I started reading and writing romances even when I was a kid. I'd sneak into that part of the library to hide and go into this, like, perfect world where everyone loved each other."

This wasn't the direction I wanted for this interview. It also wasn't the thread of the few Regency romances I'd read, where a rich, ugly nobleman tries to steal a maiden away from her young, handsome true love.

I didn't necessarily think Paige was lying about her childhood, but I strongly suspected she was manipulating me. The way any junior, in high school or college, might. I couldn't let her emotional state sway me.

I waited until Paige calmed down, resisting the temptation to pat her on the back or whisper soothing words. I reminded myself that I'd been "hired" to investigate her and everyone else. I needed a lesson from Detective Rutherford.

Once Paige lifted her head, I was ready. "Did you feel Varena gave you enough credit for all the work you did for her books?"

Paige mopped her eyes with a tissue. "Oh, yes, I was very happy working with Varena. I loved the research on the Regency period, looking up whether they had zippers and stuff like that. Making sure the family trees all were consistent from one book to the next."

"It sounds fascinating."

"And I knew eventually Varena would put my name on a book. She said, when the time was right."

"And you were satisfied to wait."

"Of course. I'm not like Laura, you know." Paige took a settling breath. "Laura Overbee, I mean. She was trying to write, too. Not romance, but poetry mostly. Lots of luck trying to get poetry published these days."

"What did that have to do with Varena?"

"Laura was always complaining that Varena went back on a promise she made when she hired her."

"What kind of promise?"

"Supposedly, Varena told Laura that if she took the job as assistant, which we all know is really just a glorified secretary, making travel plans and booking events, things like that, that she'd help Laura get published, but she never did. Laura would beg Varena even for an endorsement, but Varena just wasn't interested in the kind of things Laura wrote."

An image came to my mind of two people, Laura and Paige, their fingers pointing at each other, like the hands in the Escher drawing, each writing on the other's shirt cuff: GUILTY!

"And just to be clear, you didn't feel any resentment at the low level of acknowledgment Varena gave you? Simply listing your name with many others who helped her?"

Paige bit her lip. "No, no. I told you, Varena was like a mother to me."

She was sticking to her script. I had to rethink my theory. College juniors were more persistent than high school juniors. Too bad for me. I needed another tack, and clearly, some prep time. I knew Paige was hiding something she knew about the mysteriously delivered dollhouse, but I couldn't come up with anything to coax it out of her except a direct question.

I pointed toward my atrium. "Paige, I have a feeling you've seen that dollhouse before. Is it my imagination or do you recognize it? Is it from Varena's collection?"

Paige's eyes twitched, as did her hands, which retreated further into the sleeves of her sweater. "I told you, Mrs. Porter, I had some kind of allergic reaction. Maybe it's your plants."

"Of course. That must have been what I noticed," I said. I was almost glad when Paige's cell phone interrupted us. I could tell she was digging in and would give me nothing useful.

Paige was even happier about the call than I was.

"Bummer," she said, holding out her phone, as if I'd be able to read the small screen from several feet away. "I gotta go."

"Bummer," I said.

I saw her to the door, but I had a feeling I wasn't through with Paige Taggart.

THREE in the afternoon and what had I accomplished? Trying to be positive, I ran through all the interactions I'd had since our wonderful French-delights breakfast. I'd at least become familiar with three of the main players at the Rockwell Estate. Varena's elegant, fashionable daughter, Alicia, who commanded the respect of her household staff. Laura Overbee, Varena's aide, and Paige Taggart, her research assistant, who all but accused each other of Varena's murder.

There were more loose ends than leads, however.

There was the matter of the missing housekeeper, Corazón Cruz, and the mystery of Varena's brother. If Varena's only sibling was deceased, to whom had Corazón referred yesterday? And who did I hear arguing with Varena? (Or was her real name actually Mildred Swingle?)

I'd had only the briefest of interactions with the Rockwells' financial manager, Charles Quentin, as he closed the door in my face. Did he fall under Alicia's directive to cooperate with me, or was he above it all?

I needed to meet Varena's son, Adam. Should I rule him out as a suspect since he was three thousand miles away until last evening? Nothing said he couldn't have hired someone.

I stopped. How desperate was I, to imagine a hit man being hired by a member of a Robert Todd Heights family to murder his mother? If the police were trained to think this way, it was no wonder some of them turned into skeptics like Blythe Rutherford. It's a good thing Alicia, so determined to get to the bottom of her mother's death, wasn't spending money on this investigator she'd hired.

Calculating my score as a detective, I nearly forgot the unreachable clue in the letter hidden in the secret room of a dollhouse I could trace only to an Arizona vehicle, on the word of a ninety-plus-year-old neighbor. It was a dizzying string of facts. More in the loss column than the win, even before I counted the rift with my nephew and the possibility that my granddaughter had begun a life of crime.

"Getting your mind in order?" Henry asked, coming up behind my chair. I hadn't moved from the living room since Paige Taggart left. Neither Paige nor I had touched our coffee, now too cold to be appealing.

"I'm trying, but it's complicated."

He leaned over for a hug and I was glad to have one solid person to hang on to, one who didn't mind my saying things were complicated.

"I struck out with the secret room," he said, taking the chair opposite, where Paige had sat. "Can't find anything to open that wall, unless I tear the building apart. I think we should give Maddie another try before we do that."

I nodded agreement. "She found it once, she can probably do it again if she's not under stress."

Henry sent a meaningful look to the large clock. A look that said the time was approaching when I needed to pick up Maddie from school.

Often the trip to Palo Alto to retrieve my granddaughter was the highlight of my day. I never tired of praising her latest artistic endeavor, listening to stories of lunch-swapping with her friends, and being impressed by the newest fact she'd learned in history class.

On the drives home, Maddie served as my conscience on matters of everything from recycling to world peace, expressing her views with the simplicity reserved for the very young.

Today was different. Today the issue was not helping the poor and imprisoned, but what Maddie herself had done that might merit punishment. The state of affairs turned my stomach to the consistency of tacky glue.

"Shall I come with you?" Henry asked, as if he'd been following my train of thought.

"I think I'd better handle this alone first."

"Let's get you to your car, then." Henry lent his arm as I lumbered up from the chair, a testimony to how pathetic I must have looked. "It might not be as bad as you think," he said. "By the time you get home, I'll bet it will be all cleared up."

That was my fondest wish.

WHEN I pulled up to a spot in front of Maddie's school, I saw her sitting on a bench, by herself, hugging her neon green backpack to her chest. Not business as usual, when she'd be surrounded by her friends, chatting and laughing, until she'd bound over to my car. Today she seemed as heavy as I was, pushing herself off the bench and making her way to the curb.

She got into my car and we leaned toward each other for a kiss. At least that part of the ritual was intact. While I drove off, still pondering the appropriate greeting, Maddie extracted a book from her backpack and dropped the pack to the floor.

"Look, Grandma, I got a book on dollhouses from the library," she said, her voice strained in an effort to sound normal. "I found some in the kids' section."

Not her section now that she was eleven, she meant, but the section she'd used when she was younger.

"Did you find anything on secret rooms?" I was no more eager than she was to discuss the elephant in the car.

"Uh-uh." Maddie flipped through the oversize book on her lap. "But there's a picture of this really cool house. You can't look now, but you'll see later. The building is called a vacation home and most of it sticks out over this hill. It looks like it's going to take off and fly over the ocean right across the street from it. We used to see a lot of these along the beaches in Los Angeles, but this one is a dollhouse. I guess the ocean is fake. Isn't that cool?"

"Very cool, sweetheart."

"I think I might want to be an architect like Grandpa and build cool houses like this."

Maddie knew this would be thrilling news to me. Not only had she abandoned dreams of wearing a uniform with a gun on her belt, but she wanted to follow in Ken's footsteps. I had a feeling this was Maddie the politician softening up dumb old Grandma before she had to face the music.

"Would you rather talk about your parents' phone call now or when we get home?" I asked her. Not so dumb after all.

Maddie's knobby knees, in jeans, came together. Her shoes slapped against each other in a sideways motion. "Did you talk to my mom?"

"No, not yet. I promised I wouldn't."

"You figured it out, didn't you?"

"I think so, but why don't you tell me?"

Instead of launching into her typical articulate narration, Maddie let loose with a flood of tears. She sobbed softly, but nearly uncontrollably. I had the feeling that she'd been needing to do that for as long as she'd been engaged in an activity she knew to be wrong. My heart was breaking for her.

Between gasps, I heard the word "sorry" many times, often preceded by "very, very." It was all I could do not to cry with her.

I realized I had no plan for what to do once we started down this road. I regretted now that I hadn't called her parents immediately, no matter how much Maddie pleaded otherwise. We would have already put this issue behind us and would have been working out a solution.

I hadn't reached the freeway yet, so it was easy to find a strip mall and pull in. As luck would have it, the first parking spot I came upon was in front of a chain ice cream shop.

If I were going to punish my granddaughter, there would have to be a treat included.

Chapter 13

ONCE WE WERE settled in the pink-and-brown ice cream shop with a hot fudge sundae for Maddie and a chocolate soda for me, we'd both calmed down. Two spoonfuls in, and Maddie confessed.

"I used Mom's credit card," she said almost matter-of-factly. She looked at me, lips tight, chin up, ready to face the music.

I smoothed back a recalcitrant red curl from her forehead. "I know," I said.

"I know it was wrong, wrong, Grandma. But it was like I talked myself into it anyway." I didn't want to break the news that it wouldn't be the last time she'd make a decision under those conditions. "Dad freaked out on the phone last night. He was going to get on a plane and come and get me. But Mom just said, for now, no more computers, until we could talk."

I imagined my son beating himself up, thinking he'd done something wrong and created a potential lifer, while Mary Lou would research reasons why children steal and how to deal with it.

"Can you tell me why you did it?"

"I don't know. Except, all my friends have money of their own and I don't have any. They buy me things, like from the vending machine, or on a holiday sometimes they buy me a card. And I can never do anything back."

"You make wonderful cards for everyone on your computer. I've gotten many of them."

"It's not the same."

I didn't think Maddie would appreciate a lecture on how

much better a handmade card was than one bought in a mall shop. No matter how much parents and grandparents lectured, peers were peers.

"What about your allowance? Isn't it enough?"

"I don't get one." Maddie shouted this out, then noticed we weren't the only patrons in the small shop. She lowered her voice. "Dad says I don't need any money because I have everything I need. I have a phone for if I get in trouble and I know how to call emergency and I take my lunch and they give me money when the school needs it, like for trips, and he thinks that's all that counts."

As I listened to Maddie's rant, I became more and more sympathetic. No surprise, since I was always irresistibly drawn to take her side. That aside, I thought she had a point. I'd assumed all kids by this age received some amount of discretionary money. I tried to keep out of business matters like that in the life of my son's family, focusing on spoiling his daughter on my own terms.

I realized I had no idea if Maddie did chores at home, for example, except that I knew Richard kept after her about maintaining neatness in her room. The strange thing was that as a kid Richard kept his room in perfect order, as if he were practicing for the operating room even at eleven years old. I hope he didn't expect that of her.

Maddie spooned another mouthful of sundae. She had a special knack of getting a bit of everything—two flavors of ice cream, fudge sauce, whipped cream, and nuts—in each spoonful. She finished her reasonable defense with "Just once I wanted to buy everyone something."

"Everyone?"

"Rochelle and Shauna, my two best friends at school. And Taylor and Uncle Henry."

"Don't forget Aunt Kay. And me." I paused. "And nothing for yourself?"

"Uh-uh." She shook her head and gave me a look that said she'd never thought of doing that. I wasn't surprised.

"I'll bet you gave Aunt Beverly and Uncle Skip a present, too."

Maddie finally gave me a smile, albeit a pouty one. "I was just getting to them when I got caught."

"Too bad for them," I said, happy my son wasn't around to hear my amusement over a serious matter. But I was so relieved that things weren't worse. No one had a life-threatening illness, for example.

"I guess Mom saw her bill online yesterday and some of the charges were on it. She called me at your house, then she called you."

"Several times. She must be wondering why I haven't gotten back to her all this time."

"She probably knows what's going on."

"Probably," I said.

"I did a really bad thing, didn't I, Grandma?"

I missed the easy questions I used to get from my granddaughter. Like, why is the sky blue and how do magnets work, in which cases I went immediately to the children's encyclopedia for answers.

"You made a pretty big mistake, Maddie. I'm sure you know the right thing to do is to talk to your parents about your feelings and ask them to think about an allowance. You're the best negotiator I know."

"Yeah. I tried, but my dad is so…so…"

"A little thick-headed maybe?" I offered.

"Totally."

Dum, ta da dum, ta da dum, ta da dum.

Maddie smiled when she heard the marching band on my cell phone.

"It's Uncle Skip. I'd better take it."

Maddie's eyes lit up, then the light faded when she realized she was shut out of any "case" she might be salivating over. I'd have to remind her of her plans for a future in architecture as soon as we got over this crisis.

"Hey, Aunt Gerry." A pause. "Everything okay with, you know?" Skip asked, by which I figured he meant between us.

"Everything's absolutely okay," I said, more relieved than he might guess. I loved make-ups that didn't involve a lot of words and rehashing. A therapist might have disagreed, but long, drawn-out explanations and apologies were not for me. I hardly remembered what our tiff was about and I didn't care.

"I thought you might want to know. We're holding Ms. Taggart, your friend's research assistant."

"Paige? When did that happen? I just saw her this afternoon."

"I know and apparently she thinks you're her advocate."

"I'm not sure I understand."

"I'm not sure I do either, but she wants to talk to you and she has that right. She says you have something that will clear her."

"I can't imagine what it is."

"Only one way to find out, if you're willing to come down."

"Of course, but why is she there in the first place, Skip? Is there some evidence that points to her?"

"How soon can you be here?"

"I'm eating ice cream in Palo Alto. I'll be on my way in a minute."

"So the squirt is with you. Don't tell her I still call her that. Give her a kiss for me."

"Gladly."

Maddie, who had been following my side of the conversation intently, clapped and gave me a big smile. She was happy to receive a kiss from her uncle and me. I felt the relief in her body as she held onto my embrace, not an easy thing to do across a pink table, small as it was. Like a good girl, she cleared off our table and we headed out the door.

For now, vicarious involvement in her uncle's case seemed enough for her.

AS eager as I was to find out why the police had pulled Paige Taggart in, I still needed to take care of unfinished business with Maddie. I was ready and willing to forgive and forget. But I realized that wasn't the best solution for the long term. There was a lot more talking to be done first, especially with her parents.

Maddie seemed to agree, but her plan was different from mine. "Can you talk to Mom and Dad, Grandma?" she asked, as

soon as were safely merged into freeway traffic going south on
Route 101.

"I will, but you should know that whatever your parents decide I'm going to support them."

"I know, I know, I know. But maybe you can explain what it's
like to be a kid these days."

I was immensely flattered until I sneaked a look and saw
Maddie's wide grin and smug "almost gotcha" look.

THE police station was its busy self on a Tuesday afternoon. I
greeted officers I knew from having them in class at ALHS or
from my frequent visits to Skip. I hoped I wouldn't run into
Detective Rutherford, for no other reason than I didn't particularly care for her style.

Two female officers who had designs on Skip fawned over
his little cousin-once-removed and I left Maddie in their care. I'd
rather have left her in a drafting workshop or history of architecture class, but that wasn't an option.

Before she followed the officers, Maddie made one last attempt to work her plan. "Do you think I could go down to
the jail with you when you go to see the lady, Grandma?" she
asked.

"The lady is not in jail"—yet, I added silently—"and no,
anyway." It was rapidly sinking in that Maddie's recent interest in
architecture was targeted to soften up her grandmother in preparation for diving into the petty theft issue.

With permission from the desk sergeant—Jimmy Summers, a
B student from the class of nineteen ninety-nine—I walked back
to Skip's cubicle.

I wished I had a sweet offering for Jimmy and a peace offering for Skip, but there hadn't been time to go home first and bake
a couple of batches of cookies. One of these days I was going to
be charged with bribing a whole department of police officers,
I just knew.

I stepped behind one of the fabric-covered partitions that
made up Skip's office space, checking that June's photo was still
on his desk. I'd be sure to tell her, in case that made a difference.

Skip came up behind me and gave me a welcoming hug that felt like his own peace offering. I hugged him back.

That didn't mean he didn't have a warning for me, however.

"I'm not happy about your being this directly involved in an ongoing murder investigation, but I'm not about to refuse this request. I don't see Paige Taggart as a hardened killer who's going to take you hostage."

"That's comforting."

I wondered if my being hired by the victim's daughter counted as being "directly involved in an ongoing murder investigation." I decided not to worry Skip about it at the moment.

PAIGE Taggart, Varena Young's unthreatening research assistant, now an official person of interest in her murder, presented a sad picture in the very interview room I'd sat in last night. She was wearing the same oversize sweater she'd had on when she visited me a few hours ago at my home, except that the sweater looked dingier under the crackling overhead lights and even less as though it belonged to her.

Paige stood and I received my second police-station hug of the day, this one tearful. "Mrs. Porter, thank you sooo much for coming." Her voice cracked. "They think I killed Varena."

I gave her a motherly pat and we both took seats at the table, with me on the detective's side this time. The room was no more pleasant with a view of the opposite wall, and in addition, I detected a foul smell.

"Why do they think that, Paige?"

"The cops searched my room at school and found the handle of the sword the killer used. Like I'd leave it there."

This was the first confirmation I had that the heavy object Skip referred to as the murder weapon was one of the life-size swords from the set on the wall in the Morley room. Being good at imagining dramatic, old-fashioned scenarios of murder and mayhem had served me well as a teacher of Shakespeare, but tormented me now. I blocked out the colorful images in my mind and returned to Paige.

I wondered if her automatic reference to a third person spoke to her innocence. On the other hand, she'd all but accused Laura Overbee a couple of hours ago.

Where was the FBI's behavioral analysis unit when you needed them?

Paige continued, her voice breaking as she gave me details. It occurred to me that that was why Skip hadn't told me what evidence he had. He and Detective Rutherford were probably standing on the other side of the two-way glass, tuned in, wanting to hear how Paige would answer my genuine questions. I looked around the room for the technology that would allow them to eavesdrop. Nothing clearly visible, but they weren't fooling me.

I brought my attention back to Paige.

"The police found the sword handle in my closet, right next to my shoe boxes." Paige threw up her hands. "But I never even went back to my dorm room until after I left your house today, so how could I have put it there? And why would I keep a murder weapon, anyway? Someone's trying to frame me, Mrs. Porter. Isn't it, like, crystal clear?"

I hoped Paige would eventually drop the *likes*, which I heard as unbecoming a college student with aspirations for a career in writing. But how did I know which styles would survive the twenty-first-century–makeover of the English language?

"Can you help me figure it out, Paige?" I asked, thinking the best tactic was to let her believe I was convinced of her innocence. As I assumed the role of interviewer in a police station, I felt like an applicant to the police academy. I knew my methods were being observed and evaluated by the team on the other side of the glass.

"Well, yeah, but how am I supposed to figure it out? Aren't the police supposed to do that? Are they holding anyone else from the Heights? What about Laura Overbee?"

"Who else has access to your dorm room?" I asked. Not for nothing had I observed Skip's practice of answering a question with a more difficult question of his own choosing.

"My roommate, Tanya, but she went home to Oregon this week because her mom is really sick. And I guess, school security could get in, but that's all. I didn't give anyone a key and I'm sure Tanya didn't. But it's just a flimsy doorknob lock, you know. Anyone could get in if they really wanted to."

"Do you stay at the dorm every night?"

"No, that's just it. Laura and I both have rooms at the estate, for when we work late." Paige smiled, her eyes looking far away. "Mine is the Lady Bunting Suite. Varena named all the bedrooms after her protagonists."

How sweet, I thought. Paige continued, her expression still focused on a memory.

"Sometimes Varena starts late in the evening and dictates for hours and she wants one or all of us there. 'The muse is visiting me,' she'll say, and we all know we're in for a long night." Paige's eyes widened, her expression changing to a look of realization, as if she'd been editing a manuscript and suddenly become aware that she needed to switch to past tense.

"Take a breath," I said. Softly, lest my evaluators take my consideration of the suspect as a sign of weakness.

"I'm okay," Paige said. Unconvincing. "Last night Laura went home, but I stayed. I was all wound up and I didn't feel like driving back to an empty dorm room. When I finally got back there this afternoon, it looked like the whole Lincoln Point Police Department was in my little room, searching anything and everything, turning things inside out. And the next thing I know, here I am."

It was hard not to feel sorry for Paige, until I remembered that there was a better than even chance that she'd lied to me about being familiar with the mysterious dollhouse now in my atrium. I shook my head, playing tough. "I'm not sure what I can do for you, Paige. You haven't been completely forthcoming."

Paige hung her head and dug the heels of her hands into her eyes with what seemed an alarming pressure. "I know what you're talking about, Mrs. Porter. I just didn't know what to do when I saw the dollhouse in your house. I wasn't sure it was the right one."

"What would be the right one?" The midsize Tudor?

"It's very complicated."

I started to laugh and stopped when I realized that Paige

wouldn't get the significance of the Phrase of the Week. "Try me."

Paige dropped her arms on the table with a thud that made me wince. I hoped she hadn't hurt herself. I made a note to remind the people watching behind the pseudo-mirror that if they were going to keep her overnight, they needed to be sure she was kept safe from harming herself.

"Okay, I got this strange series of text messages and emails, all within about an hour the night before Varena was killed. This guy said Varena might be in danger but he wasn't in a position to go to the police. He said he had evidence, some documents that he put in an envelope, and hid in one of Varena's dollhouses. Then he said I should find the envelope and take it to the police."

"Did he tell you which dollhouse? Did you look for it?" It was hard to control the mounting excitement as I felt I was getting closer to the story behind the special-delivery dollhouse. If Varena's murder was directly connected to the dollhouse, everything could be cleared up at home and on the Heights.

"The messages were all really short," Paige said. "Like, I think he must have been at a café or something and the connection kept timing out. This was late at night. I was tossing around, couldn't sleep. My phone was on in the charger and when it beeped that I had a text, I opened it and that's what it said, what I just told you. I texted back and asked him all kinds of questions, like yours. We went a few rounds, sometimes by email, but when I asked him why he couldn't just tell me why Varena was in danger, and who was she in danger from, and where exactly was this envelope, he didn't write any more."

"Did you try to reach him yesterday or today?"

"Yeah, of course. When I found Varena the next day, I knew it hadn't been just some nut case on the phone. But there was nothing else from him and the account he used was closed or something. I kept looking around at Varena's houses, which are all over the estate"—here I took a minute to picture the dream acreage with dollhouses everywhere—"but I didn't have any idea what kind of house he was talking about, so how was I supposed to know? He didn't tell me the style or anything. Then when I saw one of her dollhouses in your home, I thought that might be the one." She shrugged. "I don't know why. Maybe just because it was in a different place. I thought maybe he put it there."

"So you recognized the house in my atrium as one of Varena's? You're sure of that?"

"Yes."

I had a very important question. "Where did you see the dollhouse before you saw it in my atrium?"

"Upstairs at the estate. In one of the guest rooms, the Lord Weatherly Room, where it always is. It belongs on a table that's supposed to look like a beach, with fake sand and all."

"When did you receive the last message from the man?"

"Late. Maybe midnight Sunday night. And like I said, there's been no word from him at all yesterday or today."

I thought of Maddie, who'd seen an envelope in the secret room. I no longer doubted the existence of the room or its contents, but I wanted to move step by step, for the benefit of my onlookers.

"Did you search all the houses that are still at the estate for the letter that was supposed to be there?"

"Sure. I love the dollhouses, you know."

"Yes, I think Laura told me that you're also a miniaturist. I'm surprised you didn't take a minute to look at mine when you stopped in. I suppose they're not as grand—"

"No, no, that wasn't it. First, I don't tell too many people because, like Laura, they'll assume that's why Varena picked me. And then when I saw the modern-style beach house right there in your atrium, I got flustered."

"Back to the emails, Paige. You checked all the dollhouses at some time before Varena died?"

"Uh-huh, I peeked in all of them and moved some furniture a little, but, I mean, how can you hide something as big as a life-size envelope in a dollhouse? You look in, and it's either there or it isn't, right?"

Not if it has a secret room, which apparently wasn't made clear to Paige by the mysterious man who deposited the envelope.

"Did you tell all this to the police this afternoon?"

"No, I sort of said I had some information about the real killer, but I didn't think I should talk to them too much without a lawyer, and I can't afford one, and I didn't want them to think I called one because I'm guilty and...well, the reason I'm here in the first place is that the cops got an anonymous tip to search my room and I pooh-poohed it and told them it was ridiculous to believe anything anonymous, and then here I am giving them an anonymous tip of my own?" Paige went into a frenzy of gestures, sending her too-big sweater off one shoulder. "That's why I wanted to talk to you first."

The shift gave me a chill, as if my own sweater had fallen off. The room seemed to be too cold one moment and too warm the next. I wondered if the powers-that-be were manipulating the temperature, another of Skip's "tricks of the trade" that was "just routine."

I sat back, trying to put together the pieces of Paige's story. "It sounds like a lot of trouble for someone to go to. I don't understand why the person who sent the messages didn't just take the information to the police."

"It's not like I had a real conversation with him. All I know is what was in the texts and the emails. He did say once that it wasn't safe for him to appear—that was the word he used, 'appear'—until the killer was in prison."

I let out a breath. "I don't know, Paige. There are so many questions and things that don't make sense. Why didn't he name the person he thought might harm Varena? Why did he pick you to talk to? Why didn't he call in an anonymous tip to the police himself? Or why didn't he tell you exactly in which dollhouse he hid the information? He could have done a million things that would have been so much simpler than what you're describing."

Paige's eyes grew wider with each of my "why" tick points. She seemed to be holding her breath. "I don't know, Mrs. Porter," she nearly screamed. "I wish he didn't pick me. I wish...everything you said. I thought maybe Laura killed her but I don't know now, and I'm really scared that the killer will come after me if he knows that I know about this envelope and the evidence."

It was one thing to think about suspects, evidence, and motives in the abstract, but another to picture someone lifting a heavy sword and bringing it down on a person's head. And then to have that killer on the loose to strike again. I could understand why Paige was frightened. I hoped the image in Paige's head didn't match the grisly one forming in mine.

I waited until Paige settled down. "Could you tell where the messages came from? Did the person sign any of them?"

"The address was in the form of some nonsense syllables, like spam. You know, a string like 'czd#k&h%y$.'" Paige spouted off random letters and characters, using her finger to punctuate, as if she was typing them in the air between us. "But here's the really crazy part. He signed it just, 'Varena's brother.'"

With great effort, I turned my gasp into a reasonable-sounding throat clearing. "Varena's brother?"

"Yes, but Mrs. Porter, Varena doesn't have a brother, except one who died a long time ago."

"What do you know about her brother, Paige?"

"Not a lot. Varena mentions him now and then, and once she said a character she was developing was based on him. She named him Caleb, too, except the character in the book doesn't die in an accident. Why would someone claim to be Varena's brother, Mrs. Porter?"

"I have no idea, Paige," I said, truthfully. "But I think it's time we tried to find out." I looked back at the two-way mirror-cum-window, to where I hoped Skip was standing.

I sent a questioning, eyebrows-raised look to where I estimated his head would be: Now do you believe me?

Chapter 14

SKIP'S TINY CUBICLE had now been made smaller by a roll-in filing cabinet that took up most of the opening between the partitions. I squeezed by the metal box and took a seat across from him on his rolling guest chair. I was too excited to wait for him to begin, and afraid he'd throw cold water on the investigative avenues my interview with Paige had opened up, so I plunged in before he had a chance.

"Even if you don't believe her whole story, Skip, you have to admit it's an enormous coincidence that both the missing Corazón Cruz and the framed Paige—"

"Allegedly missing and allegedly framed," Skip said, but with enough of a grin that I wasn't offended.

"Thank you for clarifying that, Detective. Now, continuing—that they both came up with a brother who's supposedly dead?"

Skip's smile broadened. "Yeah, I got the point of your look, Aunt Gerry. Sweet work with that interview, by the way." He waved his floppy notepad at me. "I even took notes."

I listened for a sign of sarcasm and didn't find one. It was nice to hear a compliment from my nephew on something other than my ginger cookies. I pointed to his laptop computer, imagining it contained an infinite number of databases at his disposal, whereas I'd been at a disadvantage without even Maddie's enthusiasm and help. "Can't you look that up?"

"Actually, we did. We came up with nothing, no brother, but we did check it out."

"You did? Based on what I told you yesterday, you tried to find Varena's brother?"

Skip nodded and sent a sheepish grin my way, a familiar expression that had marked his preteen years. "Just because I don't jump up and down when you tell me something, it doesn't mean I completely discount what you say."

"Why did you let me think so?"

He shrugged. "We have to separate the wheat from the chaff. We don't have the manpower to track down absolutely every little lead, as much as we'd like to. Part of detective work is to decide what to do immediately, what to put on the back burner, what to trash."

"You expect to be able to do it all without help from people like me, outside the department?"

"Not at all, we count on the cooperation of everyone involved. I've told you this before. Most of our cases are not solved by exotic forensic science, like on television. You know, where they trace a single blue carpet fiber to one manufacturer and then to the one store in the state that sold it between the years two thousand-six and two thousand-eleven."

"Then they go to that store and the records are there, with the names, addresses, and telephone numbers of every customer who bought that particular color carpet in the last five years."

Skip let out a raspberry worthy of the kind Maddie blew. "Our best input comes from talking to people, finding not just on-the-spot witnesses, but people six degrees of separation away. You don't just flick a switch for that. It takes time, but we don't dismiss anyone. Heck, don't I even use an eleven-year-old sometimes?"

It wasn't often that Skip spoke at length about his job this way and I enjoyed listening.

"I take it your search came up with nothing about a brother for Varena," I said, back to the case at hand.

"No brother, either alive or dead. We checked under 'Rockwell' and 'Young' both, thinking maybe he changed his name to match hers. Or maybe he's also a writer with a pen name."

Doubtful. I shook my head. "Many of the authors I read now

have pseudonyms, sometimes more than one, but you can always find out their real names. It's not a secret the way it used to be, such as when Mary Ann Evans had to take a man's name, George Eliot."

"You sound like June, going all feminist on me. Men changed their names too, like Mark Twain and Lewis Carroll."

I'd have to remember to pursue the rather pouty reference to his girlfriend at another time, but for now, something else jogged my memory.

"Swingle. Did you try Swingle?" I asked. Skip gave me a funny look. "I was looking up romance authors' bios, and…" I started. Then, to avoid a long explanation of my own attempts at research, I switched to, "Please, just try the name Caleb Swingle. It might lead somewhere."

"I told you, I'm open, and I trust you not to be frivolous about it. You wouldn't believe the calls we get." Skip took a breath. "That's not your problem, though. I'll get the computer guys on Swingle. I'm surprised you didn't use the eleven-year-old for this yourself, by the way."

I debated whether to tell Skip that Maddie was computer-grounded, and why. I thought about the special relationship they had, now one of mutual admiration. His cubicle had more pictures of Maddie than anyone else, going back to her first school photo, with untamed red curls and a pinafore that she hated.

When Maddie was born, Skip was finishing high school, and to everyone's surprise, the fatherless boy reacted as though he'd been waiting all his life for an infant to take care of. He carried her around with his large hand under her head, instructing us to be sure to do the same, as if he'd just come from a pediatrics course and was the only one trained in baby care.

It was bad enough for Maddie that her grandmother and Henry knew of her fall from grace. And maybe her father's punishment would involve having Maddie tell everyone who received a tainted present how it came about. I wouldn't put it past Richard to come up with a twelve-step program for naughty children. But Maddie had been caught, she'd said, before she could bestow a gift on Skip or his mother, her Aunt Beverly.

Maybe they didn't have to know.

I finally answered Skip. "She's been busy with schoolwork," I said.

If he knew something else was up, he didn't say. Instead, he returned to the notes he'd taken during my talk with Paige.

"What was all that about a dollhouse and a hidden envelope? Is Paige referring to the big dollhouse I saw in your atrium last night? I didn't realize it belonged to Varena Young."

I nodded. "I wasn't sure it was hers until Paige verified it a few minutes ago," I said. I briefed Skip on the appearance of the dollhouse and my inexpert canvassing of my neighbors to trace its origins. "It might have been delivered in a red pickup with Arizona license plates."

"Someone saw it?"

"Esther Willoughby," I answered. I lowered my voice, as if to soften the impact of the age of my source.

"The hundred-year-old lady across the street?"

"Ninety-something, and remember what you said about not discounting anyone?"

"You're right, you're right," Skip said, making a great show of writing down "Arizona truck" and underlining it several times.

"Maybe Varena Young's brother—going by the name of Swingle—lives in Arizona," I offered.

Skip slapped his notebook shut. "Maybe," he said. "And maybe one of Varena's dollhouses really does have an envelope that contains all the evidence we need to solve this case."

His tone hovered between sarcasm and sincerity. I decided not to push him on it. Instead, I came up with another way to push him.

"With all of these possibilities now, can't you let Paige go? I don't think she killed Varena. The story's too preposterous to be fiction."

"Easy for you to say."

"What does your gut say?"

"We're waiting on fingerprint results on that fragment of sword we found in her dorm room," Skip said, not in a gut-sharing mood.

"But she practically lived with Varena. She might have touched it at any time. I touched it, in fact."

"So you told Detective Rutherford."

"I won't leave town."

As I stood to leave, I was accosted by one more thought from my overtaxed brain.

"Since you were surreptitiously following up on my suggestions yesterday—did you ask anyone on the staff if they heard arguing as I did just before I left Varena's home?"

"Yeah, that turned out to be nothing. I looked at the interview reports the guys handed in. Two of the statements mention a brief shouting match between Charles Quentin and an unidentifiable male. If I remember correctly, one of them reported that Varena Young was also part of the argument."

I opened my mouth to speak, but Skip anticipated my question, good detective that he was. "Quentin says there was a dispute with one of the estate's drivers over the schedule. The driver verified it. So that's a nothing lead."

Maybe, maybe not. "What's the driver's name?"

Skip laughed. "Sedonis. He's Hispanic, so don't try to talk to him." He gently guided me to the exit, such as it was, out of his cubicle and into the maze of office space.

"We can finish up later," I said.

The mention of drivers provoked anxiety, emphasizing the indisputable fact of how narrow the scope of my so-called investigation was. I'd been focusing on the small number of people I knew to be at the estate that afternoon, and who had motives I'd been aware of.

But surely there were others who stood to benefit from Varena's death or who had an unresolved issue with her. Did the estate have a cook? A butler? A maid? It must have a gardener or two. The magnitude of the real job of detection overwhelmed me.

If it weren't Varena Young who'd been murdered, I'd have given serious thought to calling Alicia Rockwell and resigning immediately.

MADDIE and I had a tacit agreement that we'd talked enough

about the credit card episode and needed a break, at least until I talked to her parents.

On the way home, we reviewed her activities of the last hour, which included watching someone get fingerprinted without ink and having way too many snacks from the vending machine in the officers' lounge. We talked about the life of Amelia Earhart, whose biography she'd just finished. More than once Maddie mentioned the boy who sat in front of her in school and the éclairs from the new bakery that I promised were waiting at home for her.

"Are you ready to try again on that secret room project?" I asked her.

"Yes, yes, I thought of something else to do but I won't tell you until I get it to work."

"That's great, sweetheart," I said.

In fact, however, I was ready to tear the dollhouse apart, an inch at a time, and get to the secret room the sure way. Both Paige and Maddie claimed the existence of a room and an envelope. That was enough for me.

I weighed that assumption against the possibility that the dollhouse in my atrium was a simple one, earmarked for the library auction or another worthy cause, should the midsize Tudor come through. Paige had verified only that the house came from Varena's collection; she had no idea if it held the envelope for certain.

It would be a shame to destroy a perfectly good house on the basis of hearsay, but it was time to face the reality that it might have to be sacrificed for the sake of the investigation.

Maddie's mind hadn't been idle while being pampered by the LPPD. "Even if I can't use the computer, I can help you and Uncle Skip," she said now, a passenger in my car again. "I can sit next to you and tell you what to do."

Had no one ever explained the concept of "the spirit versus the letter" of the law to my granddaughter? "I don't know…"

"I won't touch the keyboard or the mouse. It'll be like I'm just talking to you."

"We'll see."

Maddie slumped back in her seat. "I know what that means." Someday she'd find out that expression had been working its wonders in families throughout the ages.

MY message machine was in a schizophrenic mode. Laura Overbee called to express her great relief that Varena's killer, that is, Paige Taggart, had been apprehended. Alicia Rockwell left a message asserting that Paige was most definitely not the killer, and she hoped I was still working on finding the one truly responsible for her mother's death.

A surprise call from Charles Quentin was more circumspect, offering to meet me at my convenience. He left a number for his direct line. I moved him to the front of the queue for callbacks and hit redial for his number.

Maddie came into the kitchen, and snacks and ice cream notwithstanding, attacked the cookie jar. I took the hint and multitasked. While I waited for Charles to answer, I pulled a package of ground beef out of the fridge and held it up. "Cheeseburgers?" I asked.

Fortunately, Mary Lou had given no instructions nor had she set restrictions regarding Maddie's feeding.

Maddie nodded and grinned, hoping, I was sure, that no vegetables would be involved. She got out the small grill, a container of cheese, and—her own touch—the ketchup.

I watched my granddaughter move around the kitchen, a bit clumsy when her long, skinny legs were tripped up by her bulky athletic shoes, but supremely confident. I wished I could remember the exact day that she became strong enough to lift a saucepan, tall enough to reach the dials on the range top, bright enough to put together a whole meal, even if it was devoid of anything green.

"This is Charles Quentin," said a voice in my ear. I was caught off guard by the visitor to the reverie in my kitchen.

"Good evening, Charles," I said, adopting the most formal tone possible while simultaneously clearing my throat. "This is Geraldine Porter, returning your call earlier today."

"Yes, hello, Mrs. Porter. Alicia tells me you're assisting the police detectives with their investigation and I wondered if I might have a word with you."

I liked a man who got right to the point. "Certainly. What would be convenient for you?"

"I'm afraid this whole tragedy has set us all at sixes and sevens and it's hard for me to get away just now. Can you come to the estate?"

The fiscal head of the Rockwell Estate had no time for pleasantries and no time for travel to the lowlands. Not a problem. I was only too happy to make a date for tomorrow morning at the house on the hill.

What investigator, professional or not, doesn't want to return to the scene of the crime?

MADDIE was progressing nicely with the cheeseburgers. The rolls were warming in the oven as she poured herself a glass of milk. The least I could do was set the table.

I had one more call to make in the next room before I could relax with dinner. I owed my daughter-in-law that much. I hit the number for Maddie's parents and didn't hide my relief when Mary Lou, instead of Richard, picked up.

"I knew why you were avoiding me, Mom," Mary Lou said. "Did you have to pull it out of her or did my daughter work her magic and confess in a boatload of tears? And are you now her advocate general, or whatever they're called?"

I was pleased to hear a lightness in Mary Lou's voice. I knew there'd be no such accommodation from Richard. "Let's just say it all came out over ice cream."

"What a surprise. Seriously, Mom, Richard and I have been talking about coming home now. Do you think we should do that, and deal with this face to face immediately?"

Mary Lou's suggestion was something that hadn't crossed my mind and I gave it a moment's consideration. "I'd say that's not necessary. You know I would never undermine your directives, so whatever you'd like Maddie to do or not do, she knows with absolute clarity that I'll support you one hundred percent."

"Thanks, Mom, I know that. I'm afraid of blowing this thing

up out of proportion, but I don't want to downplay it either. It's tricky."

This wasn't my first clue that I had the most sensible daughter-in-law in the world. "I'm with you."

"For now, we really do want her off the computer except for homework. Is it too much to ask you to monitor that?"

"Not at all." I paused. "She's truly sorry, as I'm sure she's told you. I know I'm easily duped by her sometimes, but I feel it's genuine. Which doesn't mean I won't enforce the ban on computer use." As hard as that will be, I added to myself.

"Thanks for telling me that." Mary Lou sighed. "She's eleven. I guess it's time for a crisis. Were you able to get a clue as to why she thought she had to steal to get what she wanted?"

Such a nasty word. I reported to Mary Lou as accurately as possible Maddie's feelings of inferiority at school since she had nothing to barter with or to be generous with.

"Then one thing led to another," I said.

"Oh, my God, that's textbook," my daughter-in-law said, and I knew she meant it literally. "That's one of eight reasons why children steal."

I was curious about the other seven, but I could ask another time. I didn't want to intrude on her near-giddiness.

"Aren't you glad your child is normal," I said, getting a laugh.

"Believe it, yes. I've spent most of today reading up on why children steal and that's one of the big reasons. Listen to this. 'If the child's school friends have pocket money, then your child could have a need for pocket money. She will feel a lack if she doesn't have it, even if you don't think the need is genuine because you provide her with everything that she wants. This type of child may be tempted to steal money just so she has money like everybody else in her peer group.'"

"Are you reading from a book?"

Another laugh. "Yes, I just happened to have one opened to that page. I have others, open to different pages, just to cover all bases."

"Isn't it wonderful that Maddie doesn't have a one-of-a-kind, incurable behavior problem?"

"You better believe it." I could hear the relief in Mary Lou's voice.

"Is Richard going to be okay?" I asked. My son the orthopedic surgeon didn't have a broad platform of behaviors he considered suitable for a child. Or for an adult, for that matter. Ken and I were thrilled that he had the sense to marry someone who could complement that approach to life.

"I'll take care of Richard," Mary Lou said. "He needs to see that it's time we gave Maddie more responsibility and that an allowance is just about a requirement for kids these days."

I smiled and felt a wave of relief, that the issue of Maddie's peccadillo (the grandmother in me would not allow a more serious designation) was at least partly resolved.

"I'll take care of Maddie; you take care of Richard," I said.

We both knew who had the easier job.

WHILE Maddie took her turn on the phone with her parents, I slipped out to my atrium to give them privacy and to be with the mysterious dollhouse.

I sat close to it, my nose touching the dividing wall that defined the top floor bedroom where Maddie had inadvertently discovered a secret passageway. I looked at every wood seam, every spackle swirl, and every paintbrush stroke for a sign or a crack in the house's armor. If intensity of staring counted for anything, something would have sprung loose.

Nothing did.

Maybe the trick was not to scrutinize every nail and line of glue, but to take a more holistic approach and view the house from afar. Maybe I wasn't seeing the forest for the trees. Or the other way around.

I moved back a few feet to get the full effect of the house, imagining it, not in the sleepy suburb of Lincoln Point, but by the shore, perhaps right on the coast in Monterey or Santa Cruz. The exterior walls seemed to weather before my eyes, pounded by spray from the churning waters of the Pacific. I could almost hear the ocean across the street from the sleek front door and smell the salty air.

Still, the house gave up no secrets, no answers to my questions. Where did you come from? What's hidden in your walls? I was ready to do a ritual dance to get the house to speak to me.

Just in time, Maddie appeared on the threshold to the living room and rescued me from the delusionary state that was so easy for miniaturists to fall into.

"Is everything okay, sweetheart?" I asked, shaking myself into the life-size world with its life-size problems.

Maddie sprinted over to me. She fell on her knees and put her head on my lap. Her messy curls cried out for attention, and I responded with what she called finger brushing, at once neatening her hair and massaging her scalp.

I felt her body slowly relax and breathe normally.

"Are you hungry?" I asked. The universal question asked by grandmothers in any crisis.

Maddie either nodded or shook her head "no." It was hard to tell since she wasn't ready to come up for a full dose of fresh, atrium air.

"The cheeseburgers must be really tasty by now, don't you think?" I asked.

Her body shook with what I knew to be giggles.

We were on our way back home.

Chapter 15

NOT EVEN A therapy session in the microwave could fix what ailed the tough, cold cheeseburgers. We dumped them in the garbage disposal and foraged for something more appetizing.

For Maddie, a quick mac-and-cheese dish did the trick. I put together a salad and offered her a portion. "Too green, too green," she said.

We sat on the couch in the living room, feet on the coffee table, each with her own dinner choice. "So, how's everything in Houston?" I said.

Maddie giggled through a mouthful of cheese-coated macaroni. It thrilled me that she hadn't lost her sense of humor. It was my contention that if you could laugh during the small crises of life, you could get through the big ones also.

Then she sobered. "I know Mom and Dad are both disappointed in me." She turned and looked at me with a touch of sadness in her eyes. "Especially my dad."

"Not necessarily, sweetheart. What makes you say that?"

"He said, 'I'm disappointed in you.'" Maddie gave me one of her priceless grins.

"Just win a Nobel Prize in medicine and he'll get over it."

"Or I can be a professional shopper online for people who don't have time to go to the mall."

"Maybe not," I said.

We hadn't had this much to laugh about in a while.

The rest of our conversation was punctuated with promises (on my part) to let her try cheeseburgers again tomorrow night, and (unsolicited, on her part) to never, ever do anything so dumb, dumb, dumb again.

Maddie reported that Richard had agreed to talk with Mary Lou and her about a suitable allowance after doing some research in their various parenting books (Richard) and determining Maddie's current fiscal needs (Mary Lou.)

With water and milk glasses drained and only crumbs left on our plates, Maddie cleared the coffee table. "Mom said I could do my homework on the computer but you have to monitor me, whatever that means."

"It means you tell me you're not going to go surfing or shopping and I'll trust you to keep your word."

Maddie gave me a wide-eyed nod that said she wouldn't dream of disappointing me. I didn't dare ask how long the ban was in effect. I had an investigation to conduct and I needed my computer assistant.

WHAT I could do while Maddie worked on multiplying fractions, for which I hoped she needed no help, was prepare myself for tomorrow's trip to the Rockwell home. The prospect of having a sit-down with its financial manager, Charles Quentin, was both exciting and intimidating.

I'd fumbled through meetings with Alicia, Laura, and Paige. With preparation, I hoped to do better with Charles. Wouldn't a good investigator determine every suspect's alibi? I myself had a great one. I'd talked to Henry on the phone on the way from the estate to his home and had spent the rest of the evening in the company of several family members. Just in case I was still on Detective Blythe's list, I was ready.

"I'm done, Grandma," Maddie said, in what seemed record time for a homework session. But then, unlike her grandmother, she loved math and thought fractions were a breeze.

"That didn't take long."

I'd hardly had time to write Charles Quentin's name at the top of a note pad, plus the numbers one through five, for the questions I might ask.

"All I did was homework," she said.

Even with my poor math skills, I could figure out that the extra hour Maddie usually spent supposedly doing homework was unrelated to the three Rs.

"I guess we can sit and read, then."

Maddie chewed that over. "Or, if you have any computer projects, I could help you without touching the keys."

I smiled. She hadn't given up on the plea she'd made on our drive home from school, that she talk me through a computer project. What I wanted more than anything was to identify the owner of the old truck that may have delivered the dollhouse in my atrium. I knew I couldn't get anywhere on that without the LPPD, the Department of Motor Vehicles, or Maddie.

Maddie was handier and far easier to deal with.

Thinking it through, with an admitted bias, I asked myself what Maddie's parents hoped to accomplish by placing the ban on her computer use in the first place. There were two goals, as I saw it. One, so she wouldn't be able to shop online for presents for the next fifty BFFs on her list. Two, to penalize her with a punishment that suited the crime.

If she talked me through what I needed, she certainly wouldn't be shopping online, so that part of the moratorium would be in effect. As far as the chastisement aspect, I reasoned that it would be punishment enough for Maddie to have to watch her grandmother fumble and not be able to step in and do it herself.

The whole question of whether punishment in general was cruel and unusual, or whether it served as a deterrent to criminals, was a much-debated topic among scholars and politicians, too heady for me to take on tonight.

"I don't know, sweetheart." What resolve I had. It went hand in hand with my negotiating skills.

"Good. Then let's go to the computer," Maddie said, jumping on my hesitation, as usual.

She made a show of dragging me by the hand to her bedroom where Richard had set up my new system. I remembered assuring Mary Lou that I'd move the computer out of her bedroom but the task seemed daunting.

Maybe I could just cut the wires.

I was miffed at the whole Internet industry anyway for having led my good and innocent granddaughter into temptation.

In a fit of guilt about not obeying my daughter-in-law, however, I held my ground, and told Maddie we'd have to move the computer from its handy spot next to her bed. I helped her unplug all the peripherals and transport everything to my dining room table where she set it up again.

While we worked on the move, I explained the key task the computer might help with. "I still don't know where that dollhouse came from," I said, pointing to the streamlined home in my atrium.

"I thought the dead lady sent it."

"Maybe not," I said. "I'd like to find out for sure."

We took seats on chairs arranged side by side in front of the screen, with mine more centrally located. I told Maddie about Esther's seeing a red pickup with Arizona plates, numbers unknown, around five o'clock yesterday afternoon.

"You want to find out who brought us the dollhouse and that's all you know?" Maddie asked. Her incredulous tone sent hope out the window.

"I was afraid there was no way to do it without access to a special database of red truck owners, but I thought you might know another way."

I hadn't meant it as challenge, but Maddie's stillness and wrinkled forehead told me she was taking it that way. In that personality trait, if few others, she was her father's daughter.

When her eyes widened, I knew an idea had struck.

"Remember when we were driving home and got stuck in all that traffic? We had to stop until the flagman waved at us?"

"Uh-huh. There's a new office complex going up at Gettysburg and Springfield," I said. "What does that have to do with our little project?"

"They always have webcams at those places. We can see if a red truck with a dollhouse on it went through the intersection on its way here."

I considered myself a veteran of webcams, having once sat with a crafter friend while she used Skype to visit with her daughter who was studying at Oxford for a term. The young student had carried her laptop around her room and showed us her sleeping alcove and bookcases, as well as the view from her window overlooking the Bodleian Library.

Even I was aware how much simpler that had been than asking for a video of something that happened yesterday, like a dusty pickup on its way to my house. But I figured the camera setup at the construction site was more sophisticated than that on Susan's daughter's computer. In any case it was worth a try.

"That's a great idea," I said. "They probably have one for security. But how do we look at it?"

"It's not just to see if people are messing up the place. They have them so everyone can watch things go up, and it's on twenty-four hours a day."

I translated "watch things go up" to "don't be upset at the inconvenience; we're bringing new business to Lincoln Point." When did I become so jaded about what made the world go around?

This time, politics seemed to be working in my favor.

I started to ask how we could access the camera's footage, which was a word that probably didn't apply to anything these days, but Maddie was already writing down the address I'd have to enter to view the video.

"You just have to Google YouTube," she said, as if she did it three times a day.

She placed the paper with the address on the table next to the keyboard. Poor child. Her fingers were fairly twitching with the desire to enter the information herself. I wondered how long I could hold out, watching her suffer. I entered the letters carefully, waited for the long list of links to show up, and dutifully clicked on the one Maddie pointed to.

A picture of the familiar intersection snapped onto my screen. I was looking at the half-completed multistory building, hardly believing how easy it had been. There was no action in the dug-out area at this hour, but floodlights along the perimeter of the project made easy work of picking out cranes, temporary fencing, scaffolding, and sheets of black tarp where walls would eventually stand.

Beyond the site I could see the hills and residential streets of Lincoln Point, as well as the hospital in the distance. The camera's reach didn't extend far enough north to reach my Eichler neighborhood, but it was interesting to have this view of my town all the same.

"Isn't it fun, Grandma?"

"It certainly is."

I hated to put a damper on the moment, but I pointed out that the actual boulevards of Gettysburg and Springfield were not visible. Once again, Maddie was on the job, explaining that the numbers down the side of the screen referred to separate cameras, each with a different view of the area.

"Try clicking the 'two,'" she said. The intersection itself, east of the construction, sprang to life.

"What do you know, it's facing the street."

I knew my surprise pleased Maddie. She grinned, having gotten over her pique at not being at the controls.

Cars, SUVs, bicycles, trucks, buses trickled by in front of me. Nightlife in Lincoln Point.

"See these arrows?" Maddie indicated a set of back and forward symbols like the ones on the remote for my DVD player. "You can look at yesterday or you can put in any date you want in the calendar, and go all the way back to when they started digging."

"How do you know all this? Have you been visiting this construction site?" Between shopping for your friends and relatives, I wanted to say, but felt the subject was still a little sore.

"Not this one, but I look at a lot of them. Like, when Mom or Dad are in another city, I look at the webcam to see the weather and stuff. Once in school when we were studying oil, we watched a webcam in the Gulf of Mexico where they were fixing the wells. And two towns over they had a webcam up when they were building the new stadium at the high school. You can even tell if people you know are walking by, if the camera swivels low enough."

I allowed myself a moment of nostalgia for the days of peeking through holes in fences to watch the guys in the hard hats.

Now we could observe them in private, all day. I wondered if today's foremen and supervisors also sat in their offices and watched their workers instead of physically walking around the site.

And who would have guessed that teaching elementary school would change so much when computers became ubiquitous? It was just as well that I retired before I had to use computers with as much facility as I had with card catalogs in libraries.

I moved the cursor to yesterday at four-thirty and saw the thick traffic of the rush hour, people trying to get from downtown Lincoln Point to their homes to the north. I was starting to get the hang of this webcam phenomenon and I liked it. I had the crazy thought that Esther Willoughby might get a lot of use out of it as she got less able to navigate her lawn and garden.

I liked it even better when a red truck appeared on the scene. I was beside myself as I peered at the faded red vehicle heading around the corner, facing me, going north on Springfield Boulevard. In its bed was a large object, something covered by a blanket or a tarp, something about the size of a dollhouse.

Maddie got up and took a spin around on one foot. It looked like a move she'd learned in a mandatory dance class, but wouldn't be using on a dance floor for a few more years.

We high-fived before I returned to the controls.

The time code on the screen told us the truck was on its way to my house (allegedly) at about four forty-five. Since the truck was clear of the bottleneck at this point, it would have taken about ten minutes for the men to reach my house, at which point they would have to uncover, unfasten, and lift the house out of the bed and onto my front step. It would take another few minutes for them to drive past Esther in her garden and reach this point on Springfield going the other way. I manipulated the arrows, under Maddie's watchful eye, and verified the timeline.

Good old Esther. This had to be the truck she saw.

"Now I just need the license plate, and maybe if I show this to Uncle Skip, he'll run it for me," I said.

"You can zoom in but you're never going to see the actual numbers," Maddie predicted.

I zoomed to the highest point on the scale, six hundred

percent. The picture got bigger and bigger, and unfortunately, fuzzier and fuzzier. Maddie was right. The license plate was an unreadable blob with not even the cactus, if there was one, identifiable.

"They do this on television all the time," I said, defending my squirrelly approach. "They zoom in and you can see the wrinkles on a person's face and sometimes even a reflection in a side-view mirror."

"Don't believe everything you see on television," Maddie admonished me, and for a moment the earth shifted. A time warp. Wasn't I supposed to be saying that to my eleven-year-old granddaughter and not vice versa?

Maddie folded her arms across her chest. I remembered assuming just such a posture when about to lecture her. "My computer teacher hates when they do that on TV because it's nuts. She says it's all wrong. She says if the digital information"—here she stuttered a bit—"isn't there, then no matter how much you blow it up, it still isn't going to be there."

"That's disappointing."

I sat back, my euphoria diminished a bit. But at least I had something to take to Skip, other than the word of the nonagenarian he'd all but dismissed. Surely there was a traffic camera at that busy intersection that the police would be able to access. That would give them a license plate, and ultimately the owner of the vehicle.

We could afford to celebrate a small victory. Maddie sensed the mood. "Ice cream?" she asked.

I scratched my head, pretending. "I don't know. Didn't we already have ice cream today?"

"Yeah, but I was too upset to enjoy it, and then you got a call and I had to leave some behind."

"Some" probably meant less than a spoonful.

"Come to think of it, I didn't enjoy mine that much, either," I offered.

Maddie jumped up. "I'll serve."

"Two scoops for me," I said.

"MOM and Dad said good night and they love me," Maddie said, drifting off to sleep under the old baseball afghan.

It touched my heart that she might have had a moment of feeling unworthy or less a treasure to us all.

"Of course they do, sweetheart. And I'm very proud of you," I said, in case there was even a smidgen of doubt in her mind. "You were a huge help to me and Uncle Skip tonight."

"And we didn't break any rules."

"No, we didn't."

Not really.

After the call with her parents, Maddie had climbed into bed more willingly than usual. It had been quite a day for her. Thinking her parents might love her less, no matter how unfounded the supposition, had taken its toll.

For me, I was proud of the way my family was handling the crisis that was, I hoped, already fading into the past. As far as I knew, this misuse of funds on Maddie's part—I hated the thought of associating any form of the verb "to steal" with my granddaughter—was the first serious problem her parents had had to face with their otherwise perfect child.

Maddie hadn't tried to defend herself unduly or to deny the allegation against her or to acquire things for herself. She'd admitted she'd lost sight of the right way to solve her money problem, that she'd done something wrong and was sorry about it. I felt strongly she wouldn't fall into that particular trap again. And I had every confidence that even my son would rise to the occasion and be willing to bend a little as they negotiated a settlement.

"Thanks for letting me help you, Grandma," she said, her voice starting to drift off. "I didn't mind just sitting there while you keyed everything."

"So it's okay if you never get to surf again?"

"Uh-huh."

That's when I knew she was actually talking in her sleep.

Chapter 16

I TOOK a cup of tea to the living room, settled on the sofa, and called Skip. It was very common for him to drop in at this hour or even later, but I couldn't wait to give him the news.

I told him about our evening's adventure in webcam land, at the same time trying to shore up Esther's reputation as an eyewitness. "There must be a Caltrans traffic camera at that corner that you can look at," I said.

"They do freeways. The traffic cameras belong to the city. Lincoln Point operates them at the big intersections in town—all three of them."

Good to know who was watching as I sailed along Civic Drive or Hanks Road in a hurry for one reason or another. "So, will you look into whose truck that is? I think this is really a key piece of evidence, Skip."

"You sure this isn't about finding out if Henry's cheating on you?" my nephew asked.

"What?" Too late I realized what a poor excuse for a joke Skip had made. But falling-flat humor was so much better than the falling-out we'd had yesterday.

"We sent Paige Taggart home, by the way," Skip said.

"I'm glad to hear that. Is there some new evidence that cleared her? Or a new, more viable suspect?"

A not-too-subtle way of finding out how the official investigation was going. I liked to think that I was among the first to learn about new developments in a case that was dear to my heart, but sometimes I had to resort to sneaky ways to get the facts from my nephew.

"We have fingerprint results. Or, you might say, no finger-print results. The handle had been wiped clean. No surprise, really, but you never know. We can usually count on the stupidity of criminals."

"So you've said. Thanks for telling me about Paige," I said, recognizing that I wouldn't be getting more than that tonight.

"I figure she'll be knocking on your door any minute."

"It will more likely be you."

"Might be. I am kinda hungry. 'Night, Aunt Gerry."

I started to dial Henry, whom I hadn't seen since midafter-noon. He'd left a couple of quick messages, but I'd been tied up with either Maddie or Paige in crisis mode. It wasn't a standard day when we didn't check in with each other a few times and I missed talking to him.

Rrring. Rrring. Rrring.

An incoming call rang through before Henry's number cleared. I clicked over to Paige Taggart. A phone call instead of a knock on my door. Skip wasn't too far off. It was hard to beat Detective Gowen and his insights.

"I'm out, Mrs. Porter. I figured it might be too late to drop in on you, but I wanted to tell you right away. I can't believe it. You can't imagine what it's like in there. I'm so relieved."

"I'm very glad to hear it, Paige."

"I can't thank you enough for coming to see me and listening to me and all. I'm not supposed to leave town or anything, but I think they realize now that someone is trying to frame me. Like, why would I bother wiping that piece of the weapon clean and then storing it in my room?"

I didn't think Paige needed to hear Skip's answer about dumb things killers do, presumably stashing the weapon being one of them. Besides, Paige was in a talking, not a listening, mood at the moment.

Over the next many minutes I found myself saying "Uh-huh" and "Really?" often as Paige went on and on about her experience at the Lincoln Point police station. I heard that she'd been "stored in a disgusting basement cell while the police tried to figure out what to do with me"; that "if it weren't for you,

Mrs. Porter, those guys never would have believed my dollhouse story;" and that "they finally gave me this little cup of water before I died of thirst."

As Paige wandered through tales of her brief incarceration, I wandered into my crafts room for a visual distraction. It wasn't unheard of that I'd put a caller on my speakerphone at times like this—such as when Linda Reed went off on a tangent about how none of her son Jason's teachers understood him, or how the nurses coming out of school these days weren't willing to work the long hours she'd put in when she was that age.

I'd even been known to do a small chore while a caller talked incessantly, not requiring input from me.

With three dollhouses on what used to be a picnic table in front of me, surely I'd be able to find something useful to occupy the large fraction of my brain that didn't need to follow Paige's every word. There was always a paint touch-up to dabble at, or a thread to be snipped, or a piece of furniture that called for a drop of glue, or a drawer of scraps to be silently sorted through.

I'd begun knitting a multicolored rug for the floor in front of the hearth that was the centerpiece of my pueblo, but the pattern required too much concentration for multitasking, especially at this hour.

One of the houses, a lovely Cape Cod that had been built by my crafter friend, Karen Striker, was finished, destined for a local school for a raffle to be held between Thanksgiving and Christmas. Henry had offered to deliver the house in the next few days. My gaze landed on the bell-shaped tag Karen had made from scrapbook paper, neatly printed with the name and home address of the school secretary who was organizing the donations. I smiled as I saw that Karen had hung the tag on the tiny doorknob of the neatly trimmed little cottage.

Something about the tag reminded me of the murder investigation, or a comment Varena had made during our wonderful, brief meeting. But before I could make the connection, Paige's voice poked through with a complaint about her time served as prime suspect.

"Then they asked me again how come I went into the room

where Varena's body was," Paige was saying. "I told them, like a million times already, that I was on my way out the front door and I heard a crashing noise coming from the hallway, down by the Lord and Lady Morley room, so I went to check."

Now I was interested. I hadn't heard this particular detail of Paige's discovery of Varena's body. "What exactly did you see, Paige?"

Paige breathed heavily. "Like I told them, by the time I got all the way down there, no one was there except Varena"—Paige paused for a breath—"but the back door at the end of the hall was open, which it hardly ever is."

"Did you look outside?"

"No, I wish I did, so I could have told the police who it was. They said, even if I caught a glimpse of what he was wearing it would help, but I just flew over to Varena. I thought she fell but then I saw her head was all bloody and…"

Paige's voice seemed to be full of a deep sadness and I wished I could put an arm around her.

"I'm sorry to put you through this again, Paige."

"I called nine-one-one and…"

What a strange mind I had. Suddenly the connection to the tag on the Cape Cod cottage came to me, as if Varena herself had tapped me on the shoulder to remind me of how she'd designated the dollhouse she planned to donate to the bookmobile fund-raiser.

"Paige, I have another question for you that has nothing to do with that room and that terrible experience. Can you help me with it?"

"Sure." Said between soft sniffles.

"You said you saw the dollhouse, the same one that's now in my atrium, at the Rockwell Estate, correct?"

"Yes, in the Lord Weatherly annex. It's a little sitting room next to the bedroom I use. It has a nautical décor. The real Lord Weatherly was a sailor in Scotland in the nineteenth century, I think."

I could hardly contain myself. I paced my own dollhouse room. "Did you see it there before Varena died? Or only after you got those texts and emails the other night? The ones about the envelope that was in one of the dollhouses."

"That dollhouse you have now was always in that room. Varena didn't move the houses around much. I think she liked to pretend she was visiting each little setup as if it was a certain street in a town, you know? And that room was the beach. We both loved the beach."

And I loved the idea of my friend and miniatures enthusiast Varena Young doing what I did often, especially on nights when I couldn't sleep—taking a pleasure trip to visit my houses and room boxes.

"Was there another dollhouse in that room also?"

"Oh, sure, there were two or three houses in almost every room, except the Morley room and the ones we used as bed-rooms."

"Did you go into the Lord Weatherly room anytime during the day yesterday, before five o'clock?" Which was the time of her discovery of Varena's body, not necessary to mention again.

"Uh-huh. I go in there all the time because I use the closet as an extension of mine. Laura uses it, too. The ones in our rooms are so small."

I swallowed hard and took a breath. "This is very important, Paige. Did you notice a tag of any kind hanging from one of the dollhouses in the Lord Weatherly room?"

I heard a low hum, the thinking kind. I hoped Paige was putting herself in the room with the fake sand and seashells, enjoying the salty breeze and smelling the ocean air, which must have been a much more pleasant mental trip than the one the police and I had recently sent her on, where her boss and mentor lay dead.

"I didn't see a tag," Paige said, causing my spirits to fall. "I noticed an index card on the table, though. Varena still used three-by-five cards for her outlines. This one had a name and address, but I didn't go close enough to read it."

Up went my spirits. Varena had told me she'd tagged the Tudor for me. I loved it that she'd used an index card, part of my stock in trade in the old days.

Paige had more to say and I was listening carefully.

"But I'm almost positive the card wasn't attached to the house in your atrium, Mrs. Porter. It was kind of halfway between it and the house next to it. Sorry, is that bad?"

"Was the other house a medium-size Tudor?"

"Yes," Paige said, her voice rising to a triumphant finish, as if I'd just won a prize for the correct answer.

I couldn't have been happier if I'd won a gift certificate to our local Katy's Krafts Korner.

A dramatic scene unfolded, as if I were watching a play in my own crafts room. Everything happened in miniature, as I'd expect.

Varena's brother, Caleb, goes to the Lord Weatherly room where the dollhouse now in my atrium was located. He opens the door to a secret room and inserts an envelope containing evidence that will incriminate someone who wants to harm his sister.

Later I'd have to figure out how Caleb knew the old dollhouse had a secret room. Plus a few other things, but for now, I had a story to finish.

Two men drive a red pickup to the Rockwell Estate. They climb the stairs to the Lord Weatherly room and look for the dollhouse with an index card that has my address on it. But Caleb has disturbed the table and somehow the index card ends up closer to the big old dollhouse with a modern style. The men take the wrong house to my address.

This scenario required that Varena arranged for the pickup before she died, which almost had to be before she met me. It was possible, but it would be nice to find out just who the men in baseball caps were and from whom they received their pickup assignment.

"Mrs. Porter." *Scratch, scratch.* I heard noises that might have been Paige tapping on her phone to get my attention. "Hello? Mrs. Porter?"

"I'm here, Paige. It's getting late and I should sign off."

"Oh, sure. I'm sorry. Sometimes I go on and on. Thanks again, Mrs. Porter. You've been such a huge help."

"So have you, Paige."

———

MY phone seemed as excited as I was, summoning me to two more calls in the next half hour. The first one was from Henry.

"I started to call you earlier," I explained.

"I miss you, but I figured you had a lot to work out today. How's my Maddie?"

I liked it that he thought of Maddie as his.

Henry sat through a summary of my day, including the tears, the parental intervention, the eventual smiles, and the duplicate ice cream sessions. Or maybe he'd wandered out to the workbench in his garage and swept up some wood shavings while I rattled on.

"Poor kid," he said, not surprisingly on her side.

"Maddie and Mary Lou learned a lot, I believe, and are fine. I haven't talked to my son yet, but I'm hoping he'll follow suit."

"As long as Richard doesn't make me give back my nice silver key chain."

I promised to do my best to protect Henry's right to his present.

The next part of our call consisted of a summary of my talk with Paige Taggart and my theory of how The Little Dollhouse That Could got to my atrium. "Do you think that's a crazy idea?" I asked, realizing the leaps and bounds it took to get from point A to point B in my proposed reconstruction.

A short pause and an intake of breath. Then, "He built it," Henry said.

"You lost me."

"Varena's brother built the dollhouse. Remember I told you I thought it was some kid's first big woodworking project? I've seen a few."

"That's how he knew it had a secret room."

"He put it there."

"You're brilliant, Henry. Why aren't you here so I can kiss you?"

"Is that an invitation?"

We laughed, considered the idea of a late date, and middle-agers that we were, deferred it to tomorrow.

"We have to find that secret room, Henry. I hate the thought of breaking the whole house down, especially now that we know Varena's brother made it for her when they were children."

"Allegedly," Henry said.

"Do you think Caleb is still alive?" I asked Henry.

"Uh-oh. Is this a trick question?"

I laughed, remembering when I desperately needed his support as I'd tried to convince Skip that Varena even had a brother.

"No," I said. "There's no right answer this time. Anyone could have signed those emails and texts to Paige."

"And your friend Corazón who told you Varena's brother was in the house?"

"That seems a long time ago. It could be that he's alive, but why tell everyone, including her own children, that he died in an accident? There was obviously a special bond if he built her a dollhouse, say it was her first, and she's collected them over all these years."

"Maybe the two became estranged and she wanted to keep it private, instead of going public with family business," Henry said.

"Could be."

"Could be."

I sensed Henry was fading fast. And so was I, as the stroke of midnight of a long day closed in. Before we hung up, Henry talked me into letting him pick Maddie up and take her to school in the morning so I could focus on my meeting with Charles Quentin at the Rockwell Estate.

"I'm not sure I'll do any better with preparation," I said.

"You've done great so far," he said.

I wanted to believe him.

"And this way, I'll get to see you, first thing in the morning, with pastry from the French log cabin," Henry continued.

Those two thoughts tipped the scales.

"You'll have to fight the traffic in town," I warned, hoping that didn't dissuade him. The éclairs we'd taken home were long gone.

"I'll get Kay or Bill to take Taylor to school, so I have plenty of time for a little detour."

"In that case...just make sure you don't speed through the Gettysburg–Springfield intersection."

"Why's that so special?"

"Big Brother. I'll show you when you get here."

THE second call on Tuesday night came from my boss, so to speak, Alicia Rockwell.

I'd checked on Maddie and was already in bed with a historical young adult novel set in nineteenth-century New York City, which was enough reason for me to enjoy it. I considered sending the call to voicemail. Surely I deserved a pleasant end to the day. Or maybe not. I felt like an employee who has been found wanting, not accomplishing what I'd been tasked to do. And if my boss was calling to reprimand me, we might as well get it over with.

"Geraldine, I hope I didn't wake you. I'm an insomniac and I tend to assume everyone else is. But I wanted to tell you how grateful I am to you for getting Paige away from the police. It's preposterous to think that child killed her mentor. My mother loved her as if she were her own daughter." I heard a soft laugh, then "Perhaps more than her own daughter. I knew I hired the right person. I hope the police are pursuing other leads. Do you know who else they have on their radar? I know they can't share too much about an ongoing investigation, but it's so hard to get information from them."

I wondered if Alicia had tried to query Skip directly. I had an idea how that would have gone. In my never-ending desire to please, to be more forthcoming than the police, I told Alicia a half truth. "I expect to be talking to Skip soon."

"Excellent. You're as good as they say, Geraldine."

Who in the world was saying that?

"Alicia, I need to ask you about your Uncle Caleb. Was he—"

"Hmmm. I don't remember anything, really, but I know from that one photo that he resembled Mother, of course. Very tall. He was in business, but don't ask me what sort. Adam might remember more. He was five at the time of the accident. We were living in Chicago then and moved out here shortly afterwards. I need to run soon, Geraldine. It's business hours in Paris. And, Geraldine, you're a gem. I know you'll get to the bottom of things."

"Thanks for your confidence, Alicia, but I—"

Another interruption, not to spoil her record. "Oh, I just remembered. You're going to the estate tomorrow to speak to Charles. I'm sure he'll be a big help to you, Geraldine. He's been with the family since we were in grade school, which is when Mother's books started to really take off. I'm looking forward to seeing you. I thought we'd leave some time for a little tour of Mother's dollhouses, if you're interested."

I could hardly keep my heartbeat in control. "I'd love to see—"

"Good, then. By now you've probably guessed that I don't much relate to the little houses. I never saw the point of making things you couldn't wear or drive. It's good that Mother had Paige. And you, too, Geraldine."

"I wish I'd—"

"My brother should be at the house for lunch, too, finally, and I must introduce you two. I have a frantic deadline to pack up three designs and ship them off to Paris, but I think I'll simply delegate the task. I hope you'll be able to stay for lunch with us."

"I'd love to."

I'd finally figured out that short sentences worked best with Alicia.

That was fine with me. I didn't have another long one in me as I allowed myself to call an end to the day.

Chapter 17

WITH MADDIE SAFELY on her way to school in Henry's shiny white SUV, and my stomach fully satisfied by a sugary French breakfast puff and two cups of an excellent Sumatra blend coffee, I had no excuse for not buckling down to the job Alicia had hired me to do. I counted myself lucky that she was so easy to please and thought I'd done well enough already.

I was glad I hadn't jokingly asked for a raise or increased benefits last night. Alicia might have taken me seriously.

Before I could do serious work, however, I needed to feed my addiction. It had been a couple of days since I'd indulged my hobby. While I'd been momentarily intimidated by the craftsmanship of the Lord and Lady Morley house, that didn't mean I was ready to give up miniatures myself.

I visited my main crafts room and picked up an unfinished mini-afghan I'd been knitting. I was about two-thirds finished, which meant I could be done in about a half hour. Just the amount of time that I could afford this morning. The instructions called for variegated yarn in nautical colors, knit in a combination shell and wave pattern, with two different blues and yellow fringe on three sides. The finished afghan would be approximately four-by-six inches, the size of the envelope that would fit in the secret room of a dollhouse, I noted.

I poured a third mug of coffee, a record for me. Normally, I switched to an herbal tea after breakfast. But there was nothing normal about this week and I needed an extra kick. I carried the mug along with the miniature afghan project to the atrium. I sat next to my small table, facing the front of the mysterious dollhouse, a life-size afghan on my lap against the early-morning chill.

I felt we'd all been very patient, and unless the house gave up its secret soon, we would have to take extraordinary measures, heirloom or not.

I have plans for you, I whispered to the house as my ultra-narrow triple-zero needles clicked away.

I HAD to admit an ulterior motive for finishing the afghan, besides finally being able to check off a task as completed. My crafters group would be at my house tonight and I was determined not to be the only one who came up empty for our show-and-tell at the beginning of the session. I folded the tiny afghan and put it on the table next to me.

The least I could do now was make notes for my meeting at ten with Varena's longtime financial manager. I closed my eyes for a moment and switched gears from the colorful threads that could be woven into a pleasing pattern to the tangle of unconnected information swimming in my brain.

Alicia had declared that Charles Quentin, whom she'd known most of her life, would be a big help to me in the investigation, from which I inferred that he was not to be considered a suspect. Too bad, because I was running out of them.

I'd all but eliminated Paige Taggart in my mind, and so, apparently, had Alicia. Paige had offered a motive for Laura Overbee—a broken promise regarding her writing. But would Laura kill Varena over something as trivial as a potential book deal? Was publishing her poetry that important to Laura? Even if she felt it was, Varena's dying wouldn't help Laura make it to the bestseller list. In fact, it would put her out of work entirely.

I wrote "Laura–3" in my notebook, evaluating her potential as Varena's murderer. I was on my way to an award for organizational skills, with a five-point scale I'd made up on the spot.

There were still Caleb Rockwell (Swingle?) and Corazón Cruz to think about. And the driver named Sedonis who was arguing with Varena and Charles shortly before her murder. Could any of them have murdered Varena?

First, Caleb. I thought about the alive, dead, and alive-again brother. Henry's suggestion that Varena and Caleb may have been estranged came back to me. For me, the idea of not speaking to my sibling, if I had one—let alone declaring him dead—was beyond comprehension. Especially if he'd built me a dollhouse, I mused.

There had never been tension of any magnitude in my family, either while I was growing up, or now. Maybe because we were a small group.

Maybe because we weren't rich. I hated to buy into the notion that the rich and famous in the Heights had more trouble, more secrets, more opportunities for destructive behavior than those of us who lived in the flats, but it was a tempting theory, borne out many times.

I wished I could call up Caleb, have him materialize in front of me, so I could quiz him. What would I ask him? Where have you been for the forty-odd years since Alicia was two years old and her mother told the family that you died in a car crash? Did you? Or were you in hiding, only to come out now and send emails and texts to your sister's young research assistant?

I looked up through my skylight at the cloudless day that was beginning. If only Varena were alive and I could ask her directly: Did you for some reason disown your brother? Did you tell anyone at all that Caleb was not really dead? Did you write it all down in a diary? Did you—?

I shot up, nearly knocking over my mug of coffee. My crazy wanderings into realms of fantasy had paid off. Varena had left behind the story of Caleb. I remembered Paige's telling me that Varena had created a character modeled after Caleb in one of her books.

I grabbed my ever-present phone, accessed my call log, and clicked on Paige's number. So what if it was a bit early for a college student. Fair was fair, and Paige had established that mere time considerations—too late at night, too early in the morning—wouldn't matter in our relationship.

The sleepy-sounding junior English major answered the phone and I immediately regretted my rash decision. The girl had had a tough couple of days and probably needed her sleep.

"I'm sorry to call so early, Paige."

"Oh, Mrs. Porter. No worries, I have a fiction workshop at nine. I was just being lazy."

I explained my little research question to the one most likely to know the name of the novel that featured a character named Caleb.

"I can't think of it offhand," Paige said. "But I keep very good records because sometimes Varena needs the information. She's... she was always wanting to know if she'd used a certain name in an earlier book, or if she was repeating a plot element. She tried to make each one different. Did you know she has more than a hundred and fifty books in print, with more than two hundred million copies sold?"

I was aware of the extent of Varena's reach in the romance field, though not the exact numbers, which were even more impressive than I thought. But for now I wanted just one title.

"She was an amazing woman," I said.

Paige cleared her throat several times. I was sorry I ever doubted the sincerity of her feelings for Varena.

"Paige?"

"I'm okay. And I knew if I thought a minute I'd come up with the title of the Caleb book. It's called *A Family Betrayed*. It came out before my time with Varena, but I can get you a copy if you want."

"No, thanks, Paige. I don't want you to be late for class."

"Let me know if you have trouble finding it. I really hope you catch whoever did this, Mrs. Porter. I miss Varena very much."

"I know you do. I don't suppose you've had any more emails or texts of interest in the last few hours?"

"No. I'm sort of glad I didn't get any, but I sort of wish I did, too."

I knew what she meant.

IT didn't take a whiz like Maddie to search for a book title and find a summary of the story. I went to my favorite book site and typed in VARENA YOUNG, A FAMILY BETRAYED.

Up popped a cover image like those I'd come to associate

with Regency romances: An impossibly beautiful woman in an emerald green, off-the-shoulder dress, a cameo on a black ribbon around her neck. A handsome man leaning toward her, his blousy white shirt open to the waist, his leather vest askew. In the next minute, you knew, he would scoop the woman in his arms. Her hair would cascade down her shoulders and onto his chest.

The cover alone was enough to send a flush to my face.

I scrolled down the Internet page to the plot summary: *Young Amanda Braxton is torn between her duty to her needy, older brother, Caleb, and her desire for the attentions of her handsome, shadowy suitor, Lucas Templeton. A dramatic series of events sends Caleb to prison and Amanda into the arms of a man who might be her undoing.*

I clucked my tongue and mentally snapped my fingers. *Aha.* I was fairly sure that what had happened to Alicia's Uncle Caleb when she was two years old did not involve a car accident. I started to make an entry on my notepad reminding me to ask Skip to check prison records. Instead, I punched in his number.

"Detective Gowen is not available..." went the recitation, in a secretary's voice. In a way, I was glad he didn't pick up. I could hold the thought that after a late night at the office, Skip might be sleeping in.

His mother and I both worried about his hectic schedule and what it might be doing to the rest of his life, if he allowed himself one. While I was at it, I decided to call Beverly, too. My sister-in-law and I didn't check in with each other quite as often as we did before meeting Nick (her) and Henry (me), but we were still best friends and always able to pick up where we left off.

I left a message for Skip, asking him to search prison records, and another for Beverly, hoping for lunch soon.

It felt good to have solved one problem and to finally start putting pieces together. Though I had no idea why Caleb might have been sent to prison or when he'd been released—days ago? months? many years?—I knew he'd been free to roam his sister's Robert Todd Heights home this past weekend.

As usual, the answer to one question had raised a dozen more. What had sent Caleb to prison, if that's what had happened? Was he wrongly convicted? Was his crime associated with whatever had gotten Varena murdered? Had he, in fact, killed his sister, his sympathetic notes to Paige notwithstanding?

It no longer seemed important to locate Corazón Cruz, except to hope that she'd either found gainful employment elsewhere in the Heights or was happily reunited with her family in Mexico. I did also wish I could thank her for setting me on a trail to find a brother everyone thought was dead.

Flashing back to Monday, I pictured Caleb's arriving at the estate, announcing himself to Corazón as Varena's brother, and being led to an upstairs sitting room. Corazón was new at the Rockwell home and couldn't have known the fiction that had grown up around Caleb. Most likely, she hadn't been briefed that the man she respectfully acknowledged as a member of the family had supposedly been deceased for more than forty years.

I tapped my pen on my notepad as I'd seen Skip do so often. I was still bothered by an army of unnamed persons of interest, besides the large household staff, who should be investigated as suspects. Perhaps I should consider other romance novelists, jealous of Varena's success. The idea was daunting. I'd never get to query them unless I hung out a shingle and hired a staff to help me.

That was not how I saw my retirement years. Poor Alicia, counting on the likes of me.

I thought back to my conversations with Alicia, who for all practical purposes had started me on this road of detecting. A wicked notion fluttered in the back of my mind. What if her big show of wanting to find her mother's killer was just that, a show, to deflect suspicion from herself?

By "hiring" me, she appeared eager to find justice for her mother's murder. And what better way to keep tabs on the true investigation by the LPPD than through the known-to-be-meddling aunt of the chief detective on the case? I realized I was her conduit for information on how the case was proceeding. Were they closing in on her? What evidence were they working with?

I recalled Alicia's laugh when she mentioned how Varena

loved Paige like a daughter, or "perhaps more than her own daughter." Was there a note of resentment in the remark? I could make myself believe anything this morning, but I decided to push away the dark thoughts of matricide. Everyone handled grief differently, and if Alicia's method seemed a more calculated, problem-solving approach than I might have taken, that didn't mean she was any less devastated by the loss of her mother in such a violent way.

The dollhouse stood mute in front of me. In some ways, it was the center of the investigation. The miniature building stared back at me. I contemplated its multifaceted history that qualified at once as a symbol of an older brother's love for his sister, as a valuable antique, as a celebrity relic, and as an example of twentieth-century modern style.

If houses could be charged with a crime, I might accuse this one at least of obstruction of justice.

I leaned forward and brushed away a piece of lint that had made its way from my laundry area to the old card table that supported the house. I had a plan in mind for the future of Caleb's long-ago wonderful present to Varena. I'd decided to give it one more day to live. My regular Wednesday crafters group would meet in my home this evening. I'd put all of them to work on the project of uncovering the secret room.

I addressed the house directly: *If that doesn't work, I'm calling in the demolition crew.*

Once I started talking to my hobby—and this was not the first time I'd spoken to a dollhouse—I knew it was time for a break. I put aside my notepad, with its pages of names and checkmarks, but mostly doodles of tiny houses and furniture, and went to my bedroom to face the toughest part of the day—what to wear?

Still conscious of the inadequacy of my wardrobe for a visit to the Heights, I did the best I could. I couldn't match the dramatic flair of Varena or her daughter, with their vibrant colors and flowing outfits, but I certainly could pull off the retro sweater-set look that Laura Overbee had adopted.

I donned a beige cashmere shell and cardigan, a present from

Maddie's parents last Christmas, and dark brown wool slacks that Beverly had picked out for my birthday. The amber teardrop-shaped pendant that Ken gave me on our twentieth anniversary seemed to work well with the ensemble.

If it weren't for my family and friends, I'd never be fit to leave the house.

I gave my bland brown hair a quick finger-brushing and headed for my garage and my dull blue car. Not even my vehicle had much color.

It was time to meet Charles Quentin, the nonsuspect.

Chapter 18

I DROVE UP the winding road with densely wooded areas on both sides to the Rockwell Estate, my mind a blur of possibilities and hope for the meetings with two new-to-me figures in Varena's life, her son and her financial manager. I'd had only cursory dealings with Charles Quentin since Monday and only hearsay about Adam Rockwell.

The road to Robert Todd Heights was familiar to me now, but for all the wrong reasons. I imagined instead a world in which Varena Young and I had bonded as friends and I'd become a regular visitor to her home. Perhaps she would also have ventured down to my humble Eichler once in a while, or she might have joined the Wednesday night crafts group, regaling us with fascinating stories of how her astounding collection came to be.

I tucked the dream away with all the other might-have-beens in my life and tried to focus on the wonderful parts I still enjoyed.

I PARKED my car in what I now considered its usual spot at the edge of the driveway in front of the main entrance. As I walked in toward the lion's head knocker, I wondered if the household had been at all prepared for the turmoil Varena's death would bring. If preparations had been made, they would have assumed a natural death at a later date, with an orderly transition of the estate. With no one associated with Varena's household suspected of murder, no remnants of crime scene tape to deal with, no police or pseudo-investigators coming to lunch.

I wondered if there was a will to haggle over? Jewelry, vacation properties, artwork, other heirlooms to parcel out? Would there be a peaceful settlement of this impressive legacy? Though it was none of my business, I hoped there would be no further drama in the lives of the Rockwell family.

Dum, ta da dum, ta da dum, ta da dum.

I checked my cell phone screen. Henry had caught me half-way to the double set of concrete stairs. I stepped to the side and sat on a granite garden bench with an elaborate *R* etched on its back and another on its seat.

"Reporting from the field in Palo Alto," he said. "Maddie is safely deposited with her peer group."

"Thanks, Henry." How old would my granddaughter have to be before I wouldn't feel a sense of relief at that message, even when there was no apparent threat to her well-being? "Did anything of a criminal nature come up as you were driving down?"

Henry laughed. "Yeah, she opened with how I might have to give back the key ring. It was all smooth from there."

"I'm glad. I'm sure every little step takes away some stress."

"Any news from the Heights?"

"Not yet. I'm just heading in to the house."

"Got your interrogation list all ready?"

I was sorry he asked. The question nearly ruined the clear sunny skies and the mixed scents of the lush flowery trim around Varena's life-size castle.

"Sort of."

"Don't worry, you won't need any."

"Thanks again."

"Since Maddie's getting out at noon today, I'm going to hang around Palo Alto. I've been wanting to get to that hobby shop in town. They might have what I need to finish that ceiling fan for your kitchen."

For a moment, I was confused. I already had a ceiling fan in my Eichler kitchen. But not in my contemporary ranch dollhouse kitchen. I'd almost forgotten that Henry had decided I needed a working ceiling fan with wooden blades, two speeds, and three lights. I didn't disagree. Future home improvement projects, with which I also concurred, included a microwave oven with a light showing through its door for the ranch home, and Westminster chimes for the doorbell in my colonial.

Even as I compared my old life-size Eichler with the larger-than-life Rockwell mansion in front of me, I felt very rich.

"I'd rather be shopping for tiny pieces of wicker," I said, referring to the decorative centers of the ceiling fan blades.

"No, you wouldn't."

"Well, once this is over, I will."

"That I believe."

There was an upside and a downside when you let someone get to know you very well.

I heard a rustling in the thicket of eucalyptus trees behind me and turned to look, standing up at the same time. My early training growing up on the streets of the Bronx made me suspicious of creatures that lived in the woods. I brushed off my slacks, signed off with Henry, and started again for Varena's home.

IT wasn't that long a distance to the steps of the house, but long enough for another call to come in. This one was from the police. I stood in place this time.

"Hey, Aunt Gerry. You did it again, with that brother thing."

Even a poorly worded compliment gave me a lift. "The thing worked out? You found Caleb?"

"We found out where he'd been all those years. In prison in Chicago. Sentenced to thirty years for embezzlement, served twenty-five. The guy is now eighty-three years old."

I soaked up the information, trying to do arithmetic at the same time. When had Varena and her brother gotten back together? I needed a calculator.

In the absence of a verbal response from me, Skip continued. "It's a pretty steep sentence for a nonviolent offender; someone must have had it in for him. We'd been looking for a Rockwell in California. And since the states don't share that well, we missed a Swingle who was in prison in Illinois and got out eighteen years ago."

Though I'd guessed Caleb's history from Varena's *A Family Betrayed*, hearing Skip's confirmation was still a bit of a surprise.

Surprise that I'd guessed correctly? Probably. It seemed a long road from my nephew's doubting my ability to understand Corazón Cruz's accent to the actual existence of a living brother for Varena.

I walked back a few steps to sit on the granite bench.

Did this new information mean that Caleb was in fact one of the men in the argument I heard shortly before Varena was beaten to death? I shuddered at the image and wished I could stop flashing back to the details of the murder.

"What else can you tell me, Skip?"

"I have a fax here with the basics. Nothing very creative in the guy's life except for his crime. He was an executive vice president for a real estate investment company and needed money for gambling debts, so naturally he took it from the company. He finally paid off all the money and a court-ordered fine a few years ago. His last known address is in Chicago."

"Not Arizona?"

"Not Arizona."

I sent a pouty, disappointed breath over the line. Or over the waves from the towers that carried cell phone messages.

"But I can tell you who recently moved here from Arizona and still has the old plates on his red truck."

I drew in my breath, now excited. "Who?"

"What's it worth?"

"Skip!"

"Just thought you might have missed my teasing while we were estranged."

I wished he hadn't used that word. Estrangement meant a thirty- or forty-year separation, like Varena and her brother had undergone.

"You're right. I'm glad to be teased. Now, who?"

"A guy we interviewed on the scene. Roberto Sedonis. He's one of the estate's drivers."

"Thanks, Skip. A lot of things are starting to fall into place."

Everything but who killed Varena.

As I clicked off my phone, I heard the same rustling noise as earlier from behind me. I should have known better than to come back to the bench. It would serve me right if a raccoon or a go-pher hopped up beside me. Or worse, a skunk. I wasn't comfort-able with animals that didn't have names and collars with ID tags.

I walked quickly away from the bench. Out of the corner of my eye, I saw a white flash that turned out to be the sun reflect-ing from an envelope. I was sure it wasn't there when I sat down, either time.

I stood as still as I possibly could, held my breath, and lis-tened. The traffic and construction noise at the intersection of Gettysburg and Springfield might as well be two counties away. Not a sound reached this part of the Heights except that from a slight breeze rushing through the eucalyptus. I looked back at the engraved bench. Should I pick up the envelope? Call Rockwell security? Run for the front door? Make a beeline for my car?

I was frozen with fright and indecision.

Two things were clear. One, that the envelope was placed there for me. Two, that it hadn't been deposited by a bobcat.

I FIGURED such a thin envelope couldn't hold a ticking bomb, and the chances of an elaborate anthrax plot against a miniaturist from a small California town seemed slim.

When I could finally unfreeze my stance, I gingerly picked up the unmarked business-size envelope, then rushed back to my car, trying to cover three hundred and sixty degrees of surveil-lance as I hustled.

Thanks to good planning and the construction-free route I'd taken to the Heights, I still had a few minutes to open the missive and compose myself before I needed to appear for my meeting with Charles.

Still, it took a while for my shaky fingers to extract the single piece of paper from the envelope.

I read the neat printing: HOLD DOWN THE RED CIRCLE. WATCH OUT FOR CQ.

Maybe the note wasn't for me after all.

Figuring out the significance of the note in the short time I had was hopeless, except that CQ must refer to Charles Quentin. How handy that I'd be calmly sitting across from the man soon, with this new directive to watch out for him floating around my head.

I decided to risk being late for my meeting and spend a minute or two putting together the new information from Skip with miscellaneous tidbits from Alicia. I needed to figure out the timeline of Varena's and Caleb's lives. If I didn't, I'd be even more distracted while trying to conduct an interview with Charles.

Alicia was told that her Uncle Caleb died when she was two years old. Around the same time, her mother's writing career began to take off and the family moved from Chicago to California.

Adding in the admittedly questionable source material I'd gleaned from the Internet, this would mean that Mildred Swingle, a high school dropout from the farmlands of the Central Valley of California moved to Chicago and wrote romances under the pen name Varena Young. When her brother went to prison—died, in her mind—she moved back to California, this time as the mistress of the Rockwell Estate in the affluent South Bay Area.

Another piece of trivia from Skip when he called to tell me my friend had been murdered: Varena had two ex-husbands. I wondered which one was Rockwell? And, how uncouth would it be to ask Alicia?

As for Caleb, now eighty-three, he'd served a twenty-five-year prison term and then worked many years at paying off the fine that was part of his punishment. Now, for some reason, Caleb was back and skulking around the woods surrounding his sister's home. When he wasn't stuffing papers into secret dollhouse rooms or upstairs in the Rockwell mansion, arguing with Varena and CQ, for whom I had to watch out.

No wonder I was dizzy.

Tap, tap. Tap, tap sounded on the window nearest my head.

"Geraldine?"

I gasped, jumped, and banged my knee on my steering wheel, almost at the same time. Not that I was on edge.

Things got better when I saw that it was the lovely Alicia Rockwell at my window, and not an especially dexterous jackrabbit.

———

AS I made my third approach on the lion's head knocker, this time with Alicia, I took a chance that she'd fire me for rudeness and asked her the freshest question on my mind.

"I'm curious, Alicia, which of your mother's husbands was Rockwell?"

Alicia laughed. "You know about my mother's dramatic habit of loving and leaving? Neither marriage lasted very long. Actually, Adam and I have different fathers, which might account for the vast differences in our personalities. I can't wait for you to meet him."

"Same here."

"Adam kept his father's name. My brother is Adam George. I think it's a shortened form of a long Greek name. Mother married my father, Bernard Willis, who, she told me, was a philandering artist. She divorced him when I was still an infant and went back to her maiden name. She changed mine at the same time. Alexandra Rockwell was her maiden name."

Of course it was.

"Thanks, that clears things up," I said.

Alicia had a lot to learn about her family history.

"Adam and I were very fortunate as kids. By the time we were in grade school, Mother's books were very popular and her publisher released three or four a year." We'd reached the bottom of the stairway. Alicia spread her arms to encompass this estate on the hill. "All of this is from romance. Can you believe it?" she asked.

I wondered if romance, fame, and fortune had also brought Varena's violent death.

ALICIA went off to make an overseas call while I waited for Charles in the same room I'd enjoyed before I met Varena Young. A tall, narrow oil painting that dominated one wall, behind the grand piano, was of a black-suited gentleman from a century ago. The imposing effect was spoiled by my new knowledge that the man wasn't a Rockwell ancestor, and that the portrait might have come with the mansion or with the purchase of the fancy frame.

While I'd waited for Varena in this music room on Monday afternoon, I worried that she might be aloof and hard to talk to.

Once I met her, I found her to be warm and giving. Now that her death had unearthed her secrets, the lies she told her family, I didn't know what to think of her.

Was she devious, hiding not just her older brother's criminal past, but perhaps her own? Or was she simply trying to protect her children from the discriminatory practices people who rose from poverty often had to abide?

Ten-twenty A.M. Charles was now officially late. My first meeting with him, when Henry and I (as Mr. and Mrs. Porter) had driven up to offer our condolences, had been short and perfunctory. He'd refused to acknowledge my need for Corazón Cruz's forwarding address and was eager for me to leave.

I remembered the only uncharacteristically polite question he'd asked on that day—had I seen or heard anything that might have upset me?

Was he asking if I'd seen him kill his boss?

Charles Quentin had better come soon, before my imagination led me to claim that I'd witnessed him standing over Varena's body with the lethal sword in his hand.

NOT Charles, but eventually I had a visitor to the room. A whiff of rosewater seemed to precede Laura Overbee as she came my way in a pale green sweater set.

"Geraldine, how nice to see you again," Laura said, taking a seat across from me. A large vase of white chrysanthemums nearly shielded her face. I shifted on the plush sofa. "Charles is running late. He apologizes profusely."

"It will give us a chance to visit," I said, with just the right amount of investigative tone in my voice, I thought. "I suppose you're busy making plans?"

I meant "looking for a new job," but didn't have the heart to be so direct.

"There's still a great deal to do here. There are two more Varena Young books coming out in the next few months and they have to be dealt with."

I gave her a questioning look.

"Promoted," Laura explained.

"You'll be promoting the book of a deceased author?"

"Certainly. The estate is owed the royalties from the books. And, of course, Varena's fans will be very excited to have a few more hours of pleasure from new releases. In fact, Missy Beaumont, another Regency romance author from the San Francisco area, has generously offered to include Varena's books as she launches her own in the next months."

There was a lot I didn't understand about the publishing business. I was happy with my status as reader. Since Laura was in a friendly mood and I was in a fact-finding mood, I did my own bit of promotion.

"I'm trying to tie up some loose ends for my report to the police," I said, with a great show of sincerity. As if Skip would take field notes from his aunt. "Would you be able to put me in touch with one of your drivers, a man named Roberto Sedonis?"

"How's that investigation coming? I thought it was all wrapped up when the police arrested Paige."

"They didn't arrest her. They asked her additional questions."

"Well, they should have just put her in jail. Did they ask her why was she down that hallway in the first place?"

I thought of defending Paige, but pulled back. Laura could think what she wanted. "The police are doing their jobs and I'm doing mine. I'm sorry to impose on you about seeing Mr. Sedonis. I'm sure your responsibilities have nothing to do with him or other employees."

Laura fairly jumped up from her hands-folded seated position on the velvety chair. "Not true. I'll find Roberto and send him over."

She left abruptly, leaving her rosewater trail. I followed her with my gaze as she walked toward the corridor that ended in the Lord and Lady Morley room.

I had no desire to visit the Morleys' house today. Not even the thought of another look at the walnut-and-maple lap harp in their miniature music room could entice me down the hallway.

I wasn't at all happy with whoever had turned my fantasy into horror.

———

I TOOK out my phone and punched in Henry's number. I'd been about to call him when Alicia had interrupted me in my car.

"Shouldn't you be at your meeting with Charles Quentin?" he asked.

"He's running late."

"He's scared of you."

Leave it to Henry to make me laugh when I least expect to.

"I found the pieces of wicker I was looking for and also a very nice pull chain," he said. "I think you'll like it."

"I'm sure I will." I also liked picturing Henry in his corduroy pants and thick wool vest, going about his business. "What's next?"

"I'll spend the next forty-five minutes or so in the library, then I'll head over to Maddie's school. We should be home by twelve-thirty. I'll take her to your house since Taylor doesn't get picked up till three. Anything you want us to do to get ready for your crafters meeting tonight in case you're late?"

"I'd better not be that late, but it would be a big help if you set up the buffet table. Maddie knows what to put out."

"Will do."

I still marveled at having found this wonderful "will do" kind of guy. We'd reconnected at the faculty table of an ALHS reunion that neither of us had wanted to attend. We'd hardly been apart since, and neither had our granddaughters.

I went through a quick internal debate about whether to tell Henry about the note I'd either received or intercepted. Maybe he'd be able to figure out what it meant for the investigation. It occurred to me that I always seemed to be giving my friend errands to do for me, puzzles to figure out, problems to solve. I'd spare him this one.

One of these days I was going to ask Henry Baker on a normal date.

Chapter 19

SOMEWHERE IN THE enormous house a clock struck eleven. For all I could tell, the sound was coming from one of the working grandfather clocks in the Lord and Lady Morley dollhouse. Thinking of my short time with them brought on a wave of sadness, as if they were a real couple who'd just suffered a loss.

Not even my doctor or my hairdresser was this late for an appointment. I was beginning to think I was being stood up by CQ. I stood to stretch my legs and considered stepping outside to get some air. But did I want to risk missing Charles? Did I want to inadvertently forgo what was probably an elegant lunch, the menu something to talk about with my favorite cook, Henry?

An even more critical question: Did I want to risk another visit from the postman in the woods?

While I was ruminating, a short, dark, formally dressed man appeared in the massive archway between the foyer and the music room.

"Mrs. Porter?" he asked, taking off a cap that screamed *chauffeur*. "Ms. Overbee said you like to talk to me?"

I detected a slight Hispanic accent, much less pronounced than Corazón Cruz's. I wasn't happy about another opportunity for Skip to accuse me of misunderstanding a member of the Rockwell household staff.

"Mr. Sedonis?"

He nodded.

"I'm expecting Mr. Quentin any minute, but perhaps we can have a short chat?"

"Mr. Quentin, he's tied up with some important people," the timid man said.

I was used to hearing that at the Rockwell Estate, where everyone was more important than I was.

I invited Mr. Sedonis to take a seat on the sofa. He declined with a shake of his head. Maybe he felt even less important than I did, less worthy of the rich, velvety fabric. Or maybe his theory was that interviews conducted while both parties were standing tended to be short.

"By any chance, did you deliver a dollhouse to my home on Monday afternoon?" I asked.

Mr. Sedonis held his cap by the edge of the brim and turned it around and around. "*Sí, sí.* I'm very sorry, Mrs. Porter."

"Why are you sorry?"

"The"—Mr. Sedonis put his hat under his arm and used his hands to make what might have passed for a rectangle—"the corner?"

I shook my head, still not getting it.

"We bang it a little."

"You banged the corner of the dollhouse?"

"*Sí*, it was very heavy, Mrs. Porter, and the doorway—"

"Is that why you thought I wanted to see you? Because there's damage at a corner of the dollhouse? I didn't even notice it. Please don't worry about it, Mr. Sedonis."

Mr. Sedonis's whole body relaxed. A smile came to his dark face. "Thank you, Mrs. Porter."

"If you could answer just a couple of questions for me?"

He would be only too happy to.

"Do you always use your own vehicle for deliveries?" I asked.

"No, but the truck that belongs to the estate, it is in the shop and the dollhouse would not fit in any of the cars, so my cousin and me, we use the truck we travel here in."

"From Arizona," I said. Just making sure we were talking about the same red truck.

He nodded.

I wondered if the Rockwell Estate—"the Swingle Estate"

didn't have the same ring to it—had as many vehicles as doll-houses.

"What time did you leave here with the dollhouse?"

"I don't get back to the estate until almost four-thirty, then we have to pack it so it doesn't fall out of the truck and that's why we get to your house so late. You are not home, so we leave it in front of the door."

It was a relief to hear that Mr. Sedonis's story was consistent with the time code on the construction site video. I had enough twisting and confusing threads to work out without having to reconcile the driver's version of events.

"There was more than one dollhouse in that room. How did you know which one to take to my home?"

"Ms. Young, she told me she put a sign on it in the room upstairs." Mr. Sedonis pointed up and to his right, where I assumed the Lord Weatherly room was. Still holding my midsize Tudor, I mused, my mind wandering off to a hoped-for tour of the dollhouses today.

"And you had no trouble finding the sign on the dollhouse?"

Mr. Sedonis made faster and faster trips around his hat, shift-ed his small frame from one foot to the other and back again, and shook his head from side to side. "I'm sorry, Mrs. Porter."

Here we go. "What happened?"

"My cousin, he's clumsy. He knocks the sign down and I ask him is he sure which house. Now I think maybe we took the wrong one? We can come and get it, Mrs. Porter. This is my new job, only six months, and I don't want to give any trouble for Mr. Quentin. I can go back and deliver you the other one today."

In any language: *Please don't tell my boss I messed up.*

"You don't have to worry about that, Mr. Sedonis. I'll straighten things out and you certainly won't be blamed for any-thing."

Once again, I had a timeline to work out. If Paige's informa-tion was correct, Caleb deposited the letter in the secret room of the dollhouse he built for his sister on Sunday evening or Monday morning. Varena must have tagged the Tudor for me before I arrived at the estate since there was hardly time between when I left and some time around four-fifteen when she was murdered.

It occurred to me that the mistress of the estate most likely already lay dead at the other end of the mansion by the time Mr. Sedonis and his cousin picked up the wrong dollhouse.

I needed a moment of silence, but there was no opportunity.

One small thing that Mr. Sedonis said nagged at me. I thought a minute and chose my strategy carefully.

"Thanks for all your help, Mr. Sedonis. You did an excellent job getting that huge dollhouse to my home with only a tiny scratch. I'm sure you have very busy days working for this big estate, don't you?"

I could practically read the man's mind: Finally, an easy question. He put his cap back under his arm and rubbed his palms together, a happy man, relieved that the formal interview was over.

He smiled broadly. "Very busy, yes, all the time."

"And I'll bet the trip to my home on Monday wasn't the first trip to town that you made that day."

"No, no. All afternoon on Monday I was in town, in the shop with the truck for the estate. I had to wait until my cousin come to get me. That's why I'm not back here until four-thirty."

"Then it must have been another driver who was arguing with Mr. Quentin between three-thirty and four?"

Mr. Sedonis turned as white as his natural complexion would allow. I thought the man was going to fall to his knees. I felt a surge of guilt that I'd tricked him into letting down his guard so he'd forget his lie to the police. It was CQ who should be held responsible, not a poor worker simply trying to hold onto his job.

Now that I knew Charles had coerced Mr. Sedonis to give a false statement to the police, I wasn't sure what it all meant. Was it too much of a leap to conclude that the argument I heard on Monday afternoon had been among Varena, Charles, and Caleb? If so, why would Charles want to hide Caleb's presence? To keep Varena's secret?

It would make sense that Charles, the longtime friend, might know of Caleb's conviction and Varena's desire to disassociate herself from him.

I was about to assure Mr. Sedonis that I would do my best not to bring his lie out in the open, when I saw a tall man with a thick shock of white hair descend the staircase in the foyer.

Charles Quentin, a man I knew to be in his mid-seventies, but who could have passed for much younger, whether from nature or design, I couldn't say.

I put my hand on the estate driver's shoulder and spoke so Charles would hear me. "Thanks for sharing your thoughts about Ms. Young with me, Mr. Sedonis. The local miniaturists club will be very happy to hear the memories, direct from someone who drove her to her favorite places."

I could hear Skip in the recesses of my head: "What a crock."

I wasn't sure Charles Quentin bought it either, but I had to give it a try. I knew I'd be devastated if Mr. Sedonis went the way of Corazón Cruz.

QUICK as a flash, the short, dark Roberto in a narrow black tie was replaced on the carpet in front of me by the tall, white-haired Charles in the most expensive-looking suit I'd ever seen. I suspected his attire was chosen to fit in with the important people who had preceded me on his calendar.

I hoped it was only my guilt-ridden imagination that saw a suspicious look from Charles, directed at Mr. Sedonis.

To me, he couldn't have been more charming. "I'm so sorry to be late, Mrs. Porter. In fact, I see that lunch is ready to be served. Won't you follow me to the patio?"

Charles didn't leave me much choice. I was sure he'd deliberately worked it so I'd have no private time with him. He came across as a man who worked everything to suit himself.

Maybe it was just as well that I wouldn't be alone with him. After all, I'd been warned to watch out for him.

I'D have been way off the mark if I thought "patio" meant a rustic, informal setting, perhaps outdoors. The Rockwell patio, at the back of the house, past the grand double stairway, was more like a conservatory where exotic plants grew than a place where you'd slap hamburgers on a grill. Sunlight poured through the structure through the floor-to-ceiling bay windows. Spread out behind it were the lavish gardens of the estate, and beyond, the rolling hills of Robert Todd Heights.

I'd have been hard-pressed to recall a setting more elegant than this, even counting all the weddings I'd been to. The white wrought iron table was set for four with exquisite china and crystal. At each place were a three-color salad of lettuce, endive, and radicchio and a selection of miniature fresh-from-the-oven rolls that emitted the most wonderful yeasty aroma.

Alicia had preceded us and now approached the entry to the spacious "patio."

She extended her long arm in a graceful gesture toward Adam, entering stage right. Another Varena, only male, causing me to conclude that genes of the men who fathered these children had been defeated by those of the mother. Biology wasn't my best subject, but at least I knew what I meant.

"We didn't allow the staff much notice," Alicia said, giving me an air-kiss near each cheek. "So, this will be a simple meal. I just wanted you to get to know Charles and Adam."

Alicia spoke as if I were her new BFF and she'd brought me home to meet the family.

I had to admit, it was convenient to have all the nonsuspects at one table.

THE very "simple" lunch of fillet of swordfish with a topping of minced olives and peppers, disks of sautéed zucchini, and jasmine rice nearly distracted me from learning more about the Swingle/Rockwell/Young family and its caretaker. With each delicious bite I pictured myself describing the taste to Henry and everyone I knew (except Maddie).

It would have been difficult for me to bring up means, motive, and opportunity for murder in such lovely, peaceful surroundings. Instead, I listened to what was important to each of my lunch companions.

From Charles: a brief history of the ownership of the estate, previously occupied by an unnamed governor of an East Coast state, bought by Varena who made a number of improvements, each one of which Charles explained in detail. I inquired politely about the origin of the plants that surrounded us in the patio. We noted how sad it was that Varena did not live to see her last planting bloom.

From Alicia: a taste of the inner workings of the fashion industry in San Francisco, New York City, and Paris. I mentioned once having worked near the Garment District during my college years in Manhattan. Alicia reminisced that her mother was always willing to be the first test model for a new design.

From Adam: a discussion of the vagaries of labor law in this state of many immigrant workers, plus an inadvertent mention of his soon-to-be ex-wife, Estelle, who was on a cruise to the Caribbean. I added that my late husband and I had cruised the Greek Islands many years ago. Adam confessed how sorry he was that he'd never taken a cruise with his wife or his mother.

I ate the last morsel of a sour cream roll with the bit of zucchini that was left on my plate. A young woman cleared away our dishes and took our orders for coffee and tea. When Alicia announced that the chef's special dessert was cognac ice cream with roasted Bing cherries and bittersweet chocolate sauce, it was almost enough to silence me on the reason I'd come here today.

So far I'd gotten nothing that would help me with the investigation into the murder of the woman who should have been sitting at the head of the table, enjoying her blooming phlox with Mozart in the background. Were Alicia and Charles deliberately stonewalling me, protecting themselves from unpleasant questions?

Now that I was pleasantly sated, I could afford to be escorted off the property, if it came to that. I started with the weakest link, as I perceived him. "Adam, do you mind if I ask you a couple of questions? I haven't really talked to you about the horrible crime against your family."

"Sure, go ahead, Geraldine. I know I haven't been much use. As my sister puts it, I'm kind of in a fog."

A stranger to the table would have guessed incorrectly that Alicia was the older sibling. Alicia was always in charge, in her posture, her voice, her manner of speaking. Adam seemed at sixes and sevens, his eyes a bit glazed, as if he'd just awakened from a long sleep.

"What do you remember about your Uncle Caleb?" I asked Adam.

Charles's throat clearing drowned out Mozart. "I fail to see why you would bring up another tragedy, Geraldine."

"What's the harm, Charles?" Adam asked. "I actually do remember some nice times with my only uncle. There was some kind of theme park he'd take us to. Or maybe it was just a circus passing through town." Adam smiled more broadly than he had all through lunch. "Whatever it was, he bought us the kind of food Mother would never let us eat. Hot dogs, especially."

"I, of course, have no such memories, but I do recall your telling me those stories. Adam. It seems they were happy times." Alicia's face took on a relaxed expression that was new to me.

I sensed that Uncle Caleb was the kind of uncle every kid should have. What a shame that, for one reason or another, he was taken from their lives.

"What do you remember about the day Caleb died?"

Charles became so agitated, I thought the table would overturn from his restless motions. If Adam noticed, it didn't prevent him from answering my question.

"It was a very strange day, not that I've ever told anyone about it. Ours was not the most open family for sharing feelings."

"Adam," Alicia said, a warning note in her voice. I expected her to send her half brother to his room at any moment.

But Adam, looking past Alicia at the outside garden, had gone back fortysomething years. "A phone call came in, and Mother told me that Uncle Caleb had 'passed on' and that we should pray for his soul. It was the first time I'd ever prayed for someone's soul and I wasn't sure how to do it."

Alicia seemed conflicted, wanting to hear this family story, perhaps not for the first time, but aware of how uncomfortable it made Charles. She folded and refolded her napkin, straightened the place setting so the silverware was exactly parallel, and finally rang a small bell I hadn't noticed before.

Immediately the young woman who'd served our lunch was at her side.

"We're ready for our dessert," Alicia said.

"Five more minutes, ma'am, while the cherries settle?"

Alicia nodded. Charles took a deep breath. I tried to focus on Adam, who hardly missed a beat.

"Mother didn't cry as I thought she would, so I remember working really hard to keep myself from crying, too. And I know we all went to the police station that day. She had to take us because there was no one around to mind us."

"I'm sure there were police reports to fill out," I said. "About the car accident," I added, looking at Charles.

"I thought I saw Uncle Caleb at the station but Mother said no, it couldn't have been. It must have been another man who looked like him. Anyway, I finally realized what 'passed on' meant. There'd be no more hot dogs."

"What a terrible loss for a small child."

"Mmm," Adam said, still not fully in the present.

"Did you know Caleb, Charles?" I asked.

Charles frowned, his thick white eyebrows seeming to connect on the bridge of his nose. "Do we really need to bring up unhappy memories, Geraldine? This family has been through enough."

"I do apologize, but I have a feeling that Adam and Alicia's uncle may have something to do with this murder investigation."

"Nonsense." Charles threw down his napkin and stood. "You'll have to excuse me. I'm afraid I'm not comfortable with this conversation."

As Charles left the patio, Alicia turned to me. "This is not what I had in mind, Geraldine. Charles is our executor and a family friend for nearly forty years. Charles is really my honorary uncle, if you want to put it that way."

That's not the way I wanted to put it, but I knew it was time to leave. We both stood and walked out of the patio, leaving Adam behind with his happy childhood memories. I suspected tomorrow's lunch would consist of hot dogs with mustard and relish from an ordinary supermarket.

Chapter 20

MY BIGGEST REGRET as I turned on the ignition in my car was that I hadn't gotten the twice-promised dollhouse tour, not from Varena, and not from Alicia. I wondered if I'd ever again be welcome at the Rockwell Estate. I pictured Alicia writing out my pink slip.

It would have been nice to try the cognac ice cream, also. My friends called me a dessert alcoholic. I never drank a drop of wine or hard liquor from a glass, but I loved rum cake, almond amaretto bars, wine jelly, and the Grand Marnier poultry stuffing my mother made for the adult table on holidays.

Driving the winding road to my home in the flats, I replayed as much of the lunch conversation as I could remember and asked myself questions I still couldn't answer.

Why was Charles Quentin so uncomfortable talking about Caleb? I revisited my charitable theory that Charles knew Varena's secret and wanted to help her keep it even in death. In terms of the murder investigation, however, the more appealing theory was that he had something more self-serving to hide. Two things were clear from my interview with Roberto Sedonis—that Charles Quentin knew Caleb Swingle was alive and hovering around the Rockwell Estate, and that he was party to an argument with Varena on the afternoon of her murder.

"Watch out for CQ" flashed through my mind and I shivered. From the idea that Charles Quentin might be Varena's killer? Or from the frightening thought that I might have been killed by a man rustling in the woods?

As for Adam George, I was convinced that he wasn't hiding

anything. I figured he'd seen his Uncle Caleb being processed in the police station. Maybe Varena had taken him there because she had no one to watch him while she made the trip to plead Caleb's case to the police or to tell her brother off or to say one last good-bye.

It might have been the lush patio setting, the gourmet meal, and the awareness that I was surrounded by dollhouses that made me vulnerable, but I'd been pulled in by Adam's charming, child-like innocence. I pushed away a thought of contacting Estelle and asking her to reconsider her decision to abandon her sweet husband.

It was arrogant enough to think I was qualified to investigate a crime. Was I now ready to pass myself off as a marriage counselor?

A big question was where Alicia stood in all this. Had her motive in hiring me stemmed from a sincere desire to find her mother's killer? She'd discounted the idea that Paige murdered Varena, and certainly wouldn't even consider that Charles was anything but a loving family friend.

If she'd had someone particular in mind to accuse, she hadn't let on. Alicia had never pointed me in the direction of an individual or hinted that she had a clue about who the perpetrator might be. Did she think I was going to consider everyone in the household simply as sources of information, not suspects? Did she expect me to uncover a random killer prowling the Heights, one who broke into the Lord and Lady Morley room and murdered Lady Varena?

I came back to my earlier thought that Alicia herself had killed her mother and that she'd befriended/hired me for purposes of misdirection. She could have been among the many Lincoln Point citizens who thought I had influence with the LPPD. What better way to assure that the police wouldn't consider her a suspect?

With little traffic to pay attention to, my mind took off, expanding on the matricide theory. I imagined the family's early years when, it seemed, Varena was essentially a single mother of two, on her own, except for possible support from her brother until he was sent away. She worked at her writing and perhaps other jobs to keep her little family together. I guessed she didn't have a lot of time for the young Alicia.

Now, day after day (just to add drama to my narrative), Alicia had seen Varena mentoring an unrelated college student, Paige Taggart, nurturing her as a writer and spending time with her at a hobby Alicia had no use for. It might be enough to turn daughter against mother. I felt a sudden need to call and warn Mary Lou until I shook myself out of the nightmare by remembering that she was a perfect wife and mother. There was nothing like a murder investigation to mess with someone's head. How did the real police do it day after day and still sleep at night?

There was the final question of the sword handle fragment the police found in Paige's dormitory room. It occurred to me that I should find out if there was a sign-in log in the building. I'd ask Skip if the police had thought to check. Couching the query in other, more flattering words, of course.

I tried to picture the seventysomething Charles Quentin, in expensive tweeds and rich leather loafers, trying to fit in as he entered a college dorm. I saw him break into Paige's room, and hide the murder weapon among her shoes. Then I saw myself taking a photo of a white-haired older gentleman and showing it to the sentry in the foyer of the dorm.

"Have you seen this man?" I'd ask.

I groaned at my inadequacy for the task of effective investigating. I knew there was a reason I'd spent a career teaching fiction and not writing it.

THANKS to the long-winded conversation I had with myself, it wasn't until I reached the well-recorded intersection of Gettysburg and Springfield that I noticed the same car had been in my rearview mirror since soon after I left the estate driveway. A dark blue sedan with a sole male driver. I couldn't see the whole license plate, but I could tell by the fact that it began with the number two that the car was an older model. The state of California was well past two as the initial number. Richard's new car boasted a seven, in fact. The age of the vehicle didn't tell me much except that it probably wasn't Charles Quentin or a Rockwell following me. If anyone was actually following me.

But if not, why did the car make a right as I did and continue up the road toward my Eichler neighborhood?

Dum, ta da dum, ta da dum, ta da dum.

I started at the sound. It was really the car behind me that rattled me, not the familiar marching tune of my cell phone. "Hello," I said to my Bluetooth device.

"Hey, Grandma, we've been home."

The friendly voice settled me. "And I've been what?"

"Away So Long." I heard the grin in her words. "Is your meeting over?"

In more ways than one. "Yes, sweetheart, I'm on my way home now." With no unwelcome company, I hope.

"There's nothing to do here."

Which I interpreted to mean, *The grown-ups in my life won't let me use the computer.*

"Maybe you and Uncle Henry can work on the new dollhouse."

"We did for a while, but we tried everything to find that room. Nuts. We even blew on everything, but I know Uncle Henry was just joking when he said we should do that. Maybe I was dreaming and there is no room."

Not a chance. "I think it will just take a little more time."

I told Maddie my brilliant idea to have my crafters group work on the secret-room project this evening. I didn't mention the demolition derby approach that was my backup plan.

"Nuts. I can't believe I'm stuck. And now there's nothing to do here."

I smiled, wishing I were there to tickle my granddaughter out of her punishment blues.

I stopped at a small intersection. The set of traffic lights, which I passed through many times a week, marked the entrance to my Eichler neighborhood. This afternoon, however, the signals sent two messages to my brain. One said STOP; the other said HOLD DOWN THE RED CIRCLE.

"Maddie, I think I have a clue about the secret room." I recited the phrase from the note I believed to be from Varena's brother Caleb. "Does that mean anything to you?"

"Huh?"

I didn't think so. What made me think the phrase had to do with the dollhouse in the first place? I repeated the instruction anyway.

"Hold down the red circle," Maddie said, slowly.

The way her voice rose at the end, I knew we'd done it.

"Duh!" she said. "I gotta go, Grandma. I got it. I got it."

It was hard to obey the speed limit and all the red and green circles for the next mile.

I forgot about the old sedan until I saw it behind me as I approached my house. Obviously I had nothing to worry about. It was my imagination that the car had slowed down before it passed me.

I DIDN'T know how long Maddie had been waiting, but there she was, sitting on the curb, shivering slightly, as I pulled up. She jumped to her feet when she saw me and ran to hug me even before the driver's-side door slammed shut.

My delight increased when she stepped back and pulled a white envelope out of the pocket of her hot pink down vest. Henry came out then, no doubt having wisely stood at the window, safe from the cold, and from Maddie's unbridled energy, until he saw my car.

"Here it is, Grandma," Maddie said, waving the speciously ordinary-looking envelope in my face. The treasure hidden in the secret room was the same size and shape as the one I'd found on the Rockwell Estate garden bench. "We decided not to open it until you got here. What do you think it is? Huh? Huh? Maybe it's a map for a buried treasure?"

Did my granddaughter really want something else to hunt down? I was hoping for a confession, signed by Varena's killer.

The three of us had something close to a group hug and walked together toward the house, agreeing that we shouldn't open the envelope in the middle of the street. Maddie talked nonstop in what we English teachers call run-on sentences.

"I finally remembered how with my laptop and my iPod and everything, that you have to hold down the button, you don't just press and let go, you have to hold, like a second, or two seconds, before it goes on, so I went around the dollhouse bedroom at all the red circles and counted, one-Mississippi, two-Mississippi. The first time on Monday I must have accidentally just leaned on the spot for two seconds, and then when I was trying to get it back, I was just tapping because I didn't know."

She finally took a breath as we entered my atrium and took seats around the dollhouse. Maddie had left the panel to the secret room open, not taking any more chances. The house seemed to be smiling, as if it had finally given birth after a long and painful labor during which its midwives were dumbfounded.

We couldn't have been grinning more broadly if we'd won a fully furnished dollhouse in a raffle.

WHAT a disappointment. "There's no note. It looks like ledger pages of some kind," I said, handing the contents of the envelope to Henry.

"I took it out right away this time, just in case," said Maddie, who still seemed not to care about the boring contents of the envelope. If there was no buried treasure, no gift certificate to Sadie's Ice Cream Shop, no special online credit card, it didn't much matter what was in it.

"Good work," I told her, giving her skinny body another hug, topped with a quick head rub that sent her red curls flying.

"I'm not too good at this kind of thing," Henry said. "All I remember from a high school accounting class is debits on the left, credits on the right."

"Which is two things more than I know," I said.

Maddie had taken out her smartphone and showed us an almost hidden button along the top edge of the phone. She pressed it quickly and nothing happened.

"See," she said. "Nothing. Now watch." She held it down, counting, one-Mississippi, two-Mississippi, and the device sprang to life with an alien-sounding groan. "Did you see that, Grandma? How it came on?"

"Good work," I repeated. I turned to Henry. "We should call Skip and get the ledger pages to him as soon as possible."

"I should have known right away," Maddie said. "This is how a lot of electronic things work."

"While you call the station, I'll start the water for tea," Henry said.

"Uncle Henry said it's not just these new phones that work that way." Maddie leaned across the small table and pulled on Henry's sleeve. "Tell Grandma how old electrical switches run that way, too, Uncle Henry."

Unlike Alicia, Maddie didn't usually interrupt so aggressively.

I finally caught on. How negligent a grandmother could I be?

Maddie had done her job and was pleased with her performance. The payoff for her was that she'd found a secret room and then figured out how to find it again. At a time when she'd been beaten down for her poor judgment and punished for her bad behavior, she needed accolades for a task well done, and I hadn't given her nearly enough.

Fortunately, I knew exactly which cabinet drawer held leftover party decorations. I made a quick trip to the kitchen and returned to the atrium with a gold paper crown I'd made for one of Maddie's early birthday parties, along with a few wrinkled but clean CONGRATULATIONS napkins from when Richard landed his current position.

"Before we do anything else, I think ice cream and congratulations are in order," I said.

"Hear, hear," Henry said.

He began a rendition of "Congratulations to you…" while I crowned my brilliant princess.

From the smile on Maddie's face, I knew the little party would stave off any thoughts of grand-matricide.

HENRY picked up Taylor and brought her to my house so the two BFFs could do homework and hang out. A combination study and play date. Not much had changed since I was in grade school except the vocabulary.

Henry and I were free to do the boring stuff.

Before we started in on the ledger pages, Henry took my phone from the counter, punched in Skip's number, and handed the phone to me. Apparently he noticed I hadn't made the call yet.

If I didn't know better I'd have thought he didn't trust me to include the LPPD in my investigation.

IN a sharing mood, I told Skip about the flimsiness of Mr. Sedonis's statement, given his utter intimidation by his boss, and mentioned that he might want to check the sign-in log at Paige Taggart's dormitory and show Charles's photo around.

"Thanks, Aunt Gerry," he said. "If it weren't for citizens like you—"

"I get it. You know how to do your job."

While we waited for Skip, Henry and I spread out the ledger pages, creased from many foldings, on the dining room table. The four pages appeared to be from one continuous record.

Neither of us could make much sense out of the pages, except to note that under the column labeled Memo was a list of people and companies that had either been paid or needed to be paid. I noted a "Reimbursement from Adam George" for four hundred ninety-five dollars, and an entry for Westbay Consultants, who were paid thirteen thousand dollars.

"We're assuming there's something illegal or incriminating here, right?" Henry asked.

I worked a half nod, half shrug with my head and shoulders. "This has to be what Caleb was talking about in his communications to Paige, what he wanted her to find. And if it's money, it must be about Charles Quentin."

Henry mimicked my gesture. "And why else would he leave it on the bench for you?" he asked.

"Along with a note to beware of CQ. I wish Caleb Swingle would stop speaking in riddles and come out of hiding himself."

In an attempt to educate ourselves, we looked in my old relic of a dictionary for a definition of embezzlement.

"'The unlawful taking of something from another that has been entrusted to you,'" I read.

Henry shook his head. "Sad."

I agreed.

We bent our heads over the ledger sheets and stared at them, as if we'd come upon a strange, coded message, which in a way we had. The first page, which was numbered page six, had headings along the top: ROCKWELL ACCOUNTING—GENERAL LEDGER (DETAIL) with a range of dates from earlier in the year.

"Let's hope the LPPD has someone who can make sense out of this," Henry said, turning away from the table.

I pointed in the direction of Maddie's room. "It's pretty quiet down there," I said. "Does Taylor know about Maddie's computer restrictions?"

"I thought I'd leave it up to Maddie to tell her."

"She's had several conversations with her parents and she seems resigned, if not pleased, with the results. That is, even with all her negotiating skills, the imposed penalty is still in effect."

"That's probably good."

"I think so, too. Shall we check on the girls or do you think they can handle things?"

"They can handle it."

"Right."

A pause.

"Let's check," we said at the same time.

Grandparents will be grandparents.

Chapter 21

BY FIVE O'CLOCK in the afternoon, the day's excitement was over.

Skip had come by but stayed only long enough to take a handful of cookies and the ledger pages with him. It had been anticlimactic for me simply to hand over the material that had been the subject of a search-and-rescue mission for what seemed like a long time.

Henry and Taylor had gone home to get her ready for parents' night at her school. Henry would be back for the crafts meeting, which he'd started to attend on a regular basis. His woodworking expertise was a great asset, for which my friends thanked me (and him).

Tonight was Karen's turn to provide our dessert, so my only task was to arrange the dining room table with plates and cutlery and set out the coffeemaker. Karen's special dark chocolate truffle cake was a fine alternative to cognac ice cream, though I could imagine a perfect world where we'd have both.

The bottom line: I didn't have to bake tonight.

Maddie was finishing her homework.

The dollhouse's secret had been unearthed and passed on to the LPPD.

I was out of things to do.

A dangerous situation for me.

I checked the clock. Was there enough time for me to make a trip to Paige's dorm and be back for the crafters meeting? I wanted to examine the sign-in sheet for Monday night. What were the chances that Charles Quentin had to sign in? What I knew of dormitory security from Richard's college days wasn't reassuring. A photo of Charles would be better. I wished I'd thought to sneak one with my cell phone.

Not that I remembered how to use the camera in my cell phone. I'd have to get Maddie to show me, for the fifth time.

I paced my house.

The plan to visit Paige's dorm room wouldn't work, and it was too soon to call Skip and ask about the ledger pages. I finally thought of something useful. If I couldn't get to Paige's dorm, I could at least call and tell her we'd found the envelope Caleb had hidden. I did know how to use the call log in my phone and reached Paige quickly.

"Hey, Mrs. Porter. Anything new?"

"We found it," I said.

Paige seemed to know immediately what I meant, and like Maddie, didn't sound as disappointed as I was by the contents of the envelope.

"I'm not crazy!" she said. "Now maybe the police will leave me alone and go after who really took Varena away."

I hoped she was right. Though we didn't find a signed confession, my guess was that we had found a serious motive for murder. "Paige, do you have a minute to answer a couple of questions?"

"Sure. I'm home for the evening. Sad, huh?"

I didn't feel qualified to comment on Paige's social life. "Does a visitor to your dorm have to sign in?"

"Theoretically, yes. But these rent-a-cops aren't the most reliable, believe me. They go out back for a smoke and forget to lock the front door all the time. A lot of kids do their homework in the foyer just to watch the door."

"Do you think Charles Quentin knows where your dorm room is?" I asked this although I had a hard time picturing the older gentleman lying in wait for building security to go lax.

"Oh, my God, Mrs. Porter, do you think it was Mr. Quentin? I didn't put it together when you said ledger pages were in the dollhouse. Mr. Quentin planted the sword handle piece in my room?"

"I don't know anything for sure. I'm just wondering who could get into your room. Would someone like Mr. Quentin be noticed if he entered the building and went upstairs?"

"Like I said, anyone can sneak in, and Mr. Quentin looks like every kid's grandfather. No one would be suspicious unless he was dressed like a scraggly old man. Oh, my God. Mr. Quentin."

I heard what I thought might be a shiver from Paige, probably remembering times when she might have stood or sat next to a murderer.

Or was I projecting my own shivery feelings?

"Has anyone else from the Rockwell Estate visited you there?" I asked.

"Uh-uh. No one's ever been up here. Once in a while Laura drives me home, when she's in a good mood and not harping on me to stop wasting time on Varena's dollhouses. Oh, another time, when I was really sick, Varena had the driver take me home."

"Would that be Mr. Sedonis?"

"Yes, Roberto. But he didn't come in or anything. No one from the estate has ever actually been in my room. Well, except for the guy who planted the weapon."

A little bell went off in my brain, signaling that something was off in what I was hearing, but as often happened, I couldn't put my finger on the problem.

Beep, beep.

My call-waiting signal. Doris Ann Hartley was on the line. I signed off with Paige and prepared myself to face the music with Doris Ann. I wasn't pleasing any of my pseudo-employers these days. Not Alicia, who wanted me to find a killer she didn't share meals with. Not Doris Ann, who wanted me to find a dollhouse.

Soon no one would trust me with important assignments. Maybe that was a good thing.

"Gerry, I'm sure you know why I'm calling," Doris Ann said.

"I do, Doris Ann. I need another few—"

"I'll bet you had a lot to do with it."

I mumbled a syllable or two, hoping Doris Ann would continue without my input.

"It's such a coup for Lincoln Point's little library. I'm thrilled that the ceremony will still go on as planned."

"Me, too."

"The head of the library association called me this afternoon to check on the arrangements. It's very exciting."

"It certainly is. Any new details?" I asked. I wondered how long I could keep up my end of a conversation when I didn't know the topic.

"Just that it will now be called a Posthumous Lifetime Achievement Award, presented to Varena Young, for her blah-blah-blah. I'm sure you had a lot to do with its not being canceled."

"I didn't even know—"

"Thank you. Thank you."

What was I doing wrong lately that everyone felt free to interrupt me? "You're welcome."

"A Ms. Taggart is going to accept the award for her."

"Paige Taggart? Not her daughter?"

"It makes sense. Varena's agent sent her speech over last week. In it, she planned to announce that her research assistant, Paige Taggart, had been—I have it right here, so I'm quoting—'largely responsible for the continuation of my series of novels and should finally have the recognition she deserves.' It's all supposed to be a big surprise to reviewers and readers and so on, but I'm sure Paige told you."

"Of course."

"I have to go, Gerry, but I just wanted to say thanks again."

"My pleasure."

When I hung up, left to my own devices, I reviewed my suspect list again. Was the plan for the Lifetime Achievement Award another reason for Alicia to be jealous of Paige? But if she was inclined to murder out of jealousy, wouldn't she have killed Paige instead of her own mother?

The same could be said of Laura Overbee. Why not kill the object of her fury?

My admiration for Paige, on the other hand, went up a notch.

I remembered searching the Acknowledgments pages of the few Varena Young romances I owned, and noting that Paige Taggart was listed alphabetically along with many other people, including the women who typed Varena's manuscripts. She'd come a long way, and apparently, earned the professional recognition of her mentor.

How hard it must be for her now not to flaunt her great success. The young woman had character. Varena had good judgment in choosing whom she'd spend time with. I wished I could have lived up to her choosing me, if only for an afternoon.

DUM, ta da dum, ta da dum, ta da dum.

We'd been finishing up leftover chicken and dumplings that Henry brought back when my cell phone rang. Maddie ran to see who had activated her marching band tune.

"Uncle Skip, Uncle Skip," she said.

Henry and I made a modest effort to clank silverware and glasses while we eavesdropped on Maddie's side of the conversation.

"I miss you, too."

Pause.

"I've been busy with a lotta, lotta homework."

Pause.

"Yeah, maybe some time, but I have a lotta stuff to do."

Pause.

"No, not so much surfing."

Pause.

"I'm fine."

Pause.

"Love you too, Uncle Skip. Here's Grandma."

I took the phone.

"What's up with the little squirt?" Skip asked. My nephew was understandably confused by Maddie's unenthusiastic response and lack of interest in helping him with his caseload.

"You'll have to ask her some time."

"I sort of did, but she didn't really answer. She's not growing up on me, is she? 'Cause I don't think I'm ready for that."

"It's complicated." As weaselly as the phrase was, there were times when it fit perfectly.

"Okay. Some other time. I thought you'd want to know the latest word on the ledger sheets."

"Yes, please," I said.

Skip gave a loud laugh. "What's going on in that house? Who are you and what have you done with the real Maddie Porter and my Aunt Gerry?"

"I'm just trying to be polite and cooperative," I said, laughing myself.

"Yeah, well, I miss the old guys."

"Come on, Skip. What about those ledger pages?" I used my nastiest teacher voice, one I called up on those occasions when a promising young student clearly didn't do her best.

"That's better," Skip said. "The LPPD has access to the state's greatest forensic accountants and they're terrific at their job. But whoever pulled those pages apparently was no stranger to accounting either. Exactly what we need is there and the key transactions are highlighted to show the fraud perpetrated on the Rockwell Estate by its financial overseer."

"In short?"

"Someone busted Charles Quentin."

I blew out a breath. Not that I was surprised, but I didn't expect such a quick, unequivocal confirmation of my theory that Charles was hiding something. No wonder he was uncomfortable when I brought up Uncle Caleb.

"How did this happen so fast?" I asked. "I just gave you those ledger sheets this afternoon."

"Funny thing, it wasn't that fast. You didn't know, and neither did I, that Varena Young had been secretly in contact with the state's white-collar-crime division with suspicions that her moneyman was cheating her. She said she didn't know how to prove it, but there was someone close to her who could help."

"Are you thinking what I'm thinking?" I asked.

"That a brother who served twenty-five years for embezzlement might be the perfect connection to have at a time like that?"

Exactly.

Caleb had certainly taken precautions, approaching first Paige and then me instead of coming out in the open. Because he was embarrassed by his prison record? Or deathly afraid of Charles?

I tried to recall the snippets of the argument I'd heard at the Rockwell Estate as I was leaving from my first visit. The exact words escaped me, but I was sure the tone was accusatory, the men accusing each other and Varena scolding one of them. There was an excellent chance the topic was Charles's extracurricular activities.

I repeated my recollection to Skip. "Doesn't it seem that Charles murdered Varena so she wouldn't expose him, and now Caleb is afraid he's after him? That must be why he's hiding in the bushes."

"A reasonable scenario, but we have to take it one step at a time."

I guess I missed that day at the academy.

"What's happening with Charles?"

"We've taken him in for questioning. The state's guys are interviewing him as we speak. Unless he can do some fast talking and explain away separate accounts and dummy corporations where he funneled some of Varena's earnings, my guess is that an indictment is on the way."

"Why would he do that? Why would he steal from a family he's been with practically all his life?"

"Let's face it, Aunt Gerry, you never can believe anyone would do something bad. Except me when I was a kid."

We shared a pleasant family chuckle.

"But Charles Quentin is not a young man. Why would he want to risk dying in prison? Besides, he certainly doesn't look poor. He has the whole Rockwell Estate, including chauffeurs, at his disposal."

"Maybe he wants his own little cabaña on the beach. Money is one motive that crosses all classes of people. The poor need it; the rich want more."

It sounded both obvious and sad.

"And you're working on the murder charge?"

"He has an alibi for the afternoon."

"Provided by a chauffeur?"

"Now that you mention it." He laughed. "It might take a while to build the case for murder, but we're on our way and he won't be going home tonight."

"I'm happy to hear that."

I could rest easy. I wished I could pass the message on to Caleb somehow.

"Nice work, by the way, Aunt Gerry, with Sedonis and Paige and the ledger and all."

"Thanks."

I liked to think I wasn't as needy as an eleven-year-old for appreciation and praise, but it felt good to hear it.

Chapter 22

IT DIDN'T TAKE long for my crafter friends to descend on the new-to-them dollhouse in my atrium. On Fridays we worked on our individual miniatures, but on Wednesday evenings we typically worked on one project together, a house or room box that ended up at a children's center or on the table of a charity auction.

I hadn't intended to offer Varena's dollhouse for the evening, since it wasn't mine to offer, but I saw right away that it was going to be difficult if not impossible to rein in my group. The ladies hardly said hello before they'd flicked all the switches and exclaimed over the thoroughly modern lighting in the house. Then they plunged in with ideas and suggestions, rummaging in their tool boxes and totes.

"It's been so long since we've had a modern style to work on," said Mabel Quinlan, our oldest member and an inveterate beader. "I think the foyer needs a chandelier and maybe a sculpture with primary colors. I'm thinking of red seed beads and yellow cat's-eyes to begin with. And some bright blue tube beads, I think."

Mabel settled at the picnic table Henry had set up along one wall of the atrium, the working area. She opened her bead case, mumbling to herself about sizes and colors. She was on her way. Who was I to take away an octogenarian's fun with small details like the ownership of the house?

Karen Striker, who was a new mother, had her eye on the nursery as everyone predicted.

"I saw this cool toy organizer that's very modern looking,"

she said. "It's just rows of bins in a sleek frame. I could probably make it with found objects. I've been collecting small pillboxes. I can paint them to go with the primary colors on the walls." And Karen was on her way.

Gail Musgrave, our city councilwoman and a new grandmother, had her eye on one of the other bedrooms, a kids' room judging by the bunk beds and shelves of toys. "I'm torn between that and the nursery. I saw this neat circular crib in a catalog. You can remove pieces of the circumference as the baby grows, and eventually it becomes a toddler's bed or two chairs," Gail told us. "Imagine! I think I can make it in miniature using one of those mesh clip containers from an office supply store."

"Or you could use the basket strawberries come in," Karen said.

"Or the netting from a sack of those small potatoes," Mabel said, sorting through her trays for the right red, blue, and yellow beads.

"Or instead of looking in your trash for materials, you could crochet the mesh and starch it," Linda said.

The meeting had officially started.

I knew Susan Giles would be the hardest to win over. Our relocated southern belle, who never met a ruffle she didn't like, was into soft curves, not the sharp angles of Varena's modern dollhouse. She'd worked for weeks sewing tiny velvet cushions and embroidering pillowslips for the lavish rooms in a flowery Victorian she'd earmarked for the children's ward at Lincoln Point's hospital.

Susan ran her finger along the edges that formed the roof and the interior doorways. She wrinkled her nose. "I don't know. A working television set in a dollhouse? This one's just not my style. But I'll think of something to contribute. Maybe I'll work on an old-fashioned games carpet for the playroom." We all approved.

Once she determined the dollhouse was not from a kit, Linda was on board with working on it and announced a plan to use balsawood with a light stain for the base of a coffee table.

"It should have a glass top," Linda said.

We all knew she meant glass, and not a piece of plastic that looked like glass. Linda would take herself to her workbench where glass and glass-cutting tools were available and the dollhouse would have a made-from-scratch coffee table.

Henry stood next to Linda, nodding, as she pointed out all the flaws he'd already noted when the house first arrived. Unlike Henry, however, who praised it as a most-likely first attempt, Linda wondered why the original recipient didn't send it to the dump. It helped that she grinned while she gave her judgment.

Once the first rush of ideas was over, but before people settled into chatting and finding materials to work with, I announced an extra attraction for the evening.

"Maddie has a little demonstration for us," I said.

Henry mimicked a drum roll with his fingers on the table.

A very smiley Maddie stepped to the open back of the dollhouse and asked everyone to gather there. What she said was, "C'mon over here, please," accompanied by dizzying waves of her arm.

She ran her hand across the back wall of the larger of the upstairs bedrooms. "This looks like an ordinary wall, doesn't it?" she asked.

Everyone knew to say, "Yes."

Only then did I realize that in my excitement over retrieving the envelope with its valuable contents, I'd never even had Maddie show me specifically where the secret room was and what it looked like. No wonder she'd felt underappreciated.

Maddie, with her usual flair for drama, ran her hand across the wall again, but this time stopped at one of the red circles and pushed it down. I could almost hear her silent "one-Mississippi, two-Mississippi."

Half of the thin wooden wall slid along a nearly invisible track, revealing another wall, painted in the same geometric design, about two inches behind it. A small passageway between the two was carpeted in red felt.

Confident that she'd never again forget how to open the panel, Maddie had stashed a chocolate cookie in the tiny hallway. She plucked it out and took a bite, then a bow. The oohs, aahs, and applause caused Maddie's smile to broaden, though I wouldn't have thought it was possible.

I felt a swell of pride that Maddie was mine, and in a way, so was the dollhouse, simply because it had finally responded to our probing.

"That's why you were asking me all those questions about secret rooms, Gerry. I'll be darned," Linda said, scratching a spot under her retro beehive hairdo.

Only someone who knew Linda well would have understood that "I'll be darned" was high praise and meant that Linda was impressed.

"Now I like it," the recently divorced Susan said. "I'd put a romantic note in that little hallway, send the house out to sea, and see who it brought me."

"Was there anything in the room when you first opened it?" Gail asked.

I started to speak, but Maddie preempted me. "Nothing important. Just an old envelope," she said.

AS the evening wore on, the featured dollhouse sported many new items. From Susan, a colorful games carpet in the loft, with blocks for checkers, backgammon, and marbles. From Maddie, working with Henry, a new picnic cooler right inside the kitchen door, thanks to my stash of molded Styrofoam packing material. From Mabel, a chandelier of clear plastic with crystal beads.

Gail made headway on the circular crib and Karen simply played with the secret room, trying different items and making up a story for each one.

I wondered what Varena had done with the secret room when the dollhouse was new. Stash away pages of her diary? Hide notes from a boy she liked? I'd have to ask Paige if Varena had ever written a novel with a hidden-treasure theme.

"Who did you say built this house?" Karen asked.

I was speechless for a moment and Henry filled in with "The brother of a friend of Gerry's."

Buzzz. Buzzz.

The doorbell was just what I needed while I thought of other details I could share about the house's architect.

Henry went to the front door and stayed there a few minutes talking to my guest. I strained to listen. Not Skip. An older male voice, but not Charles, fortunately. A voice I may have heard before. I was ready to take a nonchalant stroll to check out the visitor when Henry led him into the atrium.

The newcomer was a man unmistakably related to Varena Young, that is, Mildred Swingle.

Caleb Swingle, tall, but a bit stooped, smiled almost imperceptibly when he saw that his dollhouse was the object of everyone's attention. "I'm sorry to interrupt your meeting," he said. "But Mr. Baker here said you've all been working on my sister's dollhouse. I can't tell you how much that means to me."

I liked him already.

FOR the next hour, Caleb became part of the group, quietly explaining the kind of tools he'd worked with as a twelve-year-old, how he'd fashioned the secret room, crudely at first, then in a more sophisticated way as batteries and circuitry improved. He expressed delight with the new window treatment I'd come up with for the smaller bedroom and praised everyone's efforts to spruce up the old house.

It felt as though Caleb Swingle had been part of the group for years. There were a lot of things I wanted to know about the man and his family, but for now I enjoyed watching him bask in the praise and appreciation my crafter friends heaped on him.

The ladies of the club were so taken with the builder of the newest dollhouse, I knew I'd never tell them that he was an ex-con who'd been stalking me for a few days.

ONCE the ladies had dispersed, I went to the front bedroom to say good night to Maddie, leaving the men to continue talking. I'd already learned how old they were when they got their first serious woodworking kits (ten for Caleb, eight for Henry), what their first projects had been (a model boat for Caleb, a log cabin for Henry), which kind of glue sets fastest (yellow for both), and the best use of rubber bands (as clamps while the glue dries).

Lying on her baseball sheets, Maddie struggled to stay awake long enough to ask me the most important question of the evening.

"Did you tell Uncle Skip, Grandma?"

I didn't have to ask what she meant. "No, sweetheart. That's up to you, whether you want to tell him or not."

"Do you think I should?"

Why did a child's questions get tougher every year?

"I don't see why, unless you think you'll feel better. Uncle Skip wasn't really affected by what you did."

"Except I couldn't help him on the computer."

"True, but you were a great help with the secret room in the dollhouse. You don't need a computer to be smart."

"Did I do a good job tonight?"

"Outstanding." I ruffled her curls for emphasis.

"I don't think I'll tell anyone."

"I think that's a good decision for now. You know, some day something might come up and you might feel like telling Uncle Skip, or someone else, what happened." How many weasel words had I fit into that one sentence? "But don't worry about that now. You can explain to Uncle Skip that you're just recovering from a nasty bug and you've been catching up with homework and you're going to be your old self very soon. All of that is true."

"Thanks, Grandma."

"Did I tell you lately how smart and wonderful you are?" I asked.

She smiled. "Tell me again."

I did, and that was all it took to get her to sleep.

THE atrium was chilly, but neither Henry nor Caleb nor I wanted to move from the site of the dollhouse. There wasn't much left of Wednesday night, but the three of us continued to sit there, with different drinks, and talk as if it were the middle of the day. And as if we were old friends.

I accepted Caleb's apology for his unconventional methods of communicating and following me home.

"And for frightening me in the woods?" I asked, with a smile.

"That, too. Only when I saw them take Charles into the police building tonight did I think it was safe for me to surface."

"Understood," Henry said.

Easy for him to say.

We went back and forth from expressions of sadness at the

loss of Varena to beautiful memories of her to ugly times when, as he put it, Caleb hit bottom.

"It was my idea to break it off," he said. "I didn't want my niece and nephew knowing what a loser their uncle was. A gambler. A thief. No way were they going to be visiting me in prison. Especially Adam. He was old enough for us to have a real relationship."

"Adam has only the best memories of you."

Caleb's rheumy eyes lit up when I told him the story of Adam and the hot dogs. "I hope they'll let me back in their lives. It's going to be quite a shock, I know."

"You mean Alicia and Adam don't know you're alive?"

I hadn't meant to be so blunt, but Caleb didn't seem to mind answering.

"I didn't get in touch with Varena until about a year ago, after I paid off the debt as the court ordered. I didn't want her to think I was looking for money. She would have given it to me in a minute. And she took me back without so much as a harsh word."

"I'm glad to hear that," I said, doing my best to hold back tears.

"We talked about how to deal with the children, but then this issue with Charles came up and we decided to take care of one thing at a time."

"Do you mind telling us how Varena came to be suspicious of Charles?" I asked.

"She got a statement in the mail by mistake. Charles usually intercepted them, but somehow Varena learned of a bank account she didn't know she had, and it went on from there. She asked me to look into it before going to anyone official." Caleb's eyes watered as he talked. "Now, I think she might be alive if she'd gone to the authorities right away."

"You don't know that," Henry said, leaning over, putting his hand on Caleb's shoulder.

"If I hadn't been so stupid, I could have been her financial manager myself and none of this would have happened."

"Were you arguing with them that afternoon?"

"Yes, and I stormed out because Varena seemed to be falling for his story. I ended up sneaking back and putting the ledger sheets…well, you know the rest of the story. I knew how much Varena cared for Paige and felt I could trust her. Now, I realize, if I'd stayed behind…"

My heart went out to Caleb, a man with a great burden. I hoped Varena's children would be willing to brighten what was left of his life.

Dum, ta da dum, ta da dum, ta da dum.

Skip, one of very few people who could call at this hour and not send me into a panic that someone near and dear was in the ER.

"Thought you'd want to know we searched Charles Quentin's home and found a cloth with blood all over it. He must have used it to clean the weapon."

"He kept the bloody cloth in his home?"

"We have to test it, but I'm guessing the blood is the victim's. He hid the cloth in his garage."

"Doesn't that seem strange? A meticulous man like Charles Quentin keeping a bloody cloth around, no matter whose blood it is?"

"I thought this would make you happy, maybe help you sleep better tonight. It's what we needed to make the case against him for murder."

"I am happy. I mean, I'm glad you found evidence if that's what it is. It just seems strange, that's all."

"Sometimes we have to take 'strange,'" Skip said.

He had a point.

I gave my guests the good news, though I still held onto its strangeness. When there were no more stories, no more big questions in our minds, the party broke up.

No one ventured to ask when we might see each other again.

I LOOKED in on Maddie, who seemed to have grown more quickly this week. I wished I could take away any residual pain she was feeling from her own misbehavior and perceived alienation from the people she loved.

I knew it wouldn't be the last time something like this would happen to her but as I kissed her forehead, I invoked her good fairy and her guardian angel, just in case they might be listening.

DUM, ta da dum, ta da dum, ta da dum.

By now I should have expected a call from Alicia right at pillow time.

"Geraldine, I can't believe this. The police arrested Charles. They're saying he stole from my mother and now they're trying to prove he killed her because she found out."

"I know."

"You know? Did you put them up to this?"

I wouldn't have phrased it that way.

"The police are doing their job, Alicia."

"I don't believe this. Charles has been a father to us, a friend. What's happening to my family?"

I wished I could give her the answer, that there was good news mixed with the bad. I fell asleep wondering if Caleb would find a place in the new Rockwell household.

Or if I would.

Chapter 23

AFTER A GOOD night's sleep, I was ready to take on Alicia again. I needed to settle the disposition of the house that Caleb built and to ask nicely if I could have the Tudor that Varena had promised me for the bookmobile fund-raising drive.

I wanted so badly for Alicia and Adam to be reunited with their uncle, I'd almost spilled the beans last night on the phone with Alicia. But I knew it wasn't my place to tell her about the living, breathing Caleb.

I was less worried about Adam's reaction, feeling that Caleb would be able to win him over with a trip to a hot dog stand. But I suspected Alicia's loyalty to Charles was even greater than she'd have to an uncle she barely remembered.

With Maddie in school and Henry off to a crafters meeting of his own, I had some quiet time to call the estate. Laura picked up the phone.

"You were on my list to call this afternoon," she said, with the same uninterested attitude she'd taken with me on our first meeting. "There's going to be a special magazine article on Varena's dollhouse collection, and Alicia thought you might like to help choose which ones to feature."

Was I going to get my tour after all?

"I'd love to participate. Where will the article appear?"

"It will be in the newsletter of a romance writers group in the Midwest. I'd have to check my files for the exact name of the group."

"That's very exciting. It's nice that Varena will have so many tributes."

"I'm in a rush, Geraldine, so let me know if you can make it. Otherwise I have a couple of other people I can call."

"No, no. I'll be there," I said.

It hadn't taken long for Laura Overbee to get back to her ornery self once she no longer needed to cooperate with me. "Fine, how soon can you get here?"

I checked my watch and added an hour to change my clothes and get up the hill. "How about noon?"

"Noon is fine."

For some reason, I didn't think there would be an elegant lunch on the patio this time.

IT would have to be gusty today, making the curvy road to the estate even harder to deal with. The closeness of the trees to the narrow road caused the tips of their branches to touch at times as the shifting winds set them dancing.

I'd chosen a more casual pale green shell and cardigan instead of my cashmere sweater set for this meeting. I was annoyed with Laura and her tone. I was annoyed with myself for attributing any kind of specialness to the Rockwell Estate. The residents and staff of the mansion were like any other family in the flats, with their share of saints and sinners, graciousness and rudeness. Good and evil, when it came right down to it.

If Laura or anyone else didn't like my outfit, it was their problem. I was beyond trying to fit in or impress them.

I was still eager to see as many dollhouses as Laura would allow, but I was glad my time traveling this road was almost over. I wouldn't miss the angst that was palpable throughout the property now that Varena was dead.

I was satisfied to have helped even a little to bring her killer to justice, but I knew I shouldn't have accepted the mission from Alicia in the first place. She'd never thank me for my role in sending Charles to prison. In hindsight, I saw that she wanted her mother's killer to have been a scruffy kid from the far reaches of Lincoln Point's housing projects, someone in a hoodie who happened to get through the gate and make his way to the Lord and Lady Morley room, and…

I shook my head to get rid of the drama running wild in my imagination. The one bright spot had been meeting Caleb Swingle. I tried to recall the wonderful evening with him and my crafter friends.

Maybe I should have quit while I was ahead instead of coming up here at all. I hoped I'd at least be driving away with a midsize Tudor in my trunk.

I PARKED as usual at the edge of the wide driveway. To my surprise, the front door of the house opened and Laura Overbee walked out. She wore yet another sweater set I hadn't seen before, this one a mustard yellow that was not her best color.

She held the cardigan close against the wind and seemed in a hurry to get to me.

Uh-oh. Here it comes. She's canceling. Terrific.

Her frantic gait puzzled me, and I attributed her missteps to a combination of wind, high heels, and a desire to send me back down the hill. She knocked on the passenger window, a conciliatory smile on her face. I wondered what creative excuse she'd have for not at least calling my cell phone to alert me that she had something better to do.

I pushed the button to unlock the passenger door.

At the same time, I saw the wildness in her eyes.

Too late.

Laura Overbee was in the passenger seat of my car, turned slightly, the better to aim her gun at me.

Chapter 24

MY MIND RACED to catch up to this new reality.

I flashed back to what had been nagging me since Henry and I ran into Laura at the French bakery. I heard Laura again, as she sipped her pink iced drink and babbled about the décor in Paige's dorm room, with its bunk beds and makeshift bookshelves.

But Paige had been very clear that no one from the estate had ever been in her room. Except the person who planted the murder weapon.

Laura's startling presence in my car—hair disheveled, makeup gone south—confused me. Her wild expression and gun were in conflict with her perfect yellow sweaters and manicured fingernails.

Another picture formed, of Laura in a black sweater set on the afternoon of Varena's murder. The frightening thought emerged. She hadn't been merely efficient, changing into a mourning color for the occasion. Laura been hiding evidence of her crime. The blue set she'd worn earlier that day was probably now in the landfill outside Lincoln Point, bloodstains and all.

"Geraldine!" Laura wanted my attention.

I tried to erase the image of my own pale green sweater set, with bullet holes and bloodstains, at the bottom of a trash heap. I wondered if she had a different plan, to frame someone as she'd tried to frame Paige, and then Charles by putting a bloody cloth in his home. Would the police find my sweater set in Henry's home? One of my crafter friends' toolboxes?

"I know you'd figure it out sooner or later, Geraldine. That stupid remark I made about Paige's dormitory room. Good old innocent, naïve Paige told me you were asking questions."

I wanted to explain that the questions were simply me being me, probing. I hadn't put it together at all and probably never would have, not until she'd pointed a gun at me. She might have been able to get off scot-free. Charles Quentin would very likely have been convicted for Laura's crime, besides his own.

But I couldn't utter a word, let alone ask a heavy question: Laura Overbee, did you kill Varena Young, your boss, because she wouldn't boost your writing career?

Laura went on with no queries from me. "I couldn't believe it when Varena told me she was going to surprise Paige at her Life-time Achievement ceremony. She was going to announce that Paige had done the majority of the work on the last two books."

"Was it true?" Why did I care? If Laura's gun was real and I was reading her eyes correctly, all that mattered was, how many more minutes did I have to live?

"So what?" Laura asked, from which I gathered that Paige had indeed taken over Varena's writing. "Anyone could have written those books. In case you haven't noticed, they all have the same formula. Varena didn't give preferential treatment to Paige because she had some special talent. It was all about the doll-houses. Her own daughter couldn't have cared less about them, but Varena and Paige would spend a whole afternoon in front of one of them fixing something or painting a wall or…some other bit of child's play."

In spite of my possible imminent death I felt a thrill to think that Varena actually did work on the houses, even if only to add a notion or tuck in the draperies in a miniature living room or Victorian boudoir.

I wished I could have joined her.

Right now, I needed to engage Laura, sympathize with her somehow, to buy time. I had to figure out a way to escape.

"I can't believe they spent the day playing," I said. "I suppose you were at your desk working at some boring task." I *tsk-tsk*ed with as much sympathy as I could muster for a crazy woman with a lethal weapon.

"Are you kidding? Boring doesn't begin to cover it. I spent hours calling the airlines to make sure she had an aisle seat, bugging the hotel about her preference for down pillows, liaising with the bookstores to make sure lime water would be available, and on and on."

I surveyed the property outside my car. Where was everyone? Visiting Charles in jail? Where was Mr. Sedonis, the driver, or the chef who'd prepared the luncheon feast yesterday? How about Alicia and Adam, who'd spent a great deal of time here in the last few days?

How had Laura been able to arrange for us to be alone when I was the one who initiated this meeting?

A brilliant plan, I thought. She must have known I'd be calling sometime about the dollhouse for the library auction and simply bided her time and set her plan in motion.

What was her plan? Dare I ask?

Not yet.

I looked at Laura's eyes, which never strayed from my face.

"And now you were going to have to manage all those pesky details for Paige, too. Making the arrangements, and then watching Varena and Paige fly off together on tour."

Laura's eyes went wider than ever, as if she'd never thought of that particular angle. Maybe I'd gone overboard with my scenario.

"I tried to talk to Varena that afternoon. She was on her way to the Morley room to get back to you. I walked with her, hoping she'd hear me out. Do you know that the great lady wouldn't even give me a measly one-liner that would have meant the difference between a contract or no contract? All she had to do was introduce me as a writer to her own publisher."

"You can still—"

Thud.

The gun crashed against the dashboard as Laura whipped her arm around. She'd apparently had enough of my soothing voice.

"What are you going to do with me, Laura?" I blurted out.

"I wish I didn't have to do anything with you, Geraldine, but you're too smart for your own good."

"No—"

She grabbed my arm with her left hand. I closed my mouth.

I wanted badly to tell her how I'd thought Charles murdered Varena and that I could be persuaded to return to that theory, if only she'd put her gun away.

"You're going to turn around and drive down the hill at a normal pace," she said, with a calmness that worried me as much as her lunacy. "There's a spot about five hundred yards ahead on the right with a path that leads into the woods. You'll just pull over and we'll get out." She laughed, pleased with her own strategy. "For some reason, you decided to take a stroll today, perhaps do some bird watching, and, oh dear, you were shot. Security at Robert Todd Heights isn't what it used to be, and some ne'er-do-well got in."

Laura laughed again while I bit my lip, thinking. Under no conditions was I going to drive the curvy road behind me with a crazy woman holding me hostage.

I came up with my own strategy.

"Turn the car on, Geraldine." Stern now.

I checked the interior environment and rehearsed the movements in my head. I still had my seat belt on; Laura hadn't buckled up. A good thing.

I turned the key and shifted to Drive.

Laura seemed to be satisfied that her plan was underway.

I wished I'd read the manual for my new car more carefully. I shouldn't have skipped the parts about how long to accelerate how many feet, and what all the airbag features were.

I had to take a chance that I knew enough to free myself from the car and Laura.

"Go, Geraldine. Back up and go down the hill."

Not a chance.

I hit the accelerator as hard as I could. The car leapt into action. At the same time I reached down with my left hand and put my seat as far back and at as much of an angle as I could, until I was reclining enough to take a nap.

Or to receive minimum impact when the airbag inflated.

Which it did, when I hit the granite garden bench head-on.

The bang was as loud a noise as I'd ever heard close-up, like a shotgun in a movie. The air filled with dust and whatever pre-sumably harmless gas that had been inside the bag, setting us both to coughing.

I'd successfully pushed myself nearly out of range of the bag, but Laura, unrestrained and taken by surprise when the deployed bag assaulted her, got the full force of the blow. I saw blood coming from her nose and now she seemed unconscious, leaning on the airbag as if it were a pillow.

I used the window of opportunity to rush from the car, grabbing my cell phone from the side pocket on the door. I ran down the hill, glad that I'd worn casual flats.

It took three tries to hit the nine-one-one buttons correctly.

I didn't dare look back until I reached the guard's gate at the entrance to the Heights. "I crashed my car and someone is hurt up there," I said to the young man on duty, my breathing labored.

I grabbed the gate and hung on to it as if I'd just crossed a finish line.

Chapter 25

ALICIA ACCOMPANIED the men who delivered the midsize Tudor to my home on Sunday afternoon. She hoped it was a satisfactory donation. She'd already called Doris Ann at the library and told her how wonderful it had been to do business with me.

I hoped that positive performance evaluation didn't inspire Doris Ann to assign me another mission that involved negotiation.

Alicia took a seat in my living room, seeming relaxed for the first time since I met her. "I can't tell you how grateful I am, Geraldine," she said. "I'm so sorry I made it difficult for you at times."

"I didn't feel—"

"I knew you'd be able to determine who killed my mother. And who was cheating her, I might add. It's hard to imagine Laura and Charles, two key figures in my mother's household, now sitting together in a jail cell." She waved her hand. "Well, in a manner of speaking."

If a relationship had to be built on misunderstandings, I supposed it was better that they all worked in my favor, with Alicia constantly overestimating my role in resolving the issues of the Rockwell Estate.

"I really didn't—"

"You're much too modest, Geraldine."

It seemed there'd be no end to the misunderstandings and interruptions.

"And neither Adam nor I can possibly thank you enough for facilitating our reunion with Caleb. It has meant the world to all of us."

That, I would in all modesty take credit for.

"Say the word, and I'm ready to cut you a check for whatever you say," Alicia added.

Any amount of money I wanted? Was I about to pass up an unprecedented opportunity? Most people hoped to hit the lottery or receive a windfall from an expected source. There must be something I could do with a check from the Rockwell Estate. I just needed a minute to think.

The Rockwells had already rewarded me handsomely. Alicia had insisted on replacing my damaged car with a new one. I'd had a grand tour of Varena's dollhouses, by Paige Taggart, who loved them as much as Varena had, and the estate chef had sent over a full gallon of cognac ice cream.

Ken and I had paid off the mortgage on our Eichler long ago, Maddie's college years were well funded, and I had all the sweater sets I needed.

I shook my head. "Thank you, but I don't need anything," I said.

Alicia pointed to the Tudor, temporarily set up on my dining room table. "The library bookmobile drive has its donation. Wouldn't you at least like a dollhouse for yourself?"

I heard a light tapping sound from the atrium just behind us. Maddie, drumming her fingers on the Frank "Lord" Wright house with the secret room.

I gave Alicia a smile and a questioning look.

"Consider it yours," she said to Maddie. "I know my uncle Caleb adores you and he'll be thrilled that you like it."

"Thanks," Maddie said, grinning broadly.

I could have sworn she made a little curtsy, jeans and all.

BY Sunday evening, it had been a week since I'd spent normal time with my family and friends. We convened an impromptu potluck supper. The meal was distinctly non-gourmet, with ham, steamed green beans, buttermilk biscuits, and plain vanilla ice cream.

Skip and June were behaving like a couple again, which

pleased me, never mind what had been wrong in the first place. Skip had done me the great favor also of tracking down Corazón Cruz and assuring me that she was alive (I'd begun to suspect Charles of more than embezzlement) and happy in her Mexican hometown.

All was well.

"It seems like forever, Gerry," Beverly said. "What have you been up to?"

"You don't want to know, Mom," Skip said.

"She had a long to-do list," Henry said.

"She's been Away So Long," Maddie said.

Maddie was right.

It was good to be back in the flatlands, where I was just Gerry.

Gerry's Miniature Tips

Wallpaper
Outgrown baby and children's clothing with small-figured print makes perfect wallpaper for a dollhouse. A half-and-half mixture of glue and water makes good wallpaper paste.

Realistic Fruit
To make the "dimpled" skin of oranges, lemons, grapefruit, or limes: After making the clay ball of the appropriate size and color, lightly roll the ball on a piece of Velcro or sandpaper.

Bake as usual, according to the instructions on the package of polymer clay.

Water Spout
Need a water spout for the "rain" that's collecting in the gutters on your dollhouse roof? Use a drinking straw with an accordion bend at one end. Paint if necessary.

Stones for Walkway
Tear up gray cardboard egg cartons into random shapes for a walkway, patio, or siding for a stone house.

BBQ Briquettes (or Coal)
The hard way: make small black shapes out of polymer clay and bake in the usual way. The easier way: strike a few matches, either from a box of stick matches or from a matchbook. Wait until the ends cool and cut them off. The easiest way: cut up a stick of artist's charcoal and roughen the edges of each piece by rolling on sandpaper.

Yard

Expand your property line by putting your dollhouse on a large piece of plywood or particleboard. You can have a front yard with a lawn and flowers, a backyard with a swing set, pool, a vegetable garden, and a BBQ area. No zoning problems, so go for it!

Footstool

Small leather jewelry boxes such as those that hold earrings or cufflinks can simply be used as is. Plunk them next to an easy chair and you're set to relax.

Richard Rufer

About the Author

Margaret Grace, author of five previous novels in the Miniature series, is the pen name of Camille Minichino. She is also the author of short stories, articles, and ten mysteries in two other series. She is a lifelong miniaturist, as well as board member and past president of NorCal Sisters in Crime. Minichino is on the staff at Lawrence Livermore National Laboratory, and she teaches science at Golden Gate University and writing at Bay Area schools. Visit her at www.minichino.com.

MORE MYSTERIES
FROM PERSEVERANCE PRESS
🕭 *For the New Golden Age* 🕭

JON L. BREEN
Eye of God
ISBN 978-1-880284-89-6

TAFFY CANNON
ROXANNE PRESCOTT SERIES
Guns and Roses
Agatha and Macavity awards
nominee, Best Novel
ISBN 978-1-880284-34-6

Blood Matters
ISBN 978-1-880284-86-5

Open Season on Lawyers
ISBN 978-1-880284-51-3

Paradise Lost
ISBN 978-1-880284-80-3

LAURA CRUM
GAIL MCCARTHY SERIES
Moonblind
ISBN 978-1-880284-90-2

Chasing Cans
ISBN 978-1-880284-94-0

Going, Gone
ISBN 978-1-880284-98-8

Barnstorming
ISBN 978-1-56474-508-8

JEANNE M. DAMS
HILDA JOHANSSON SERIES
Crimson Snow
ISBN 978-1-880284-79-7

Indigo Christmas
ISBN 978-1-880284-95-7

Murder in Burnt Orange
ISBN 978-1-56474-503-3

JANET DAWSON
JERI HOWARD SERIES
Bit Player
ISBN 978-1-56474-494-4

What You Wish For *(forthcoming)*
ISBN 978-1-56474-518-7

KATHY LYNN EMERSON
LADY APPLETON SERIES
Face Down Below
the Banqueting House
ISBN 978-1-880284-71-1

Face Down Beside
St. Anne's Well
ISBN 978-1-880284-82-7

Face Down O'er the Border
ISBN 978-1-880284-91-9

ELAINE FLINN
MOLLY DOYLE SERIES
Deadly Vintage
ISBN 978-1-880284-87-2

SARA HOSKINSON FROMMER
JOAN SPENCER SERIES
Her Brother's Keeper
(forthcoming)
ISBN 978-1-56474-525-5

HAL GLATZER
KATY GREEN SERIES
Too Dead To Swing
ISBN 978-1-880284-53-7

A Fugue in Hell's Kitchen
ISBN 978-1-880284-70-4

The Last Full Measure
ISBN 978-1-880284-84-1

MARGARET GRACE
MINIATURE SERIES
Mix-up in Miniature
ISBN 978-1-56474-510-1

WENDY HORNSBY
MAGGIE MACGOWEN SERIES
In the Guise of Mercy
ISBN 978-1-56474-482-1

The Paramour's Daughter
ISBN 978-1-56474-496-8

The Hanging *(forthcoming)*
ISBN 978-1-56474-526-2

DIANA KILLIAN
POETIC DEATH SERIES
Docketful of Poesy
ISBN 978-1-880284-97-1

JANET LAPIERRE
Port Silva Series
Baby Mine
ISBN 978-1-880284-32-2

Keepers
*Shamus Award nominee, Best
Paperback Original*
ISBN 978-1-880284-44-5

Death Duties
ISBN 978-1-880284-74-2

Family Business
ISBN 978-1-880284-85-8

Run a Crooked Mile
ISBN 978-1-880284-88-9

HAILEY LIND
Art Lover's Series
Arsenic and Old Paint
ISBN 978-1-56474-490-6

LEV RAPHAEL
Nick Hoffman Series
Tropic of Murder
ISBN 978-1-880284-68-1

Hot Rocks
ISBN 978-1-880284-83-4

LORA ROBERTS
Bridget Montrose Series
Another Fine Mess
ISBN 978-1-880284-54-4

Sherlock Holmes Series
**The Affair of the
Incognito Tenant**
ISBN 978-1-880284-67-4

REBECCA ROTHENBERG
Botanical Series
The Tumbleweed Murders
(completed by Taffy Cannon)
ISBN 978-1-880284-43-8

SHEILA SIMONSON
Latouche County Series
Buffalo Bill's Defunct
*WILLA Award, Best Original
Softcover Fiction*
ISBN 978-1-880284-96-4

An Old Chaos
ISBN 978-1-880284-99-5

Beyond Confusion *(forthcoming)*
ISBN 978-1-56474-519-4

LEA WAIT
Shadows Antiques Series
**Shadows of a Down East
Summer**
ISBN 978-1-56474-497-5

ERIC WRIGHT
Joe Barley Series
The Kidnapping of Rosie Dawn
*Barry Award, Best Paperback
Original. Edgar, Ellis, and Anthony
awards nominee*
ISBN 978-1-880284-40-7

NANCY MEANS WRIGHT
Mary Wollstonecraft Series
Midnight Fires
ISBN 978-1-56474-488-3

The Nightmare
ISBN 978-1-56474-509-5

*REFERENCE/
MYSTERY WRITING*

KATHY LYNN EMERSON
**How To Write Killer
Historical Mysteries:
The Art and Adventure of
Sleuthing Through the Past**
*Agatha Award, Best Nonfiction.
Anthony and Macavity awards
nominee.*
ISBN 978-1-880284-92-6

CAROLYN WHEAT
**How To Write Killer Fiction:
The Funhouse of Mystery & the
Roller Coaster of Suspense**
ISBN 978-1-880284-62-9

**Available from your local bookstore or from
Perseverance Press/John Daniel & Co. at (800) 662-8351
or www.danielpublishing.com/perseverance.**